THE
VIEW
FROM THE
WIDOW'S WALK

Anne Yates Burst

ayburst@yahoo.com

For Tom...my Tarzan

THE
VIEW
FROM THE
WIDOW'S WALK

1

Her head throbbed, her back hurt and she couldn't seem to figure out what had happened, or what she was doing there - or why. It was a warm day for early spring, little bugs kept buzzing around her head, the asphalt had a slight tar scent and a subtle breeze came and went in warm, little waves. She couldn't seem to think about any of it. She just sat there, cross-legged on the edge of a narrow blacktopped road staring straight ahead.

The rattle of a car sounded on her left, and the woman turned to watch an old, rust-covered Buick slowly come to a grinding halt in front of her. She just sat there and stared at it. The passenger door opened, and a teen-aged, straggly-haired girl looked over at her.

"You OK? You been settin' there long?"

"I don't know."

"Where you going?"

"I don't know."

"Well, I just passed a fancy car in a ditch back there...was that yours?"

"I don't know."

"You sure don't know much!"

The teen sat up and looked around. In both directions the road looked deserted, cutting through acres and acres of not-yet-ready-to-pick cotton. There was only one reason for the nicely dressed young woman to be sitting on the side of a seldom used back road in southeast Georgia.

"Come on lady, you can't just keep settin' there. Maybe you was in an accident. Maybe that's your car back there. You think?"

"I don't know."

"Well, hell... I can't just leave you settin' here all by yourself. It just don't seem right! Get in and we'll go see if that was your car back there. OK?"

"OK."

Slowly the young woman got to her feet, obviously in pain, and stumbled to the car. Hanging heavily onto the car door, she got in the front seat but couldn't pull the door closed. The teen, mumbling something under her breath, got out, walked around and closed it. She spotted a sweater on the weedy ground and picked it up. It felt very soft and was a perfect match for the gray tweed slacks the woman wore. She threw it in the open car window.

Turning around in the middle of the road, the girl drove back a quarter of a mile to the ditched black Mercedes sports car. Not only in the ditch, but now they could see it was jammed against a small pine sapling that had snapped in half from impact. Loose white airbags that had activated were draped around the car's interior.

The young girl got out and walked to the woman's door and opened it.

"You want to get out?"

"I don't think I can."

"Oh...well, guess I can look around for you. Did you have a purse with you? Luggage? Was anyone else in the car?"

"I don't know."

Shaking her head, the teenager climbed down into the ditch through tall weeds and slippery red clay to open the front door of the Mercedes.

"Well, here's a purse...does it look like yours?" Getting a blank look from the lady, the teen struggled back up the incline and passed the woman the purse, suggesting she look inside for her driver's license.

"Is it your name? Look at the picture."

After a bit of searching, the woman produced a leather wallet. She opened it carefully and looked, blankly, at the picture with a quizzical gaze. "Is this my picture?" she asked, hesitantly.

"Jeez lady, yeah, that's you, without the big bump on your forehead and the black eyes. I'll see what else you left in the car. The keys are still in there; I'll check the trunk for you."

The trunk held three suitcases and a carry-on shoulder bag, all matching and expensive-looking. The girl piled them all in the back seat of the old Buick. She then looked throughout the Mercedes and found nothing. Starting to leave, she remembered the glove compartment. There, she found a large envelope and a folder, all with the same name as the driver's license. She gave them to the woman who was sitting, quietly watching the girl with nervous interest.

"Well, now what?" said the girl as she got back behind the wheel. "What do you think we should do? I could take you..."

"No! I need to get away from here! We've got to leave this place right now. Please!"

"But don't you want to call the police?" The girl was starting to wonder what she had gotten herself into. "Go to the hospital? Call somebody?"

"No, let's just leave and keep going...just keep going. Please. Right now!"

"But you can't just leave your car here. Somebody needs to do something...Elizabeth!"

The woman slowly turned her head and looked at the girl. "Elizabeth? Elizabeth? I'm Elizabeth?"

"Yeah, you are Elizabeth and I'm Stella. What's wrong with you?"

"I don't know. I feel very odd. I don't remember anything...nothing...not even my name! But I'm frightened! I have a very bad feeling...like... maybe someone is after me. But I don't know who or why. Can we go now? Please! I'm afraid to stay here!"

"Go where?" Stella asked.

"Anywhere! Where were you going? We can go there."

"Ha! Now that's kinda funny 'cause I don't know where I'm goin'. I'm leaving home... for good. Today is my sixteenth birthday and I've waited a long time for this day. I stole the car from my crazy, drunk-of-a-father and when he sobers up he's gonna be looking for both it and me. My plan is to be far away by then. I've been saving my money and all my stuff is in the trunk. Shit...I don't have time to lollipop around, lady!"

Stella turned the key to the beat-up Buick and took off in the direction she was originally traveling. Elizabeth leaned her head back and closed her eyes.

The next little town in Georgia was coming up. Stella thought she might be able to get ice for Elizabeth's head. She had to get a lot further down the road before she could think about stopping, and Elizabeth didn't yet seem to care about anything but sleeping. Stella's get-away plan, two years in the making, all depended on speed. What was she thinking? Picking up a hitchhiker!

2

It was late afternoon and they were coming into Americus, Georgia, an old town that still looked like an old town with lots of red brick and big oak trees. Stella was getting worried about Elizabeth. She had heard you were not supposed to sleep after a hit on the head. They needed to stop and eat and drink something, and talk. They definitely needed to talk.

Stella had no idea who this person was. Taking her abusive father's beat-up old car to get a head-start on her get-away was part of Stella's plan, but picking up a passenger was not. She did not know where Elizabeth had been going, but Stella kept heading south. That was her plan. Go south till she found a place she liked and could get a job.

She could not have left an injured woman sitting alone by the side of the road; but for Stella, time was crucial. Many miles had to be put between her and the life she was escaping before she ditched the car and started traveling by bus or thumb.

Elizabeth, Stella was sure, would want to go back home after she was feeling better and thought about her situation. People who dressed like she did and drove such a beautiful car had nothing they needed to escape. Stella could drive Elizabeth to the airport in Tallahassee for a flight back to Atlanta. She would leave the car there and maybe catch a bus to Daytona Beach. She felt she had done all she could for her accidental hitchhiker. She had to return to her original plan. She sure hoped Elizabeth would be thinking more clearly when she woke up.

"Do you want coffee or a coke, Elizabeth?" Stella thought that caffeine might help Elizabeth focus. She had limped into the hamburger place on her own and seemed a little better...not that she looked so hot. The bump on her head was still there and turning a lovely, eye-catching shade of purple. A pair of black eyes set the face off very nicely, if you liked Picasso.

Stella had already ordered two Big Macs for them and one order of fries to split. She had no idea if Elizabeth had cash with her. Spending her own carefully hoarded money, made the teen very nervous.

"I'll have coffee."

Elizabeth started for a booth in the corner but turned to go to the ladies' room. At this time in the afternoon the restaurant had very few people about. She returned, extremely agitated, as Stella sat down with the trey of food.

"I can't believe the way I look!" Elizabeth whispered. "My God! I look like someone beat me up! What is happening to me? I look terrible. I can't remember anything. Besides my name, I don't know who I am or where I am or what I'm doing here! Oh my God! What's happening to me?"

Putting her hands over her mouth, Elizabeth desperately looked around the rather empty room. Turning back to the table, tears flowing slowly down her cheeks, she looked at Stella, stared at her sadly for a minute or two, then reached out and covered her new friend's hand with her own.

"I don't know what to do, Stella. You are the only person in the entire world I know."

Stella paused in her chewing. Shit, she thought, this couldn't be for real. My big moment, my big get-away, two years in the planning, and I have to pick up a hitchhiker with no memory. This lady is twenty-nine. I saw her driver's license. I'm only sixteen. I don't even have a driver's license! I can hardly take care of me. How in hell am I going to take care of both of us? Shit!

By this time Elizabeth was having a real aquatic event, tears sliding and splashing into her uneaten burger, sobbing, moaning. She had had a bad day! A uniformed, curly-haired girl,

14

cleaning off tables, came over to ask if there was anything she could do. Stella told her they had received some bad news and maybe a glass of water would help.

Why do people always think a glass of water will help, thought Stella. It never helped me. But it was delivered and Elizabeth drank some, dipped her paper napkin into the water glass and wiped her face, over and over, as if she was washing all her bruises away. When she had recovered enough she looked sadly up at Stella with big, watery, red-rimmed, blue-green eyes. She was a colorful character, you had to give her that.

Desperately, Stella tried to figure out what to do. "Elizabeth, we have to decide on something to do for you. Maybe you should see a doctor here in Americus and let him help you. Or call a friend or someone in your family? Damn it, lady, you need more help than I can give you!"

"This sounds weird, I know," said Elizabeth, "but the only thing I feel sure about is I want to hide. I want to get away! Maybe it's this stupid amnesia, which I hope is temporary, but I don't want to go back or let anyone know where I am. If I recover my memory, maybe then; but right now, I just want to keep going!" Elizabeth sat with her elbows on the table, both hands cradling her chin. "I'm sorry, Stella, I don't think I'm being much help."

"Well, one of our problems is money," replied Stella. "I only have so much, and until I get a job it's got to last me. Check your purse, see if you have some?"

Elizabeth checked her wallet and found $54.32. "I have a check book but no idea how much is in there, and credit cards, but that would leave a trail wouldn't it? Oh God, listen to me, I sound like a crook!"

Rummaging around in her brown leather bag, which, of course, matched her shoes, Elizabeth froze! She looked around to see if anyone was watching, turned her body to face the wall of the booth, and with an astonished look on her face, furtively pulled out a thick, huge handful of money! Stella and Elizabeth looked at it and then each other!

"Oh my God! Where did this come from?" whispered Elizabeth.

"Jeez," said Stella. "I could have gotten two orders of fries!"

3

Elizabeth felt the blood drain from her face. Suddenly, she was dizzy and hot all over. Her left hand went up to shield one eye as she looked through her fingers at Stella.

"Do you think...um...does it seem ...eh...possible that...oh my God, Stella...do you think I could be...a bank robber?"

Stella, at sixteen, had not survived her last few years without learning important diversive tactics. After a few seconds of shocked silence she leaned across the table toward Elizabeth and said softly but firmly, "Put the money back in your purse, Elizabeth, put the strap over your shoulder. We gotta blow this pop stand. Follow me!"

Stella held the restaurant door open as her new friend limped through, then opened the car door as Elizabeth, in colorful zombie mode, sat down. Carefully backing out of her parking spot, Stella pulled out onto the road and peeled rubber!

For the next ten minutes nothing was said. Stella was trying to get on the route south. All she could think about was getting away from Americus and heading south. South seemed safe. Stella wanted to get the hell out of Georgia!

Elizabeth sat at attention in her seat, staring straight ahead, both feet flat on the floor and a death grip on the purse in her lap.

Stella finally spoke up, "Uh, Elizabeth...um...just how much money was in that envelope?"

"A lot."

"Well, can you give me a clue?"

"I don't know."

"Uh, maybe you could count it? There's no one here but us. Don't you want to know?"

"No."

"You want me to count it for you?"

"No, you're driving."

"Well, maybe it's not real money. Maybe it's just play money or counterfeit money."

"Now you're suggesting I'm a counterfeiter?"

"No, I'm not. I just think we need to know how much and what kind of money it is. Could it be you're a whiz at Monopoly?"

"I'm afraid!"   Elizabeth started to tear up again, melting against the seat back. "What if I am a bank robber or a counterfeiter or a murderer or a kidnapper? Maybe I'm a mob enforcer, and this is what I've collected and the mob is looking for me!"

"Let's not get carried away here, OK? I'm gonna pull off the road at the next shady spot and we'll take a look. We're safe. Hell, nobody knows where we are. We don't know where we are."

"Yes, we do." Elizabeth was sniffling and looked around. "We're in the middle of a pecan grove somewhere in south Georgia."

A late afternoon sun was shafting through the canopy of trees as Elizabeth managed a rueful smile at Stella. "You do it! I can't."

Stella took the purse out of Elizabeth's reluctant hands and slowly reached for the large, seemingly full, manila envelope. Reaching in she pulled out lots and lots of one hundred dollar bills. Swallowing hard and looking at Elizabeth, she reached in and pulled out more!

"I'll tell you this, Elizabeth, you're one hell of a bank robber!"

"No, no, don't say that! Don't even joke about it!....Is there any more?"

18

"Just this check looking thing…Holy shit!!!"

Stella passed the 'check looking thing' to Elizabeth. There, in her hands, was a cashier's check, in her name, for $2,990,000! Elizabeth leaned back on the car door and, in utter bewilderment, stared, wide-eyed at Stella.

"What have I done? Where did this come from? Who am I?"

"Well, Elizabeth, there's one thing for damn sure! You are either a very wealthy lady or an exceptional crook!"

Stella started to slowly count the money…all hundred-dollar bills…all crisp and new. Never having seen a one-hundred-dollar bill before, she had no idea if they were good or not. She put them in piles of ten. She ended with ten piles! Stella looked at Elizabeth who was watching her with a baleful look.

"There's ten thousand dollars here. …I guess…with the cashier's check…that rounds out to a nice even three million! I agree with you, Elizabeth. Who are you?"

4

Elizabeth and Stella sat for a long while, each one pondering this new situation. Finally Stella realized it was getting late and they had to get on down the road, preferably out of Georgia, to an airport to leave the car. That had been Stella's plan, and she was sticking with it. She figured Elizabeth was unaware that Stella had no driver's license, and she sure didn't want to get stopped with all that cash in the car. Since Elizabeth seemed to have no idea about anything, Stella just kept heading south.

They went through Albany and it started to rain, still not a word from the passenger side of the car. Stella wondered if they could use some of that money for a motel. Both could use a good night's sleep, especially Elizabeth. She had been in a bad accident that morning, and tomorrow she not only would feel very sore but her multi-colored face would probably look worse.

"Elizabeth...are you still here?"

"Don't ask me any questions. I don't have any answers." Elizabeth seemed a bit out of sorts.

"We need a place to spend the night," said Stella. "I can't make it to Florida, in this rain, before sundown. Do you think we can use some of that money for a motel? The sign we just passed said Camilla, Georgia, six miles."

"What if we use this money and it turns out to be counterfeit? We would both go to jail!" Elizabeth did not seem real excited about her money.

They were coming up on a convenience store/service station, and Stella swerved into the parking lot.

"Give me one of those bills and I'll check it out. I'm damn good at this sort of lyin'."

Stella jumped out of the car and ran into the store. Sodas, potato chips, chewing tobacco and other healthy snacks and smokes were stacked around on boxes. The place seemed to have everything but a broom.

"Hi, I wonder if you can help me?" Stella said with a big smile. "I want to buy two sodas, but every time we stop people tell me they can't break a hundred-dollar bill. This lady I baby-sat for gave it to me for helpin' with her sick baby, but I can't buy nothing with it. Ya think it might be counterfeit? It's the first one I've ever had, or ever seen for that matter, and I don't know how to tell."

The good old southern boy behind the counter reached out for it. "Lemme see that thang. They teach us here how to tell what ain't real cause they don't want to get took. Take it out of my pay for sure. Yeah, you see this here line righten ther? Tha's what makes it for sure it ain't a faker. Also, if it's crisp like this'un here, you know it's a good'un. Man! Don't seen many of these things 'round here. But I can't sell you two sodas, neither. Damn clean out my whole dern cash box givin' you change. Sorry 'bout that. You got to go to a big place to spend 'at kind of money, but it's a good'un!"

"OK, thanks." Stella was out the door and back in the car in seconds. Elizabeth, with her lips pressed together in apprehension, sat waiting.

"It's good! Elizabeth, it's good!"

Elizabeth just put her hand over her mouth and stared at Stella.

"We need a place to sleep, Elizabeth, and eat and shower and think about all of this. Can we use some of that money? My original plan was to sleep in the car the first night or so 'cause I don't have money to waste on sleepin'."

"I'm still afraid of it, but if we want a place for the night,

I guess that's the only thing to do."

Stella pulled into a chain motel and parked. She looked at Elizabeth. "You know, I've never checked into a motel before. To be perfectly frank, I've never stayed in a motel before. If you want me to check in you'll have to tell me how."

"Well, let me see." She pulled the visor mirror down. It was cracked in three places but reflective enough for her to groan and realize, visibly, she had not improved much since lunch. She gave Stella basic instructions and told her to pay cash for the room now so they could leave early in the morning.

After showering and having 'dinner' from the food machines in the hallway, they both felt a little better. This had been a hard day for both, emotionally and physically. Stella had finally, after years of planning, made her one-chance-in-a-lifetime escape from her terrible home situation. She had been driving about twelve hours with few stops.

Elizabeth had been in a bad automobile accident that morning, leaving her badly bruised, apprehensive and unable to remember her past. In her state, the three million dollars she had found was just something else to worry about.

They were finishing the last of their candy-bar dessert when Elizabeth came across the other envelope in her purse. It came from the same law firm as the money and cashier's check. This was already open but she could not remember what was in it. With a great feeling of trepidation, she read the friendly note from the attorney explaining, in simple terms, the contents of her deceased husband's will!

5

Dead silence! Elizabeth looked at Stella, tried to speak but couldn't get words out. "I, uh, um.... don't, um remember...

Stella laughed. "I'll say this for you, Elizabeth, you certainly make a fascinating travel companion. Now you find out you're a widow before you knew you were married! I don't know much, being only sixteen, but I think this amnesia thing is working very well for you. I've known you only for one day and it's been the most exciting, terrifying, exhausting, amazing, unbelievable, goddamned day of my life!"

Elizabeth's face took on a sad, woebegone expression. In a very small voice she whispered, "I don't remember being married."

"That doesn't surprise me in the least. If you can't remember where three million dollars came from, why the hell should you remember being married? But it might explain all that money and that check. Whata ya think?"

Elizabeth went and sat in the chair, putting one pillow in her lap and tucking her feet under another. Stella felt she was trying to build a little barrier between her and whatever else the letter had to say. Elizabeth read quietly. After a very long five minutes she looked up.

"It seems my husband, John Stuart Dandler III, died less than two weeks ago. His father, John Stuart Dandler Jr. died three months ago. His father left three million dollars to each of his four children and another three million each to their spouses, but the bulk of his estate went to my husband, his only son. When he died, two months later, it was all left to me, in trust, for our first-born son. If no son, then the estate is to be shared equally by all surviving members of the family."

Elizabeth took a deep breath. "He, the attorney, wants me to come in so he can meet with me. He says it is very complicated. I wonder if I went?"

Stella threw a leg over the side of her chair. "Of course you went. Hell yes, you went! When is that letter dated?"

"A week ago."

Stella snorted. "Where do you think you were going... besides south? I wonder what that attorney told you. I bet it had something to do with you drivin' somewhere before you came to that abrupt stop!"

"I have no idea. No idea! Ugh, why can't I remember anything? What if my memory never comes back and I don't know why I felt I had to leave? This makes me feel very insecure. If you can't remember being married and feel no anguish at finding out you are a widow, what kind of a person are you? It's scary!" Elizabeth looked over the pillow at her new, and at this point, only friend.

"Stella," continued Liz, "I know you had plans for your get-away, but I really would like it if you could stay with me while I try to figure it all out. So far, I don't know what I would have done if you had not come along in that rattletrap car. I'm frightened to be by myself. I'll pay you minimum wage, I'll handle all expenses and we'll pretend to be sisters or cousins or something..."

Stella shrieked, laughed out loud and waved her arms. "Yeah! Employment! Awesome! Thanks Lizzie. I would be thrilled to continue our journey of unplanned, amazing adventures. This is totally cooler than any soap opera I've ever seen. And it sure beats my great plan of going to Daytona and trying to get a job. Shit, Lizzie, I can't wait to see what happens next! Or maybe this is just how your life always is? Do ya think?"

"Lizzie? Lizzie? Now you're going to call me Lizzie?"

"Get real, Lizzie, sisters or cousins don't call each other

by four syllable names. You can call me Stell. OK Sis?"

"Oh God, I've created a monster. But if truth be told, I've only known you one day and I have found...well...I just feel comfortable with you. You don't scare me and right now I'm afraid of someone. I just don't know who. Or why."

Stella hopped up and went for Elizabeth's luggage. "Maybe some of the clothes you packed will help us figure out where you were going. I'll look through this suitcase and you look through that one."

Opening one of the suitcases, Stella was amazed, "Wow, great clothes, Liz! Do you really wear these things? Looks like an ad for a cruise line. It all feels so soft and such pretty colors. Oh, look...this scarf matches the colorful purples and greens of your face!"

Stella turned around to Elizabeth and was startled to see her standing by her suitcase, holding a white envelope, with an odd expression on her face.

"Oh shit! Now, what have you found? You OK, Elizabeth?"

"This looks like a letter from a law firm in Key West, Florida; and the name, Key West, sounds familiar for some reason."

"Are you going to open it up or just stand there hugging it? This might answer some of your questions. But you take your time, Lizzie, I'll just sit here and wait. So far, you haven't disappointed me. I just hope I don't lose my new job before I get paid!"

Elizabeth slowly took out the letter. She read it through, sat down, read it again and went and stared out the window.

Stella, not the most patient person, decided to wait this one out. She reached over the table and daintily reached for the last little bit of Elizabeth's Baby Ruth, like she had all the time in the world.

Elizabeth finally came back from the window, sat on the sofa, and said, "Well, now I know where I was going. Evidently, I had a grandmother, my mother's mother, who died recently and left me her house in Key West."

6

Trying to figure out Liz's past life was like putting together a giant puzzle. A big piece had just fallen into place. In the process of trying to regain her memory and figure out what to do, Elizabeth had learned of all these major events in one day. She had lost three people close to her and in doing so had inherited huge, financial gains.

All of these events had happened over the past six months, but Elizabeth was learning about them all at once. She could not recall these people in her past. It seemed overwhelming. It was overwhelming. They went to bed so exhausted they couldn't even talk about it. But at least they knew where they were going.

Stella felt a destination gave them a security of sorts. She felt safer with some sort of direction. This was so much more exciting than what she had planned. That had been a simple, survival plan; this could be a future. When Liz decided she did not need her any more, at least she would be in a wonderful place to begin her own new life. She had heard of Key West, the Island City. Who thought she would ever be going there? She had a little smile as she fell asleep.

Elizabeth lay in her bed thinking of her grandmother. She couldn't remember her or picture her but felt warm and comforted by trying. She must have liked her, she decided. I wonder what her house is like? Did I ever visit her there? Where was my mother? Was she there also? Elizabeth drifted off with a small happy feeling and a large number of questions.

"Oh shit!" Stella yelled as she jumped out of bed the following morning. "It's ten o'clock! How come we slept so late? Oh jeez! Get up Elizabeth! It's ten o'clock! Why is it so dark in here?" Stella was up, loudly pulling back curtains, letting in the morning sun.

Elizabeth turned over and glared at her roommate. "It's the blackout curtains, Stella, keep it down. If you want to pretend to be my sister you have to clean up that potty mouth. What's so bad about ten o'clock?"

"Who ever heard of blackout curtains without a war? That's not fair! I wanted to leave early so we could get rid of my car in Tallahassee. If my Dad finds me with that car I'll look worse than you! Hurry Elizabeth!"

"OK, we'll get down the road a bit before we have breakfast," said Liz, looking like she had no idea where to start.

"We'll get all the way to that goddamned Tallahassee airport before we have breakfast," Stella mumbled under her breath. She was not out of her precarious situation yet.

About two hours later they pulled into the airport. After unloading Elizabeth's perfectly matched luggage and the many cardboard boxes, mostly advertising beer or wine, that held Stella's worldly goods, the teen went to park the car in some obscure area. She had planned to leave the car at an airport so her father, if he found it, would think she had flown far away.

Walking back to Elizabeth she realized that, for the first time in years, the weight of her unfortunate life was now off her shoulders. She could totally relax and enjoy whatever came next. She knew a new life had begun and whatever it brought was going to be better than what she had left. Totally. Stella took a deep breath and smiled.

Elizabeth, on the other hand, was concerned about the multi-million dollar cashier's check she was still carrying around in her purse. She had slept with the purse in bed with her last night. Actually, it was nerve-racking, carrying around three million dollars. They needed to rent a car, but she did not want to use her credit cards. When Stella returned, Elizabeth had a cab waiting with all their stuff inside and was sitting in the front seat talking with the driver. Stella squished in the back seat and shared space with Liz's fancy luggage.

The taxi driver seemed a bit uneasy about all of Stella's boxes in his trunk until Elizabeth passed him a one-hundred dollar bill and asked to be taken to one of the largest banks in Tallahassee. He took them to an imposing façade on Monroe Street where she asked him to wait for her. Stella would wait with him. He seemed in a better mood.

Half an hour later, Elizabeth emerged with a relieved grimace of sorts. She had deposited her $2,990,000 into a checking account and had changed some of her hundreds into twenties. Now she felt relieved and had the feeling of getting on top of things, even if things were still all confused. At least, she was not casually toting a fortune around in her purse.

Oddly, she could remember everything she needed to function but people and events in her past were still a blank. She had the ability to open a checking account but she was unable to remember her husband. It was a very 'Alice in Wonderland' feeling.

Next, they went to the BMW dealership and again the taxi waited. After speaking with a salesperson, Elizabeth finally had the cab unloaded and paid the driver. He shook his head but seemed very happy as he leaned over and whispered, "I don't know what you two ladies is up to but I wish you good luck!"

Soon the two women were driving down College Avenue in a cream Mini Cooper convertible with the top down and Elizabeth driving. She slowed in front of a large pale yellow brick Georgian-style house. It seemed familiar. Had she attended FSU? Maybe she had lived in that sorority house. Maybe...maybe... maybe. She seemed to know where to find a nice hotel.

"Stella, I think we need a place to rest, relax, get organized, make plans. We need to regroup and think about what we're going to do. OK?"

"Suits me, Sis. You may not be able to remember your past but your present seems awesome to me. I like your taste, man, you got style!"

7

In their hotel room, with a balcony overlooking the pool, each woman lay sprawled on her own double bed. Elizabeth was exhausted. Stella was hungry.

"I'm starving! If I had a bathing suit we could have lunch by the pool and go swimming." Stella was not one to let opportunity pass. " I can see people eating down there in their swim suits, under umbrellas. Awesome! Did you bring a suit, Liz? Of course you brought a suit...and probably a matching cover-up, sun hat and clogs to go with it."

"I may have more than one, Stell. Borrow anything you want and go eat, swim, whatever. I'm going to take a nap. I'm not hungry. Just sign the room number on whatever you buy. And before you leave, could you pull the blackout curtains?" With that, Elizabeth turned over and was out.

Stella, amazed at Elizabeth's casual attitude about her beautiful clothes, was fifteen minutes later seated under an umbrella clad in a fabulous yellow, two-piece bikini with matching cover-up and cork clogs.

She ordered a tuna sandwich, as it was one of the few things on the menu she recognized. Also it cost the least and she did not want to waste Elizabeth's money. After all, how could you eat a Salade Nicoise if you didn't know what a nicoise was. This was a life Stella had only seen on television. Amazing! This may not be permanent but she would try to learn as much as possible so she wouldn't embarrass Liz. She wondered if that totally cool pool dude would teach her to swim.

Elizabeth slept till mid-afternoon and woke in a murky, dark room by herself. She was confused... was it daytime, nighttime, where was she? Sitting up, it took a while for it all to come back. She was still woozie when she heard the key in the lock and Stella walked in.

"How are you feeling, Liz? You OK?" Stella went to the windows and pulled back the blackout drapes. Light flooded in and Elizabeth lay back down, her arm over her eyes and moaned.

"Are you OK?' Stella asked again. "You haven't had more than a sweet roll and coffee all day. You need to eat something. Yesterday, I know you had to push to get here, but now you can rest and recover from all that bashing around you did to yourself in that car. Why don't you take a warm shower and I'll order room service for you? You can sit on the balcony and dine and rest at the same time."

Stella's teachers had always told her she was a quick learner, and she was proud of being able to throw out 'room service' and 'dine on the balcony' like she knew what she was talking about. (Who said soap operas weren't educational?) It might be a steep learning curve, but she was totally going to like her new job!

Half an hour later, Liz, wrapped in a terrycloth robe (compliments of the hotel) was seated on the shady balcony dining on vichyssoise, a small Caesar salad and hot tea with lemon. Stella realized this job might require her to learn a whole new language. Vichyssoise? What the hell was vichyssoise?

"Tomorrow I want to take you shopping, Stella, you need new clothes for your new 'position' and we both need to get our hair done and maybe a facial and a manicure. What do you think...maybe a pedicure? I can get heavier makeup to cover my bruises. I think staying here a few days and relaxing before we start south for Key West would be good for me. If I can get an appointment, I could see a doctor about my memory loss."

Stella jumped right on that. "I totally think you need to see a doctor. I'd feel better and I know you would. We could call first thing in the morning...and about all that shopping and hair and face and stuff...well, guess I'll just have to think about that, totally...duh."

Elizabeth laughed. "It's such a good feeling to feel so free. I just wish I knew what I felt free of. Maybe I don't want to know. We have money, we have a car and we have a place to go, so let's buy a map, plan our trip and act like we know what we're doing. When I start remembering, we may have to alter some things, but I was going to Key West before the accident so we might as well continue. What do you think, Sis?"

"Cool! Sounds like a plan to me and I love having a plan. 'Specially if it includes new clothes, new hair and all that other stuff. It's all amazing! I sure like being your sister, Liz!"

"Thanks, Stell. Night."

"Night." After a while, when Stella thought Liz was asleep, she sneaked out of bed and quietly opened a portion of the blackout curtain. She did not plan to miss any of tomorrow.

8

Stella was strolling around the shopping center, styling... new clothes...new hairdo, new shoes...new everything. Even underwear! Yeah, she was totally styling.

She and Liz had eaten breakfast early around the pool, and left for the mall to be there for the ten o'clock opening. Dancing around her shoulders now was her newly cut, dark brown hair. She loved it! It bounced when she walked.

Kevin, the hairdresser, had told her she had beautiful hair, good bone structure and absolutely gorgeous, gray-green eyes. Wow...her dad always told her she had ugly cat eyes. Kevin had even commented on her long, dark eyelashes. Maybe he just wanted a return customer, but Stella ate it up! No one had ever commented on her looks before, at least not positively. She would take what she could get. She felt a least two inches taller.

Liz looked better too. At the beauty salon she had her makeup done and bought the cover-up that covered the bruises. Stella had thought she was pretty but it had been hard to be sure when she had two black eyes and a purple bump on the forehead. Wispy bangs now covered her bump and her eyes looked so much better, still blue/green, but without the red, purple and black circles. Stella thought Liz looked like a model but she had more curves then models. People turned to look at her as they passed, but Liz never even noticed. Stella, on the other hand, did notice if they turned and looked back at her. It was a totally new experience and she was loving it. It was awesome!

They had also bought new cell phones and could now communicate if they were not together. Liz picked Stella up at the mall, after seeing the doctor at the walk-in-clinic, and they went back to the hotel. Knowing they looked better than yesterday, they went to the terrace lounge and ordered iced tea and lite-bites.

"The doctor could fine nothing wrong with me that needed immediate attention," Liz reported. "He thinks my memory will return but says nothing will speed it up. Some times familiar things, like people or places help, but not always. He wants me to go in for a full check-up when I get to Key West. My ankle was a minor sprain and is doing fine. So I guess I'm good to go."

"Cool," Stella commented. "You know that you are going to have to drive most of the time now, even if we take back roads. We should plan this trip in small pieces so you won't get too tired. Tallahassee is a long way from Key West. Florida is one hell of a long state when you stop and think about it."

Elizabeth was studying the map. "Let's take route 27 and see how far we can go. We can stop any time we want, but for some reason I'm anxious to get to Key West. I don't know why. Maybe I'll feel safe there. Maybe I'm excited about what kind of house my grandmother left me. I love old houses. Maybe it's a beat up old house we can fix up!"

"Ha!" laughed Stella. "Knowing your luck, it's probably a huge, elegant mansion on the beach with its own squad of hunky lifeguards! But anything will be an improvement for me. I'm excited about it too. I don't think I ever lived in a real house... without wheels."

The next morning, in their brand new sporty Mini Cooper, Liz and Stella were traveling down route 27 with the top down and radio blaring. They had discovered a decided difference in music preference. Stella was a big country music fan, and Liz preferred jazz and NPR News. They each had on visors and shades. Stella was dressed in a new pair of lime green short shorts and a pink tank top. Being able to work on her tan while traveling was, to Stella, awesome!

Liz could not believe the change in Stella. She just glowed. Everything was new and exciting for her. Liz realized Stella was smart but had not had many chances to experience the things that Liz just took for granted. And she was funny. Sometimes Liz felt she didn't mean to be funny, but she was.

Last night she had asked what vichyssoise was and refused to believe it was essentially potato soup! She had eaten potato soup all her life, she said, and it didn't taste like that, look like that or cost like that. Stella was always aware of the bottom line. Even after counting all that cash in Liz's purse, she still was not easy spending money. She had pinched pennies for too many years to suddenly become cavalier about it.

Liz was feeling wonderful and free even though there was still a dark veil over her past. She wondered how long she and her husband had been married. Had she loved him? How could you forget someone you loved? Had he loved her? She hoped the answers, when they came, were not going to be too awful. Getting to Key West before she remembered anything seemed like an important goal. Why she thought she would be safe there she wasn't sure, but she did. That, in itself, was a mystery.

9

They stopped around Leesburg for an early supper at a barbeque restaurant. Liz wasn't too sure about it but Stella was thrilled with the thought of barbeque. Inside, Stella ordered vichyssoise as a first course. The waitress, looking perplexed, said she was sure they did not have that on the menu. Then Stella, smiling serenely, ordered the pulled pork sandwich, slaw and fries. Liz, keeping a straight face, ordered the same. Both ordered sweet tea, the staple of the south.

Stopping at the next nice motel, they checked in and went for a swim before bed. Liz was still working on her sore muscles while Stella was practicing her new swimming technique. Liz went up to bed early but Stella stayed in the pool, swimming back and forth, from side to side where she could stand. She didn't feel quite ready for the deep end yet but she was determined. Whoever heard of anyone going to Key West who couldn't swim? I mean totally cool, it was not.

In Tallahassee, when she was buying her bathing suit, she could not make up her mind between the lime green bikini with pink polka dots or the chocolate bikini with baby blue polka dots. The clerk had said, "Land sakes, sweetie, you're going to Key West! You'll need both." She could see already that was true!

They started out the next morning in the rain. By ten, the sun was flirting through the clouds and it started to clear. Liz drove a while and then Stella spelled her for a bit. They decided, if stopped, Liz would say she was teaching her to drive on the highways. They did not know the driving or learning age in Florida; they were just hoping for the best.

Liz would get tired of driving after three or four hours. She still was not yet over her accident.

They decided to stop in Clewiston for the night. All around them were miles and miles of sugarcane fields and Mexican cantinas for the workers. The historic, colonial looking Clewiston Inn was the obvious place to stay. Dinner was served in its famous bar with the panoramic Everglades painting. Liz and Stella were amazed at the lifelike mural depicting the Everglades, with all the indigenous animals and birds, on all four walls. After dinner, they went for a short walk and then to bed. Stella was going to catch up on her sleep with this job. Liz couldn't keep her eyes open after nine o'clock.

The next morning, after one of those belt-busting, diet-be-damned, southern breakfasts of fresh orange juice, cheese biscuits with butter and marmalade, grits and gravy, two fried eggs, bacon or sausage and baked apples with heavy cream, they were off. Clewiston sat on the southern end of Lake Okeechobee and was a straight shot south, a little over a hundred miles or so, to the first of the Florida Keys.

It was a colorless day, overcast; and the scenery was monotonous, just miles and miles of sugarcane, as far as the eye could see. Liz was driving and Stella was staring out the window.

"What are you thinking about, Stell? Are you having second thoughts about leaving home?" Liz asked.

"Are you kidding me? I've never been so damned sure of anything in my life! I will never ever want to go back!" Stella turned to Liz. "My life was in an old, rusty trailer with a drunk for a father. My mother died of cancer four years ago. My father did not want a small child around so he farmed out my brother, Kirk, to his brother, Uncle Charlie, and his wife, Aunt Cindy. He was left with me and has been yelling at me, slapping me around, blaming me for everything...not enough money, his getting drunk, the leaky roof. Even my good grades made him furious. He was constantly on me. Nothing I did was ever right. He was

42

getting more paranoid by the day. It got to the point that he felt the government was always watching him, waiting to pounce for unexplained reasons. He always kept a loaded shotgun by his bed. And he was getting more physically abusive as I got older."

Stella went on. "He had been telling me for some time that the day I turn sixteen he was yanking me out of school and putting me to work in the factory. I needed to start paying my way, he told me...wanted me to start paying him rent, buying food, putting more time into keeping house for him. He told me that was what girls were suppose to do."

"That is terrible!" Liz shook her head. "I just can't imagine! How did you manage to get away?"

Taking a deep breath, Stella stared out the window. "I had an English teacher, Mrs. Peterson, who always told me I was smart and I should try to get a scholarship to college. One day I met with her and had to explain that instead of college, my Dad was going to make me quit school at sixteen. I told her I was planning to leave home, get a job somewhere, get my GED and try to get into a junior college."

"She thought I was too young to go out on my own", continued Stella, "but realized that staying in a physically dangerous home without going to school, was no good either. She couldn't take me in 'cause my father wouldn't have stood for it. To help all she could to prepare me for leaving, she taught me what she called basic life skills...proper English, table manners, etiquette, how to handle money, how to dress for an interview. She even told me to watch soap operas and notice manners, how people spoke, and emulate them. She wrote me a letter of recommendation, telling about my good grades, my perseverance, my positive attitude and my determation to improve my unfortunate life situation." Stella laughed. "That was sure true!

"When the time came, she gave me ten twenty-dollar bills to put with my small savings and asked me to write or call collect to keep her informed. I hated leaving my little brother, Kirk, but I knew his situation was not nearly as awful as mine. Uncle Charlie wasn't a bad guy, not great, but he never hit him or anything and Aunt Cindy was OK. She was a tad overweight, but she laughed a lot. I promised Kirk I would come back for him as soon as I could and we would make our own family. Mrs. Peterson would never believe my good luck! I can't believe it!"

"You can send her a post card from Key West," Liz said, smiling. "I'm sure glad you picked me up off the side of the road, Stell; we'll just keep on going south and see what happens. Maybe we saved each other. Who knows?"

10

"Wow, Liz, look at that sign...Key Largo...the first key... awesome! I can't believe we are finally here. I'm so excited I think I'm going to expire!" Stella sat back with her hand over her heart. They had been traveling the last twenty miles through the bottom of the Everglades, past signs that cautioned 'crocodile crossing', past turquoise-painted traffic barriers and were now only one hundred miles from Key West.

Liz laughed. "I'm excited too. I feel like this is the start of my new life...this is the right thing for me to be doing... speeding down a highway that goes straight out to sea! Stella, it is awesome! I agree with you. Totally!"

They laughed and joked as they went. Over bridges, over islands, US 1 was a serendipitous string of exotic sights.

"Look at that water! What a gorgeous color!"

"Look at that cute guy in the surfer shorts! Hot!"

"Ah, Tea Table Bridge. Isn't that a cute name?"

"Catch the dude in the convertible! Can you get closer to his car?"

"Oh my gosh, look at those beautiful boats out there."

"Did you see that girl? She was totally falling out of her bikini!"

"Well, I guess we know where your interest lies. Come on, Stell, look at this fabulous scenery."

"I am looking at the fabulous scenery. Wow! They don't make boys like this in North Georgia! Shit, Liz, that guy looked like Brad Pitt!"

"Watch it, Sis. That word is not going to Key West with us. I mean it. Wow works just fine. In fact, I'm totally cool with wow."

"I don't know, Liz. These are some serious hunks and they demand some serious language. I mean, really, awesome doesn't cover everything you know. Look, look, he's waving...act cool, pretend you don't see him!"

Brown pelicans sat around on piers and dived into the water. The air smelled salty. Liz started getting that familiar feeling again. Was it the salty scent of the ocean? The further they went, the more certain she was that this was not her first trip down this chain of islands...Islamorada, Matecumbe, Duck Key.

An hour of so later, they were leaving Marathon and driving onto the Seven Mile Bridge with an end so far away you couldn't see it. Off to the side of the bridge was a tiny island called Pigeon Key with a small group of old yellow houses. It was all so new, so different, so utterly amazing, Stella could not sit still! But Liz had a homing feeling and was anxious to get to Key West. On Big Pine Key they slowed down to the forty-five MPH speed limit for the safety of endangered Key Deer.

They passed Summerland Key, then Sugarloaf, and stopped for lunch at Mangrove Mama's, tucked in at the side of the road. This turned out to be a very casual restaurant with most tables outside in the shade of palms and banana plants. In the center of the tables along with the condiments were little cans of mosquito spray...just in case. The fresh grouper sandwich was delicious...and conch fritters to dip in two different sauces. They were in the lower keys now and really could experience the salty tang of the sea breeze as it wafted through the mangroves.

Finally they were passing Boca Chica with the Naval Air Station on the left with fighter jets practicing their landings. Liz was getting a breathless feeling. They crossed over the final bridge and a sign greeted them, 'Welcome to Key West!'

At last, thought Liz. Stella was whooping and waving her arms but Liz just felt relief. Finally, they were here. The road split to the left and right and Liz went left...around Roosevelt Boulevard, where the ocean lapped against the seawall, then past an old brick Civil War fort. It was while passing Smathers' Beach that Stella got really excited.

"I think I've died and gone to Heaven. This is totally amazing! When can we come back here? Liz, I mean it! Look at all those people playing volleyball in the sand. Can we stop and just look? I've never seen anything like this before."

"Not now, Stella, we have to get settled first. When I called the attorney yesterday, his secretary said reservations had been made for us at the La Concha hotel on Duval Street. She said it was close to his office. We meet with him at four o'clock this afternoon. I promise, after we know what we are doing, we'll go to the beach, OK? That beach isn't going anywhere. Look for Duval Street on the map. Why do I feel like I know where to go? Am I going the right way?"

"Yep, the next street over is Duval. I can't believe all the beautiful old houses. Jeez, look at that one...it's pale pink with green shutters! Awesome! I hope ours is pink. Pink is cool! Look at all the fancy woodwork on the porches and the huge trees with flowers. And look, there's 'Cheeseburgers in Paradise'! Oh my God...this island is totally awesome!"

Liz pulled off Duval Street and under the porte-cochere of the La Concha Hotel. At seven stories high, it was the only tall building in Key West. After checking in, Liz needed to take a nap. Stella, of course, had to check out the pool deck, lobby, dining room and 'The Top' lounge, which had an unbelievable, seventh-story view of the entire island city. She had to bring Liz up here...what a panorama!

Liz was nervous about the upcoming meeting. Would she find out more about herself? Would she really own a house here on the island? Would her memory come back when she saw it? Who was her grandmother and who, for that matter, was she?

"Do you want to go alone?" Stella asked. She knew that sister stuff was only for fun.

"No, I appreciate the thought but I might need moral support. After all, you're still the only person I know. I feel like we're in this together for good or for bad, but I'll tell you Stella, the suspense is killing me!"

11

Liz and Stella walked around the corner of Duval and Eaton Streets past the beautiful, old St Paul's Episcopal Church, and down the street to the law firm. The attorney's office was in a beautifully restored, two-story, gingerbread house. They entered a very traditional looking living room with Oriental rugs and camel-back sofas. There was an empty desk by the window and an open doorway.

"That you Elizabeth? Come on in. I let my secretary go at four so we have all the time in the world!"

Liz froze! Somebody knew her! Her face got a funny look; was she going to cry or expire? "He knows me!"

Stella put her arm around Liz. "It's OK. He sounds friendly. Let's just walk in calmly and sit down and..."

A short, plump gray-haired man came barreling out of his office. "Jesus, Joseph and Abraham! It's been a while. Look at you! A beautiful young lady! By Jove, you look like your mother... those same turquoise eyes. She was a looker! But, then, so was your grandmother. I was in love with both of them but one was too old for me and one was too young."

Winslow Morganstern bustled about and ushered both ladies into his office. "And who might you be young lady...a friend, or relative...?

"Hi, I'm Stella Ashcroft, a friend of Liz's."

"And as I was saying, your granny was a peach. She and

49

I were friends most all my life and I've always handled her legal needs. We were buddies. When my wife died, she and your grandfather, Carl, just took me over and we became a threesome. Then when Carl died, Edie and I, we were a twosome. Had some fun times, I can tell you that, no hanky-panky through!"

Liz sat spellbound, unable to say a word.

" I remember your mother used to dress you in turquoise all the time. Said it was your special color. I see you are still wearing it."

"Um, huh, Mr. Morganstern…"

"Mr. Morganstern! What's this Mr. Morganstern business? You always called me Uncle Winnie."

"OK…Uncle Winnie. I have to tell you right up front that I have amnesia and don't remember you, or my mother or my grandmother. Stella is the only person I know and I just met her a few days ago. I wrecked my car, hit my head and woke up on the side of the road with no memory. Stella picked me up and later we found your letter about my grandmother's house and here we are."

Of course, Uncle Winnie had a lot of questions for both Liz and Stella. Being an attorney and old family friend, he delved deep and finally got the whole story except the amount of money Liz had inherited. He didn't ask. He wanted to make sure Liz was going to see a doctor soon. It had been a week since the accident. He got up and fixed himself a whiskey and water, serving Cokes to Liz and Stella.

"We will let all that go for now and I'll tell you about your grandmother's property. It's really a nice, large sized property for the island. Key West homes were built in the eighteen hundreds when everyone walked, so small properties are the norm. Two and three story homes are built here within feet of each other but with plantings of bamboo and tropical trees, they are very private. It's also what makes Key West feel so cool and shady."

Uncle Winnie opened a drawer and took out a large map of the island. "I have marked Edie's property in yellow. You can see it's four lots that go from Southard Street through to Gumbo

Limbo Lane. That is why it's considered a large piece of property. There is a little house, behind the big house, that faces the lane and that is, also, part of Edie's property. In Key West there are lots of little lanes that go into the interior of the bigger blocks. Usually the smaller homes are built on the lanes but they do not often belong with the big houses built on the streets."

He explained further that Edie had been living in the little house and had the larger house rented. The two houses shared a large, tropical garden with indigenous trees and a small swimming pool. He thought Liz might want to live in the small house for a while until she got her life figured out. He explained that after Carl died, Edie had the cottage redone, specifically for her, and moved out there.

"It's a bit modern for my taste, but then Edie was always one for adventure and change. She loved to travel, so a smaller home was preferable to the larger; and she liked getting the rent money. I have already called Earl and made the appointment to see the entire property tomorrow at ten. He's the tenant and takes great interest in the history and upkeep of the home."

"Can you tell me about my grandmother or my mother or somebody in my family?" asked Liz. " I can't recall any of them."

"I'll tell you a bit…it might help you remember. Your mother, your grandmother and your great-grandparents were 'Conchs'. They were born here in families that originally came from the Bahamas, particularly the Abacos where they had been part of the English Loyalist group after the Revolutionary War. Many of them emigrated to Key West in the early eighteen hundreds and settled the island. Your great-grandfather was an attorney from Candor, New York and was in Key West, during the Spanish-American War, when he met your great-grandmother. Your history goes way back on this island. I'm sure it will start coming to you. I'll help all I can."

"Tell me about my mother." Said Liz, looking very unsure and worried. "It's all very strange…I can't remember anything about myself…how can I forget my own mother! I feel so stupid."

Uncle Winnie reached across his desk and took Elizabeth's hand. " Don't worry about anything, Lizzie girl, you're home now. You're safe. And about your mother…she was beautiful…she was

51

happy…and she absolutely adored you. She was a golden girl…full of fun and swirling blond curls."

"She met your father while she was home from college for Christmas at a Midshipman's Ball, given for seniors of the Naval Academy here on their winter cruise. When she met your father, Lt. Paul Collins, from Philadelphia, that was that…talk about falling in love! Six months later they were married in the Old Stone Church. I was there and it was a wonderful wedding. They walked out of the church, under crossed swords, the happiest couple of the world.

"Your father made a career of the navy," continued Uncle Winnie, "and part of the time was stationed here. This is where you were born…in the naval hospital. But he was stationed in San Diego when he became ill with cancer. Edie would go out to help your mother, I think you were about eight, but your Dad never recovered and died about a year later. Your mother came back here with you, to live with your grandmother Edie and grandfather Paul. You may not remember it, but this is your home.

"You lived here in the big house with your mother and grandparents until your mother died, also of cancer…but hers was very fast. Less than four months after she was diagnosed she was gone. You were around sixteen and continued to live with your grandparents until you went to college. Your grandmother and you were very close, very creative and often worked in the garden together. That is why it looks so good today."

12

Uncle Winnie picked Liz and Stella up in front of the hotel the following morning. It was a short ride to the property. Everything in Key West was a short ride, as the island was only three and a half miles long and a mile wide. Finding a parking place was a primary concern anywhere you went, but this house came with on-site parking for four cars.

The house looked big, but tucked behind a huge, old, sapodilla tree and palms, it was hard to tell. A large porch ran across the front filled with white wicker, colorful cushions and green, lacy ferns. Liz noticed the porch ceiling was painted a pale aqua. As they climbed the front steps the front door flew open and a tall, gray haired man emerged, attired in white Bermuda shorts, blue linen shirt and leather thong sandals.

"Oh my goodness, it is so good to meet you, Elizabeth!" He took her hand in both of his. " I don't feel like I even need an introduction. You are the spitting image of your grandmother...a bit younger of course, but those same beautiful eyes and that golden hair! Do come in, come in and see this absolutely divine house you have inherited. I understand you used to live here?"

"I guess I did?" Liz looked at Uncle Winnie for confirmation.

"Yes you did, when you were about nine or ten, after your father died. You and your mother came back to live in her family home." Uncle Winnie turned to Earl. "I didn't get a chance to tell you, Earl, but Lizzie is suffering with amnesia, caused by an automobile accident."

"Key West is a blank for me," said Liz. "The only thing that seems familiar so far is the aqua ceiling on the front porch. I felt like I'd seen it before. But so far...well, maybe something else will hit me as we walk around. I love this porch! It's just fabulous...has a very happy feeling."

"My dear, don't you worry about a thing. I'm sure your memories will all come tumbling back. Phillip and I have changed things quite a bit since you were here. You will meet Phillip in the kitchen. He is the chef in the family and he's preparing the most scrumptious luncheon for us."

"Earl, I don't believe you met Liz's friend, Stella." Uncle Winnie introduced them as they walked around looking at the house. Liz would stop and stare or touch certain things, like the banister rail, as she moved through the rooms. She looked rather perplexed and obviously was trying very hard to find something that would jog her memory.

"It is a beautiful home, Earl, and I can see that you take wonderful care of it. Perhaps if I could see my old room. Do you remember which one it was, Uncle Winnie? "

"Oh yes, the one overlooking the back yard. It has a little balcony with French doors and a big royal poinciana tree right outside. Earl and I will go join Phillip in the kitchen. You and Stella go look around upstairs. Take your time. Maybe Earl and I can talk Phillip into a Planter's Punch."

Stella thought this was the most beautiful house she had ever seen, but she knew her experience was limited. Liz, she could tell, was distressed to know she had actually lived here but could not remember any of it.

Upstairs, Liz slowly walked around her old bedroom and then out to the balcony standing for a while gazing at a tree. Suddenly she whispered to Stella. "Stell, I think I remember that tree. I used to climb up there sometimes." Liz sat down on the deck of the balcony, still staring at the tree, tears starting to flow slowly down her cheeks. "I remember, oh Stella, I do remember!

I used to throw pillows from my bed on this deck and lie here in the shade and read. And in the spring the poinciana would be a mass of orange flowers, like big bouquets of little orange orchids, and I would break off whole bunches of them for my room. Oh my god! I am so excited!"

Stella sat down next to Liz and passed her a tissue from her pocket. "I'm glad for you, Liz, in fact, I'll just adopt your life. It's the best life I could ever dream of but you can't remember it and my life wasn't worth shit but I can't forget it. I guess that is what Mrs. Peterson called irony."

"Stell, could you rephrase that?"

"Sorry," Stella answered laughing, " but this house just boggles the mind!"

They walked around the bedrooms, each opening onto a balcony or the upstairs porch, which was located over the first floor porch. The house was larger than she had originally thought and after another visit to her old balcony, Liz and Stella went down for lunch and to meet Phillip.

"Wow!" said Stella, staring at the hunk stirring something on the range.

"Don't get too excited," replied Liz under her breath. " He may prefer a different menu."

" I know, but you have to admit cute is cute!" Stella sighed. "And he is totally awesome!"

13

It turned out Phillip really was a chef...executive chef at Louie's Backyard, a well-known restaurant on the ocean side of the island. Earl said he practiced all his new dishes on him. "You absolutely never know what he will serve and I love the mystery as long as it doesn't kill me!"

Today Phillip was serving something with Florida lobster, it was served over a bed of browned seaweed with caramelized onion slices and avocado. Phillip was cute but also very serious about his food. He was writing a cookbook on island cooking and did not share his recipes.

Liz did not want to dawdle over lunch, and Earl seemed to sense this. After a delicious dessert of guava duff with a creamy butter-sugar sauce, they went out to the back terrace.

"This is the neat part of the living arrangement here." Earl explained, gesturing to the garden. "Few yards in Key West have much space, but this is a quadruple lot; both the guest house and the big house share the garden, the pool and the fruit trees. Privacy has been planted in, but it's still an open feel to the space. Edie was very particular about her renters. She had to get to know you before she'd even consider renting to you. I feel privileged to live here. There is a sense of history and obligation about residing in an old house...even if you don't own it."

Liz looked around in amazement. You could not see one house! They had all been landscaped away with tall bamboo, palms, old tropical trees and lush under-planting. Had it been this way when she lived here? She couldn't remember helping her grandmother plant the garden.

Liz, Stella, Uncle Winnie and Earl strolled through the tropical paradise.

"I always felt cool back here," Uncle Winnie commented. "Any little breeze is captured by the big leaves, and the soft sounds of leaves moving and bamboo clicking is very soothing."

There was the pool...a lap pool, under a huge sea grape tree. And there was the other house, one story and painted a dark, leaf green with mahogany shutters. Because of the color and the plants you hardly saw it as it blended into the landscape. What an unusual idea, Liz thought. This place just keeps getting better and better.

Earl led them inside the cottage. Liz was mesmerized. "This is just fabulous!" She exclaimed, looking around in awe.

Earl gestured, "It's all ready for you to move in. The maid came yesterday to refresh the place and I've done a little stocking of the fridge and pantry. It is all yours, literally. If you're OK here, Win and I will leave you two and go back to work. When you're ready to pick up your things at the hotel let Phil know and he'll run you back. Call us if you need anything. Welcome home, Liz!"

Liz and Stella stood in the middle of an open, white, modern home and looked at each other. "Well, I tell you what Lizzie," said Stell, amazed! "You hit another one out of the ballpark. This place is to die for! It is awesome! Kinda reminds me of my trailer."

"Can you believe it?" Liz kept turning around and around. The little house was a gem, everything was white. The soft looking, linen sofas were white, the rattan chairs had plump, white linen cushions and on the white walls hung large, brilliant abstract paintings. The white tile floor had a big, sisal rug between the two sofas and sitting on the rug was a four-foot square, glass and chrome coffee table filled with bright flowers, large books and a gorgeous piece of white coral. A skylight was located directly over the table.

The dining-library area had a whole wall of book-filled

shelves with bamboo chairs surrounding a round, glass-topped table. Floor-to-ceiling windows filled another wall, bringing in the garden. It was breathtaking.

The kitchen was all white...white Corian counters, white cabinets and chrome appliances. Over the kitchen counter was a large panel of glass that overlooked the garden, the pool and a private terrace. The house had one large bedroom and bath off one side of the great room and two small bedrooms with connecting bath off the other side.

"This is perfect. Amazing! I mean, totally the coolest!" Stella yelled from one of the smaller bedrooms, "Which bedroom do you want me to have? Or are we still in business together?"

"Take which ever one you want, Stella, and yes, we are still in business together."

Liz was looking around her bedroom. All white with a touch of the palest blue in pillows and a soft, pale blue rug on the white tile floor. Over the bed was a stunning, large watercolor of blue flowers with dewdrops on the petals. Someone had placed on the bedside table a small bouquet of blue plumbago in a cut glass vase. There was also a silver framed photograph of a smiling, blond lady holding a small child in her arms. Instinctively she knew this was her mother holding her. This had been her grandmother's room...she was the one who kept the picture here.

14

Liz and Stella walked out the front door of their little house that faced Gumbo Limbo Lane. It was a tidy little porch with rockers and blooming vines winding through the carved wooden railing. The ceiling of the porch was painted the pale aqua hue of all island porch ceilings. The shady lane was lined with little homes that looked similar to theirs...some with white picket fences, some with hedges, not all in perfect condition. Lots of bicycles were chained to fences and multi-hued cats napped in shady locations. Chickens, in beautiful shades of iridescent orange and black, made occasional appearances and then were lost in the foliage.

Many of the homes were painted pastel colors with white trim. It was a surprise to find that from the lane, their house was a very pale shell pink that blended with the other white or pastel homes. This lane went to the middle of the block and stopped at the smooth, gray, multi-trunk of a very old, very large Spanish lime tree.

Liz and Stella were charmed with the lane and amazed at how their house was painted to blend with both settings. From the lane you could only see pale pink. Wherever it changed, was disguised with large plants and trellises. They were both glad they lived here rather than the big, more formal house. This was perfect for two women. They would have to get bikes, though, as it obviously was the preferred means of transport on the island. And Stella was anxious to get to the beach.

They retrieved their luggage from the La Concha and moved into their little pink cottage on Gumbo Limbo Lane. Liz was going to take a nap. Stella couldn't wait to unpack and put her new things in her new drawers. She had never had her own room before. She could wait for a while, but she was going to have to do a little redecorating. She needed to add some color to the white of her room. What was wrong with a little pink and lime green? Maybe mango walls and white trim would be cool. Or, to be really cool...maybe she could paint each wall a different color!

That evening they walked down the lane, met some of their new neighbors and walked around the block on sidewalks cracked and broken from the roots of nearby, ancient trees. They could smell spicy Cuban cooking odors, garlic and black beans and hear Spanish being spoken behind hedges and walls. Liz was trying to get the feeling of the area and looking for memories. Key West, in the very late afternoon, with long shadows and cool breezes, mixing the delicious cooking odors with exotic scents of opening, night blooming flowers, was enchanting.

"This is just too perfect, Stella...too perfect...I keep waiting for something awful to happen. I just can't relax yet. I need to find out about my former life, maybe hire a private detective. I'll talk to Uncle Winnie about it. I also need to see a good doctor here and get a check-up. Maybe you need one too. When was the last time you went in for a check-up and a dentist? And we need to check into schooling. Get back to real life."

"But what about my job? I need to be here with you to be your assistant."

"I want my assistant to be healthy, educated and sixteen. You will still be here with me. We are family now. It seems everyone I was related to died. We can depend on each other so don't worry about your job. You're doing it." Liz gave Stell a hug.

The next morning Liz was fixing breakfast in her new kitchen when she heard splashing in the pool. It looked like a man swimming laps...back and forth. Who was he? Neither

Earl nor Phillip had black hair and she could not figure out..."Oh my God! Stella, come here! There's a naked man in our pool! Look! He's swimming back and forth. Oh my goodness! Now he's getting out and...oh my God...now he's toweling off like he owns the place! Maybe I should call the police!"

Stella was staring and giggling. "Man, this is great! Don't call the police, Liz, he may be a friend of Phillip's. Wow! He doesn't know we're here and I have to say he is amazing, totally... um...cool. He's not naked either...he has on a watch. See, he just checked it. Maybe he does this every morning...wouldn't that be awesome! Don't let him see us. We don't want to scare him away."

"Well, he does have a great body and is fairly good-looking, but we don't need this every morning. Besides, you're only sixteen. We are not going to live next to an X-rated swimming pool! I prefer to drink my coffee in peace."

Stella was whispering, "Ha! Look at you! You can't take your eyes off of him. He may be too old for me but he sure looks perfect for you. Why don't you go out there and ask him in for coffee...or you could take it out to him. Yeah, that's a better idea...take him a cup of coffee and find out who he is!"

The mystery man had by now donned a pair of gym shorts and strolled out of sight toward the big house. Liz and Stella kept staring at the pool. "I'll have to ask Earl if it's one of their friends. He can keep his pants on next time."

"Ah Lizzie, don't be a spoil sport. You wanted to get back to real life, what is more real than that! I mean totally!"

15

Liz and Stella took their coffee out to the front porch and sat in the rockers. The little alley was a quiet microcosm of island life, moving in slow motion.

They had been told a ninety-five-year-old-women lived by herself across the lane behind masses of tropical leaves and flowers. She sat on her porch now but you could hardly see her. Earl had explained that everyone called her 'Aunt Norma', and Meals on Wheels came by each day around noon. She had been a friend of Edie's, and the people of the lane checked up on her often. She had her Master's Degree in music and the gingerbread trim on her porch columns was in the shape of violins. Evidently, she would still teach, for free, anyone who wanted to learn to play the violin.

"We've got a lot to do, Stell. First, I'll go up to the house and ask if Tarzan is a regular morning event or just the welcoming committee. I'll get the name of a doctor for me, and you. I need to talk to Uncle Winnie about finding out about my past. And we need to check on the schools...see what paperwork you need to get in. And maybe we need to see about getting bicycles. Every one of these houses has a bike in sight except Aunt Norma's."

"She probably zips around on a motorized wheelchair. I bet she's a character. She's over there right now trying to figure us out." Stella was intrigued. "See, she has on a bright yellow blouse and a yellow sun visor. You can see her through the leaves."

An hour later, Liz was slowly walking through the garden. If she remembered the poinciana tree maybe she would remember climbing some of these. Maybe she had had a swing when she was young.

As she approached the terrace she stopped..."Oh my God!" There sat Tarzan, as big as you please, in gym shorts, reading the newspaper, his towel draped over one shoulder.

"Hello there." He put down his paper, smiling at her in a questioning way. "Taking a tour of the garden?"

Liz had turned pink all over. He obviously had no idea he had had an audience this morning. He kept looking at her.

"You look a lot like Edie's granddaughter Lizzie."

"Yes."

There was a long pause. "I remember you. Are you living in the cottage now?"

"Yes." Liz seemed to have lost the ability to speak. She had no idea what her husband had looked like but this man was very appealing. Evidently, she had not noticed much about his face this morning. He had a stubble of beard on tanned, rugged features and a great smile which was changing rapidly into an expression of chagrin.

"Oh...well... I think I get the picture now...let me apologize. I had no idea the cottage was occupied. That will not happen again. I'm Steven Sandford, and I knew your grandmother. She was a lovely, fascinating woman. We will all miss her."

"Thank you, but I don't remember her at all. I was in an automobile accident last week and have amnesia. I can't remember any of my past, people or places. I'm hoping being here will help trigger some memories. Uncle Winnie says I used to live here but so far, nothing...except that poinciana tree. Of course I don't remember Uncle Winnie either. Should I remember you?"

" I can't think that you should. We may have played together as children, briefly. My father was a Navy doctor and your father was a Navy Commander, and they were stationed here at the same time. I think your parents met in Key West

66

and married here. Most of my information came from Edie who served as a second mother to me when my parents were transferred to Japan. My senior year was just beginning and she let me live with her. I always appreciated that...made a big difference in my life. You and your mother came at the end of my senior year. You were about nine or ten and I was a very busy guy of eighteen so we didn't have much in common. Soon after you arrived, I left for college."

"I appreciate you telling me about my family. Nothing is ringing a bell but the more I know the better I will be. It's awful, living in a kind of vacuum, trying to get out."

"Have you seen a doctor?"

"Only a walk-in-clinic doctor. He said I needed to get a full check-up when I got to Key West."

"Let me make you an appointment with my doctor. He's good with head problems. I've had a few since I got here, even a bit of amnesia; but I feel I'm getting better."

"Were you in an accident too?" Liz was just noticing scars along his right arm as his towel slipped off his shoulder

"Well, I guess you could call it an accident, but it's a long story. Are you staying in the cottage alone?"

"I have a sixteen year old girl with me. She picked me up from the side of the road after the accident, and we have been together ever since. As crazy as it sounds, she is the only person I know. I can't even remember my mother."

"I'm sorry to hear that. I'd like to know more about your amnesia. Maybe you and your friend could have dinner with me tonight? I'm staying here, and Earl says there is a new restaurant just down the street. We can walk over."

"That sounds wonderful."

"Should we meet here on the porch at six?"

"That would be great...you're being very nice so...I won't tell you my friend was in our kitchen this morning too!" Liz was smiling as she walked away.

16

Steve, Liz and Stella met on the terrace of the big house. They walked down quaint streets lined with old houses built in the graceful, Queen Anne style so prevalent on the island, to Michael's. The food, especially the seafood, was good and locals were always in attendance. Locals often were people not from Key West originally, but lived on the island while they wrote their books, plays or rested between openings. Quite a few famous people kept a home on the island for winter retreats. Key Westers were used to well-known people and treated them as normal. 'You write, I sell condos, so'...seemed to be the general philosophy.

They were dining in the courtyard, under an old banyan tree. It seemed such a romantic setting and Liz was noticing the beauty of the island because she was trying so hard to see something she remembered. Steve and Liz ordered white wine. Stella, never one to be outdone, ordered ginger ale served in a wine glass.

Stephen was explaining his relationship with her grandmother and the house. He had graduated from Key West High School while his parents were still in Japan. Edie had told him as he left for college that the small back bedroom would always be his, that he could come back any time and feel like it was his home.

"She was the sweetest lady. When she moved to the cottage, she told me the bedroom was still mine, and her renters had to agree to that before she'd sign the lease. Phil's fine with that but Earl has more of a Lord of the Manor complex. He wanted to buy the whole piece of property from Edie, but she wouldn't sell. She always said it was for her granddaughter."

"Are you in Key West very often?" Liz asked.

"In recent years, I've been here only once or twice but lately, I've been here more. I got in late last night and did not know you had arrived. Earl should have put a note on my bed to warn me. I think Earl likes to pretend I don't exist." Steve laughed.

"I think you'd be rather hard to miss." Stella said with a grin. "Do you swim every morning when you're here? Is the water cold in the morning? How many laps do you swim?"

"Well, in order of your questions...yes, just cool and about thirty or forty. I've found doing laps helps my muscles stretch and my head to clear. In fact, I recommend it for everything. Maybe it will help your memory return, Elizabeth."

"Maybe. I'll try it. The setting under that huge sea grape tree is so inviting. That whole garden is just delightful. The more you walk around in it the more you realize all the thought and knowledge that it took to get this casual result."

"Your grandmother designed it all herself. The large trees had to bear fruit or flower and plants had to have beautiful large leaves. The exception was the gumbo limbo. That was her favorite tree, so she loved living on Gumbo Limbo Lane. Did you notice that little house has two color schemes...one for the lane and one for the garden? She wanted to blend in with the houses on Gumbo Limbo but did not want a pink garden house. I think she solved her problem very well. You can hardly find where the colors change."

"She has lots of unusual palms too," Stella added

"Yes, she has some very rare and exotic palms, and it's all laid out for privacy. She had a gift. But I have to ask you a question, Liz, now that you are the new owner. Do I get to keep my room for a little longer?"

Liz laughed, "Now I know why you asked us out for dinner. Right now, while my memory is on vacation, I plan to keep everything like it is... with the exception of a new rule for bathing attire!"

"I will be most happy to acquiesce to the new rule," Steve replied. "Thanks Elizabeth."

Stella asked. "If I'm out there tomorrow when you finish your laps, Steve, will you give me a swimming lesson? It is totally embarrassing to live in Key West and not know how to swim. I know all the cool kids know how to swim." Stella grinned at Liz. "And I, too, will wear a bathing suit."

"Why don't you come too, Elizabeth?" asked Steve. "I'm doing it because my doctor recommends it for post traumatic stress syndrome. He feels slow, repetitious laps help you into a Zen-like mental state and clears out a lot of stuff that's clogging the mind. It really might help you recall things."

"Does it help to forget things?" asked Stella. "I'll have to try it. By the way, Steve, you see that cute boy over there?" Stella indicated with a jerk of her head. "Do you know him?"

"No, don't think I do."

"Well, he is seriously cool. I mean, like totally. Don't anyone look at him when we leave. OK?"

Steve gave Liz a questioning look.

"Don't ask. I think it's a girl thing."

17

"Hey, Stell, you're kicking me in the face!" exclaimed Steve the next morning, amid much splashing generated by the physical effort of gyrating arms and legs. He was trying to teach Stella basic strokes.

"Sorry, but your face is in my way." Stella was trying hard to look like Steve and Liz had as they smoothly swam through the water. Her technique was a bit looser and a lot splashier than ideal, but she was getting there. The lap pool was only four feet deep so that helped give her confidence. At least she wasn't going to drown.

Liz was bringing the coffeepot and three mugs to the wrought-iron table on their secluded terrace. She had on a one-piece, red tank suit that looked fabulous on her and a red sarong cover-up. She was about five feet six, slim and fit. Her blond hair was naturally curly, and now, wet, it curled up all over. Without make-up, you could still see the light bruising on her face. It was her eyes that made her face so memorable. They were large and a unique color of blue/green...depending, often, on what she wore. Stella thought she should paint her bedroom aqua to match her eyes.

Stephen lifted himself out of the water. Liz couldn't help think of the last time she'd seen him do that. He came over and sat down at the table. Today he was wearing board- shorts in black and brown.

Liz poured him a mug of coffee and asked if he needed sugar or cream.

"No thank you, black's fine. I love a hot cup of coffee after a swim...it just starts a perfect day. Sometimes the day goes downhill fast, but at least it started well. I think your bruises look a lot better then yesterday, Liz."

"Thanks, I guess. I'm not used to wearing make-up but I think I have a few more days of it. I don't look so much like a raccoon now though."

"Hey look!" Stella yelled. "I can swim the whole length of the pool. Wow, I am amazing! When I start high school maybe they will have a swim team!"

Liz and Steve both laughed.

"Can you believe that last week she was taking care of me, driving for two days, making the decisions, everything! She was the mother...I was the sick child! Now I believe we are back to normal. Stella is sixteen again, and I'm glad."

"Don't forget the doctor's appointment I made for you tomorrow," said Steve.

"Right, and I'm seeing Uncle Winnie at three today. I want to know about my life before, and then again, I don't. I've been happy since we got here. But should I be happy if my husband died just about a month ago? I can't even remember him. I don't think I had children, but what if I find out stuff I don't like or makes me feel like I have to go back? Right now I just want to stay here, in my own little house, and do nothing important. Just sit on the porch like Aunt Norma. I just want to chill."

Steven laughed. "You picked the perfect spot to do it. Oddly enough that's why I'm here...to chill...on doctors orders no less."

"Really? What happened to you?"

"Well, it's not really a long story so I may as well tell you. I was married. My wife, Allison, and I graduated from Emory Medical School at the same time and decided to delay our specialty training and join Doctors Without Borders for a year, after which we would come home and finish our training. Ali wanted to be an OB/GYN and I was going to be a pediatrician."

74

"We were sent to southern Sudan. It was hard work and in many ways, anguishing work, seeing all the need and only being able to help with a small part of it. Although we were in a hospital unit with supplies, it was never enough. But you just did what you could and tried not to think about the rest.

"We were there about nine months when we got word to evacuate immediately. We broke down what we could, loaded the trucks and took off. I was sitting in the middle of the truck cab, with my arm around Allison, who had asked for the window seat. We were going to a pick-up place where a plane waited.

"On the way, a roadside explosion hit the side of the truck and...killed Allison immediately. I was covered with burns and shrapnel wounds. The driver was not too badly hurt. At least he was functioning. He loaded us into the back of another truck and we managed to get to the plane. I was still holding Allison. Until we landed, I held her." Steve paused and took a few deep breaths.

"Then, they took her from me. I was very weak at the time from blood loss and they took me to an emergency unit where they knocked me out. When I came to, I was on my way to a hospital in the States. I did not know what had happened to Ali. I was kept in a woozy state for some time and had five operations in the first few weeks. My parents came from Japan to be with me, but they had never even met Allison as we had had a very small wedding right after our graduation. Her parents had called the hospital, but I was still out of it. By the time I could think again and called to talk to her folks, they had already buried her.

"My parents and I went to Albany to see her family and visit her grave. Not much to see...a new grave... no marker yet... no grass...no feeling of reality or closure. Her parents were very kind, but I still had months of treatments to finish and Edie kept calling me. She had been calling me the whole time I was in the hospital. She wanted me to come back to Key West.

"I think she knew she was dying and wanted to make sure I came back to the island even if she wasn't here. She made me promise, when I was finished with my treatments, I would come here to recover. The day of her funeral I was having one of my last operations. Win called to tell me about it but I don't remember much.

"My parents wanted me to come to Japan to recover but I didn't want to go there. To return to Key West...sit in the shade... try to get my life back together was all I could think about." Steve looked at Liz with a small smile. "So after six months of therapy, I came back. That's why I'm here."

18

They sat there for a while, gazing into the garden.

"That is a very sad story," murmured Elizabeth quietly. "I'm so sorry about Allison. It sounds like she was a wonderful person."

"She was. And it is sad. My doctors say I need to try to get over the sadness, not the memories, but the sadness. I'm hoping that being back in Key West, where I was once very happy, is going to be helpful. It's been about eight months and physically I'm as good as I'm going to get. I've got all my limbs and all my parts work...of course, the doctors say I should not expect to sire children, but shooting blanks is better then not shooting at all." Steve gave a little, rueful smile. "I'm trying to get over the guilt and the nightmares and the constant 'if onlys' and the only way to do that is to have a purpose. I just haven't found one yet that works for me but I'm trying. I've just..."

"HELP!!! Come quick!" Stella was screaming! "What is that thing? Shit! Will it bite me? What is it?" Stella was still screaming as Liz and Steve went running in her direction.

"Oh my God! What is it?" yelled Liz.

"It's OK, Stella, don't panic! That is a very large iguana but he will not hurt you! I've never seen him here before. There are quite a few on the island now; usually they live in trees and eat the leaves." Steve laughed. "Just consider them large green lizards."

"Oh my stars! He must be three feet long! I hope he doesn't live in our garden. Are you sure he's harmless?" Now Liz was concerned. "He is the ugliest thing I've ever seen! He looks like a small dinosaur up there on that limb. Yuk!"

"If you see him again, Stella, give him a name and he won't seem so scary." Steve was amused at Stella's wild and verbal reaction ,but iguanas were scary if you had never seen one before. They were becoming a growing nuisance in south Florida.

"I'll name him Scramdamnit. Maybe he'll take the hint." Stella was not amused.

"He certainly improved your speed through the water; maybe not your technique, but your speed in the back-paddle was great!" Steve was still laughing. Stella was climbing out of the pool and running toward Steve.

"Keep that thing away from me! This is not one bit funny. I about had a heart attack!"

Still laughing, Steve was thinking, maybe this is what I've needed. Being around people whose problems were so different... people who accepted him without the kid gloves. He hadn't felt this free of sorrow in a long time. Stella, without knowing it or trying, made him laugh. Liz, without any conscious effort, even with her bruises and amnesia, was still very beautiful...and, obviously, in need of help. She made him feel like a man again.

Dr. Hu had told him he needed to get an interest. Helping Liz find out who she was could give him some sort of purpose, and it would be interesting. He would talk to her about it. Maybe something like this could help them both.

Stella asked Liz if she could use her new computer to look up iguanas. "If I'm going to be living among those things I need to know something about them. Do people think they're cool or gross? I'll have to ask Phillip that question. He would know about things like that, I mean totally. Do people eat them? Or shoot them? Or what?"

Liz and Steven returned to their table and coffee. "Nothing like a little excitement to get the blood flowing." Steve was still smiling. Liz poured more hot coffee.

Steve continued. "I know you are seeing Winslow this

78

afternoon, Liz, and if you would like my help in any way, I'm available. It would be helpful to me, and I certainly have the time. Seems like someone needs to go back to Atlanta to find out about you and your life there. I've been wondering why no one has been looking for you."

Liz thought it over and sighed. "I feel so safe here I just want to pull the covers over my head and hide, but I realize I've got to know about my past before I can go on. I need information about my husband, his family, photos of him and the house I lived in. Did I love him? I'd like to know all of those things. Did the papers carry an article about a missing Atlanta woman? Maybe you could find some answers, and no one would know I was looking. Surely my car was found!"

They talked it over for a while. Liz thought it might be helpful if Steve came with her this afternoon. He and Winslow were friends, and three heads were better than two. Unfortunately, no one was a private detective.

"Before we meet with Win," Steve said, "let's see if the computer has anything on your husband. Hey, Stell, if you're finished with the laptop bring it out, please."

"All I know is his name and that he is dead," offered Liz.

Stella brought out the computer. "Iguanas are all over the Caribbean. That is awesome!"

"A name is enough," said Steve. "Here we go...John Stuart Dandler III...whoa...that him, Liz? Looks like we have an important person here. Do you know this guy?"

"Oh my God! Is that him?" Liz didn't recognize him. He had been in the Georgia State Legislature and there was a lot of information about him, including pictures. Liz was in some of the photographs and looked absolutely stunning...straight hair, perfect attire, bright smile.

"Maybe that was what I wanted to get away from. I know, deep down, that I'm trying to run from something. I also know I would hate that artificial, always perfect, type of life." Liz looked at Steven. "Does it say anything about me?"

Steve typed in Elizabeth Dandler. "Yep! Look at this! You were a busy girl. Looks liked you did it all...charity events chairperson...after school projects chairperson...Save Our Water, chairperson. No wonder you were so tired."

Stella was hanging over their shoulders. "You looked so different then, Liz. I like your new look better. I like your curly hair."

"The strange thing is," said Steve, " that there has been no mention of you missing...in newspapers or on TV. Somebody has to be covering this up."

19

"It does seem very mysterious as to why there has been nothing mentioned about you since the death of your husband." Win, Liz and Steve were discussing her odd situation over iced coffee and guava tarts in Winslow's office.

"Surely someone would have reported you missing," Win went on, looking at Liz. "It's been about a month since John's funeral. Newspapers and TV would love a story like this, but there's been nothing. Someone has to be answering questions about you, where you are, how you are coping with the loss of your husband, because lots of people would be interested! You were too involved in Atlanta society for your friends not to notice you are not around anymore."

"I don't feel I even know that woman but you would think she had a few friends." Liz was unable to offer any reasons or helpful insights. She had decided by now that maybe her subconscious didn't want to remember. The glimpse into her former life was depressing.

" If your husband had three sisters, I'll bet they are the key to this. They are mentioned in his will, as is his male child. They would, at least, want to know if you're pregnant!" Steve felt John's sisters might be the key to the puzzle. "I bet they don't know about your Key West house," Steve continued. "Even if you had told your husband, he may not have mentioned it to them. If they knew, they would be here by now."

81

Winslow sat back in his chair, arms folded over his chest. "I agree with you, Steve, going to Atlanta is the best way to get to the bottom of this. You will have to think of some reason to be asking questions. Maybe you could interview the sisters about their brother and his career. But be careful. They are looking for her too... probably very actively if not publicly." Win sat up. "But, Edie did tell me once, Liz, she liked your husband, but did not like his family. She said they were very controlling."

Liz and Steven left Win's office and strolled down Eaton Street under the shade of large tropical trees. Mini bikes passed, driven by crazy, laughing tourists. The Conch Train was going down Simonton with the driver reciting the history of the island... "and the banyan tree in front of the Old Stone Church is over two hundred and fifty years old." When you lived in paradise, you were required to share it.

"Let's look at bicycles," Steve suggested. "There is a bike shop on the next corner."

Inside the shop, Liz looked for something to remember. Smells seemed to trigger her memory, and this had a pleasant odor of new rubber and oiled wooden floors. She had a feeling she had been here before.

She found an 'island bike', one that had a basket for shopping, a seat for comfort, and nice fat tires for a slow, meandering speed. Besides all that, it was a luscious shade of mango yellow. They asked the shopkeeper to hold that one and a pink one until tomorrow when she would come back with Stella. Steve had been amused by her excitement over the bike colors. No one was going to run over them by mistake, that was for sure.

Tomorrow she would go see Dr. Hu. After that she and Stella would buy the bikes and then go shopping. Liz needed new clothes. Everything she had with her, even though casual, was not casual enough for Key West. She needed cotton shorts, tee shirts, a straw hat and slip-on sandals. Maybe a mango colored sun visor to match her new bike.

Liz was pondering again her present conundrum. She now had money, a great island house, and new friends. All

82

because of a past she could not remember. She knew she had to unlock her past before she could relax and enjoy her future and she was very curious about that nice-looking man in the pictures. How in the world could you not remember a husband who looked like that? Why had she been running away? Nothing made any sense to her and it was driving her crazy! She kept waiting for something to trigger her memories of this past but nothing, not even John's picture, was helping. Would she ever find the key? And if she did, would she be opening Pandora's box?

20

Liz was sitting on the terrace, behind their little house, waiting for Stella to get ready to go. She didn't know what the appropriate attire was for bike shopping but Stella would find it. You could depend on Stella to be cool. You could also depend on her to make you wait.

"I'm ready, Liz. What do you think?" Stel turned around and posed. Her shorts were white and pink stripes, the tee shirt, lime green and the sun visor was bright yellow. "Cool, right?"

"Totally." Liz laughed. "Sit down a minute. I want to talk to you."

Stella sat. Her heart started pounding! Here it comes, she thought, Liz doesn't need me here any more. Well, I've done the best I can and I can take it. I'll just smile and thank...

"First, I want to say that I think our little family, you and me, is going very well. We should think about it as a long-term arrangement so you know where you stand. I can't adopt you because of your Dad, but I can be your guardian for school or any other thing for which you might need a parent or guardian. If you agree with the idea, you could be a distant cousin or something and I will be your official guardian. Wherever I am will be your home, and you will finish high school and go to college."

Stella, who had sat up straight, waiting for the bad news with determination, just about fell off her chair! She got up slowly, tears of relief sliding down her face and hugged Elizabeth.

"I don't know what to say. I thought you were going to tell me to leave. This is the happiest day of my life! Thank you, Elizabeth! I mean totally, thank you...thank you...thank you! I'll make you proud of me. I will...I really will."

"Well, Sis, I'm happy about it too. I think you have been very good for me. You've given me a sense of purpose. This running around with no memory makes me feel like I'm floating off into thin air. You've been my anchor and I like having you around. And, before you get too excited, there is something else I need to tell you. I'm not sure how I feel about this but...I'm going to have a baby!"

"Oh my God! Uh...you're kidding right?" Stella was staring at her.

"Nope. Dr. Hu believes I'm two and a half months pregnant! The baby will arrive around December. I guess I'm not really surprised. There has been so much happening that I have just let my suspicions slide, but now I know for sure, it seems very weird. I can't remember the father of my baby...I'm just assuming it's my husband...who else could it be? But that is not the baby's fault and I am excited about having a little baby. Now we'll be a family of three. Can you imagine that, Stell? We'll have to get a little pink or blue bike! We'll redo the other bedroom as a nursery. We'll..."

"What's all the noise and laughing? Sounds like a party." Stephen walked onto the terrace. "What's all the hullabaloo? Something good must have happened."

Stella yelled. "You will never guess in a million years!"

"Then tell me." He looked at Liz.

"I'd like to keep it a secret a while longer but it's too amazing...I'm kind of in shock! I'm having a baby... in December... just in time for Christmas. What do you think of that, Stevo! Isn't that the most surprising news you have ever heard? I'm having a baby and can't recall a father!"

Steven looked at Liz and laughed. "You sure know how to keep life from getting boring, Lizzie. It is surprising...I'll have to teach him to swim."

"Him! It's going to be a girl and I'm going to teach HER to

86

swim," responded Stella.

"I'm getting her a little pink bathing suit with ruffles and a matching sun hat and we'll call her Sugarpie. I'll take her over to visit Aunt Norma and we can get her a pink stroller with a pink sunshade with fringe. She will be one totally cool baby!"

"Why don't I take you girls out for dinner tonight to celebrate? We can go to Louie's. I'll call Phil to get us a good table outside and we'll toast Little Johnny with orange juice and little blue umbrellas. Maybe we should include Winslow. This news is going to make him feel like a grandfather. Even with the unusual circumstances, he will be thrilled!"

They were going to make it a special evening. A dress-up, island event and Liz and Stella were excited! Stella wore her new Lilly sundress of pink and lime-green floral print, short with tiny shoulder straps and pink, flat sandals. Liz, who always seemed elegant even when not trying, appeared in a simple, sleeveless, white linen sheath with a clunky African shell necklace and white, strappy heels. Now that her tan had overtaken her bruises, she had a warm peach glow.

Louie's Backyard was one of the places in Key West where you could dine right on the water. Located in an old two-story, gingerbread house, it had been converted into an elegant restaurant. Outside in the "back yard", under tall trees and palms that draped over candlelit tables, was the most charming dining area and bar in Key West. You couldn't see the actual sunset but often saw a moonrise in a sky swirling with cerise clouds and scattered with silver filigree If flowers occasionally fell on your entrée from an overhanging blooming tree they did not charge extra. You went to Louie's for confirmation of the good life.

Liz was mellow, kind of excited about the baby, but waiting for the unknown to come out of hiding. Steven was flying to Atlanta tomorrow morning to delve into her strange and unremembered background. What would he find?

21

Rain was coming down in sheets as his plane landed in Atlanta. Steven took the MARTA rail into the Buckhead section of the city and checked into a hotel. Debating about taking a nap or going out in the storm, he opted to stay inside until time for his appointment with Bailey and Calhoun. This was the law firm that had written Liz about her deceased husband's will.

He had decided to use the approach of a free-lance reporter for a business magazine; and if med school or the Sudan had not given him any inside knowledge of reporting, he would soon find out. He had certainly watched enough detective shows while in the hospital to have a PhD in covert demeanor. He could picture himself in trench coat and dark sunglasses. But they usually were not needed at the same time. Today, maybe just the trench coat was appropriate.

Buying a pad of paper and a pen, he walked three blocks to the law firm. The rain was letting up. A bit of sun was slanting through big oak trees and drops randomly fell from water-laden branches. He loved the fresh cool earthy smell after a rainstorm. That was a surprise to him. He had not noticed much of anything since Allison's death.

Taking a deep breath, he realized that maybe, given time, he could at least consider a future without her. Not that he'd ever get over her but he didn't feel that usual gut-wrenching guilt about enjoying this walk alone. Dr. Hu had been right. He needed a project outside of himself.

After a five-minute wait, he was ushered into the law office of Chris Calhoun, a very imposing looking attorney. He could have done the commercial for Patek watches.

"I was happy to meet with you, Dr. Sandford. My affiliation with the Dandler family goes way back. It was a tragedy for our state that both father and son were lost to us. It was no surprise when John Stuart passed. He had been in ill health for over a year. His wife had often filled in for him in public events. But it was shocking when, three months later, Johnny died. I don't believe the family will ever get over it!"

"Has his wife been filling in for him?" Steven asked.

"I have not seen her since the funeral. Talked to one of Johnny sisters, Mary, and she intimated that Elizabeth was having trouble adjusting to his death and was staying in New England with a good friend of hers. It had to be a terrible shock for her. They were very close". He walked over to the window, turned around and went on speaking.

"There's even been talk of her filling his seat for the duration of his term and maybe running for it in the next election. She would probably win too! She was very involved in civic and social circles. Everyone liked her and, of course, she is very attractive in a soft, elegant way. Women loved her. The Dandler family is not going to let this seat go. They've been a power in the state of Georgia for too long."

Steven asked various questions about 'Johnny' and his life and found out he was a very popular man. He excelled in everything he did, had many friends in all walks of life and would have been certain of re-election.

Steven thanked him for his time and insight and left the building feeling like a true reporter. He had actually learned something. In fact, he had learned a lot. He knew when they found Liz, the pressure on her would be great. She had been running away from all of that when she crashed the car. No wonder she could not remember. No wonder she felt threatened by her past. Even if she could not recall it, she instinctively knew she would not want to be a part of it. But was this the only reason she did not want to return?

Next he would try to talk with the sisters. Chris Calhoun suggested he speak with Mary about her brother. Steve still felt the sisters held the key to the mystery. He called the number

90

Chris had given him and after talking with Mary, they decided to meet the next afternoon.

That evening at the bar in the hotel, Steve let it be known he was writing a magazine article on the life of John Stuart Dandler III. This must have been the watering hole for the after-five executive group as they all knew each other and all had known 'Johnny'. Best of all, they started swapping stories about him. Talk about hitting pay dirt...dirt being the key ingredient of the tales.

Steven found out, without any proof of course, that old Johnny was quite the playboy. Amid a great deal of laughter and cocktails, everyone seemed to have a favorite story about Johnny, and all were sordidly funny, not the image that Chris Calhoun and computer files had given. It seemed he came by it naturally as his father had a reputation for skirt chasing. Good thing Chris Calhoun didn't drop in for a drink. On the other hand, maybe what he knew and what he said were two different things.

He wondered if Liz knew any of this. She was much better off in Key West right now. This was turning out to be a sad, sordid tale of a family in crisis, with Liz its only hope. It was not a good position for a woman who disliked public life and might now be carrying the immensely important heir to the Dandlers' future.

22

Mary Dandler Cox lived on Habersham Drive in a beautiful red brick Tudor mansion. A dogwood-lined drive led to the front door, which was answered by a black maid in a white uniform. Mary, when she arrived, gave off an aura of importance. She let you know, without saying a word, that nobody was as important as Mary. After a little polite conversation and an explanation of the reason for the visit (she had already checked with her attorney), they discussed her brother.

By the time she finished telling her story of Johnny, Steven figured he would be elevated to sainthood in the very near future. At University of Georgia he had been the football quarterback, student body president and outstanding student. He had made a flawless transition into the business world...being taken into the vast, family business of Worldwide International Financial Investment. He had married and gone into politics...first the state house, then it was going to be the governor's office, then a run for the presidency. The family had had it all planned out.

"How did he meet his wife? Is she from Atlanta also?"

After a pause, Mary smiled in a tight-lipped sort of way. "No, unfortunately she is from Florida but people seem to like her."

"Mr. Dandler's death must have been a terrible shock for his wife. They were so young. How is she coping with all of this?"

"It has been a shock, but she is getting through it. She is visiting friends in New England now. We thought a different environment might be helpful. When she returns, she will be taking over Johnny's position in the State Senate. After all, she is a Dandler and people expect it."

"Is there any way I could speak with her? Maybe call her in New England?"

"I don't believe so."

After leaving Mary's house, Steven realized that they had to really be scrambling trying to find a woman, who had wrecked her Mercedes, left it on the side of a road, and simply disappeared. It was a sure thing the sisters did not know of Liz's Key West connection.

Obviously, Liz had wanted to get away. She had told no one in Atlanta she was leaving and was taking back roads through Georgia. She had made the decision before her accident. She was going into hiding and maybe a new life. Liz probably knew of their big plans for her and decided to take her three million and disappear. All the rest of the money and the fancy, political life they could keep. Steve doubted Liz had the same memories of her husband that his sister had related.

Finding information on Johnny had not been difficult. Now, he wanted to know about Liz's life. It would really help her if she knew her own background. He tried calling the organizations with which she was involved. He got nowhere until a sweet magnolia-sounding lady admitted she and Liz were best friends. She'd meet with him. Maybe he knew where Liz had gone.

"She was the kindest, nicest person I ever met." Bethanne Benton was a waterfall of information. "I've known her for years and years. We were sorority sisters at FSU and double dated. I was with her when she met Johnny. He was quarterback when Georgia was playing in the Gator Bowl and Liz was Gator Bowl Queen. They met at a party and pofft! That was it! I declare, I've never seen anything like it."

Bethanne laughed at her memory. "They were inseparable

after that. They kept that road between Athens and Tallahassee hot, I can tell you. I was in their wedding, which was held in Atlanta. His family had money, and was footing the bill so I guess they held it where they wanted. It was a very posh society event. The only family Liz had was her grandmother.

"I married and moved to Atlanta a year later and we were so excited to be living in the same city. It seemed odd, though, every time we made plans they had to be canceled. It really bothered her that his friends and political events were all they had time for. She'd call and complain about it but...you know... what can you do. It was like she had married that whole family, not just Johnny."

Bethanne looked him in the eye. "I want to know where Lizzie is. I just don't buy this New England crap. I know all of her friends and, believe me, Liz doesn't know anyone up there. There's something wrong...and I'm not the only one concerned. Liz isn't the kind of person to let people worry about her. We have E-mailed and called. Nothing. Do you know anything?"

Steven was tempted, but instead asked for Bethanne's address. "If I hear of anything while I'm doing this story I will be in touch. Try not to worry."

23

Steven was flying back to Key West from Orlando, where he had changed planes from Atlanta. The flight from Orlando to Key West only took an hour. If you drove, it took all day. From the airplane, the view was incredible...a necklace of tiny, green islands haphazardly thrown into a sea of pale aquamarine, streaky lime and deep turquoise with cobalt blue swirls. It always thrilled him to see it from the air.

Throughout the keys, boats navigated by the color of the water. It seemed simple...the darker, the deeper. Unless it was a rocky bank covered with dark eelgrass, which often led to a shallow bar of sand where permit lurked, or a small coral reef, or coming in around sunset, when the setting sun made the water a mirror of the sky. The Bay side could really be tricky. Steven loved it.

Now, at thirty-six, he was starting to think again of the future. Maybe he'd be a charter boat captain. Why not? He could be whatever he wanted. He would start his life over again. Key West was helping, just like Edie promised. He was occasionally feeling a positive thought or two. His life, before the roadside explosion, had always gone in an agreeable direction and he was naturally a glass-half-full person...if he could just get that back again.

That evening, Liz, Win and Steve met on Liz's terrace. They were going to discuss Steve's findings and Liz needed moral support. She wanted Stella there too. Finding out about her life before the crash made her feel very nervous.

Stella had made mango smashes from a recipe she had cajoled out of Phillip. As everyone settled at the table, Steve reached over and put his hand over Liz's.

"It's going to be OK, Liz. I will start with your past then you can relax. You are not a bank robber!" Everyone laughed. Liz felt a little better. At least, she was among friends.

Steven then told what he had learned of Liz's past starting from graduation from FSU until her disappearance. How she and Johnny had met at the Gator Bowl...her structured life as a politician's wife...her friend, Bethanne Benton.

"Bethanne? That sounds familiar! Bethanne! She was in my wedding? Where was I married?"

"In Atlanta. The Dandlers held a very large and elegant wedding for their Crown Prince." Steve paused, letting Elizabeth take it all in. She sat still for a while.

"I know you will think it strange that I don't remember Johnny, but I think I remember Bethanne! Was she about Stella's size with brown hair and blue eyes...and a real southern accent?"

"That's her! She is very concerned about you. She wants to hear from you. Evidently, the story that is being told about your disappearance is you are visiting friends in New England... recovering from your grief. Bethanne says she doesn't believe any of that crap. You don't have any friends in New England."

Liz started to laugh. "I do remember her! She always used that word, 'crap.'" Liz had her fingers over her mouth... staring into space. "I can picture her. Oh, I'm so excited! Go on tell me more!"

"Mary Dandler Cox," Steve paused to see if that name triggered anything. "She's Johnny sister, seems to be the spokesperson for the family. She explained to me that when you were ready, you would return and assume Johnny's seat in the State Senate. They expect you to take over his political future."

"Oh my God! I would absolutely hate that!"

"I don't think they care. Their plan is to keep the House seat and, because everyone knows and likes you, that makes you

98

their best option."

"Anyone for more mango smash?" Stella picked up the pitcher. She was trying to make Liz feel better. Liz leaned over and hugged her. "Yes, thank you, I'll have some."

After a deep sigh, Liz said to Steven. "Tell me about Johnny."

"I'll say this for your husband, he was a very popular guy. Everyone thought the world of him. His sister thinks he was a saint in the making, and his friends tell that he was the life of the party. He was successful in college and successful in the business world. Of course, his position in that world was handed to him on a platter. He was his family's shining star. You were important in your role as his wife."

"I hate to ask this," said Liz, "but did he play around?"

"I hate to answer that, but it seems like he did. The way I read it, you and Johnny fell madly in love in college. After your marriage his family took over, and he became as much of a puppet as you. When his father died, his sisters got serious about the family's ambition. The fact that Johnny had a massive heart attack so young might be tied in with all of that. He was trying to be someone that he did not really want to be."

Steve went on. "The sisters probably started on you right after the funeral. They wanted you to act like a Dandler, carry on for Johnny, march to their drumbeat. But you had no reason to do that since Johnny was gone. You might have felt some feeling of loyalty to him but not to the sisters.

"I bet you left even before his will was read. You were now financially independent through the inheritance from your father-in-law. You knew you had a house in Key West. Uncle Winnie could have handled everything else. So you just left, not telling anyone you were leaving or where you were going." Steve paused.

"Once you arrived here, my guess is you would have notified them. Explained you were finished with their political life. You would have had distance between you and the family and Win to back you up, but on the way to Key West, you had that accident."

99

24

Winslow was sitting on the lounge, feet up, with his drink in hand. He had opted out of the mango smash. "How did this gothic tale become your life story, Elizabeth? You were such a sweet, simple little girl." Win shook his head. "It is amazing where love can take you."

Win continued, "What we need now is to think of a way to unwind this ball of slippery string. There is a lot of money involved here. They can't stop looking till they find you. You are critical to their lives. You hold all the chips. Old man Dandler left most of his fortune to his son. He, in turn, left it for his son. Here you sit, pretty as a picture, carrying what could be a multi-millionaire. Yes sir, Lizzie, you sure grew up to be interesting!"

"But I don't want all that money. I'm perfectly happy with my three million dollars and this house. To me, it's more then I ever dreamed! I like my life here. I've decided we're island girls, right Stell? We are not going back to Atlanta. And I'm having a precious island baby, not a multi-millionaire." Liz paused, looking worried... "What if they find out about the baby and try to take him away? Should I change my name, back to my maiden name? And what if..."

"We will just hang tight for a while, Lizzie," said Uncle Winnie. "We will think on it, mull it over and check with an Atlanta attorney friend of mine. I don't want my name used as they might trace it to Key West. We need to know more before we can make decisions." He paused and patted Liz's hand. "Don't worry about your baby, Liz. It is your baby...you are the mother... they can't take him away from you. Don't even think about that... Now, what are the plans for dinner?"

"I'm cooking." Stella jumped up. "Liz feels fine in the morning but smelling food in the late afternoon makes her queasy. She sure can eat though. We are serving Grouper Phillippe with papaya and avocado salsa and a salad of baby greens. It will be served on the terrace in twenty minuets." Off Stella went into the kitchen. Between Phillip and the beautiful new kitchen, she was becoming a cooking addict!

The evening was delightfully cool with a little breeze sneaking in from the ocean. On an island, there was always a breeze from one direction or another. In the summer, Key West was usually cooler than central Florida or even Atlanta for that matter. As they sat under a darkening blue sky dotted with pink wads of cotton, Liz wanted to know if she could contact Bethanne.

"Not yet," answered Win. "Let me talk to my friend first. There are Georgia laws to contend with...inheritance laws, estate taxes, marital laws. Let's get our eggs in a carton before we make a move. By the way, Earl still wants to buy this property from you. I've told him I don't think you want to sell but he still insists."

"I do not want to sell! I love this place! Why does he keep asking?"

"He has trouble with people not agreeing with him," said Steve with humor. "Earl has a great sense of entitlement. Things are always supposed to go his way."

The meal was wonderful, and Stella was thrilled at the compliments. People saying nice things to her, about anything, was still a novel experience. She insisted on doing the dishes by herself. Win left for home. Liz and Steven were left sitting in the ebbing light.

It was peaceful. Stars started to show themselves. Leaves rustled.

"When I was in Atlanta," Steve said, "it rained and I walked

102

through the rain and felt, for the first time since Allison died, like it was alright to enjoy it. Maybe I could feel happy again... without all the guilt. You and Stella have been good for me and going to Atlanta got me out of myself." Steve was silent for a while. He leaned forward and took Liz's hand in his. "Whatever is happening between us feels good too. I feel my life slowly returning and I hope it's going to include you."

"What a strange threesome we are," Liz answered. "Stella, wanting to forget her past. Me, trying to remember my past. You, trying to make peace with your past. We are all looking for a new life on this island. We can help each other find whatever we are looking for. We just have to consider it a new adventure." Liz leaned over and put her head on his shoulder. "I'm not going anywhere."

Steve put his arm around her. They sat close for a while, looking up at the stars. Orion was starting to appear over the trees. That was another thing Liz liked about her new life. At night, you could see stars.

25

A few days later, Liz was trimming a passionflower vine that bloomed profusely but threatened to consume the front porch. Tropical foliage was never timid. People living on the lane had different ideas about how their vines, plants and trees should be maintained. That was one of the beguiling charms of Key West...everyone did his or her thing and people were usually tolerant of other ideas. Conformity was never a Key West issue.

Mr. Garcia was their next-door neighbor. His idea of beautiful was a white painted house with bright blue trim and lots of flowerpots, usually filled with his three cats. They spent most of their time in the sun, curled up in his pottery, taking catnaps. His flowers either adapted to blooming while wearing a fur coat or died...but everyone loved his cats and their occasional, 'Lord of the Landscape' visits.

Liz was talking to the mailman, Hector, when she heard Stella calling her from inside the house. There was something odd about her voice! She found Stella sitting on the sofa with a phone in her hand and a very worried and perplexed look on her face.

"What happened, Stell?"

"Mrs. Peterson just called to tell me that she found my brother, Kirk, this morning, curled up on her porch sofa, sound asleep, with his dog next to him." Stella paused as if to get it straight in her mind. "He's only ten and when I left, I told him I would return for him as soon as I could afford it, and if he ever had trouble he was to go to Mrs. Peterson's house. I'd written our phone number on the post card I sent her. He's there now because Uncle Charlie, whom he's been living with since our mother died, is getting a divorce, and neither he nor Aunt Cindy want to keep him. He overheard them talking about sending him back to his dad, and he knows that would be very bad.

"Mrs. Peterson said I'd better come for him before our dad heard about it. She's hiding him at her house until I figure out what to do. Kirk can't stay in town or my old man will find out. Dad doesn't want him but will take him and mistreat him just to be mean! I've got to get him but I haven't saved enough yet...and how will I get there...and..." Stella broke into tears, putting her head into a pillow, sobbing.

"Don't cry, Stell, we'll go together and get him. We'll leave right now. He can live with us and don't worry about money; we've got lots of that, right? Remember? You counted it."

"But that's yours. I can't use your money for my problems."

"Stella, honey," Liz put her arm around her, "we're a family now and we help each other with problems. I think this is a very important thing to spend my money on. We'll talk to Steve when he comes for lunch...which looks great, by the way, you must have just finished putting it on the table when Mrs. Peterson called." Liz sat down at the table. Presentation was as important to Stella as the food and her natural, from the garden, stick and leaf centerpieces were always fascinating. "Let's eat while we discuss it."

"Permission to come aboard?" Steve walked in, dressed in khaki cargo pants, a black tee shirt and flip flops...proper attire for lunch on the island. He looked good but then, Liz thought, he always looked good. "What's the matter? Someone spatter mud on your pink bike, Stell?"

"Hi Steve," said Liz. "No, Stella had some bad news today and we're trying to figure out what to do about it."

"What happened Stell?" Steve sat next to Stella and took her hand. "Can I help?"

Stella got all teary again and Liz explained about Stella's

brother and their problem.

"I think I can accommodate that problem. The three of us will go...two and a half drivers, lots of tissues, and room for a boy and a dog. What do you think, Stell? Can you put up with me for a few days? "

"Are you sure, Steve? It's a long way." Said Liz.

"I have just been waiting for another trip. If going to Atlanta helped me so much, a trip with you two ought to cure me. If we can wait a few days maybe Stell can get her learner's permit. What do you say, Ladies, am I in?"

Stella sat at the table boo-hooing while Liz answered that she thought it was a terrific idea. She had to get a sonogram tomorrow, but she would be ready after that. She would call Mrs. Peterson and apprise her of their plans and ask her to keep Kirk hidden for a few days.

"Come on, Stell," said Steve. "Let's eat your beautiful lunch and then you freshen up and we will go down and see about a driver's license or learner's permit. I'm sorry about your brother but we'll bring him back with us and he will love it. I know you'll be happy to have him here and you know what? We need a dog around here!"

"I don't know why you both are so nice to me. When you see where I used to live you may not want me around anymore." Liz gave her another hug. "Don't even think that. When we see where you lived we will say, Wow, wasn't she smart to get out of there on her own? We will be proud of you! We'll still be family, OK? We're just getting a little bigger, OK? Sis?"

"OK." Said Stella softly.

26

Stella and Steve went to see about a Learner's Permit. This was a change for Stella. Having someone volunteer to help her do something was completely out of her realm of experience. She liked it that Steve thought she was funny. Sometimes he actually bent over double, laughing. He just did not understand why you always had to ignore a cute boy. I mean, really, you had to be cool.

Stell thought he was very good looking, in an adult kind of way. His close-cut beard covered a lot of scars on the right side of his face. She thought it gave him an attractive, intellectual sort of look, especially when he wore his glasses. His right arm and hand were scarred but didn't look bad. Steve often exercised his hand when he sat around talking. It wasn't back to a hundred percent yet he said.

They came home with a Driver's License Study Manual for Stella. She started studying right away. Tomorrow she would pack. She was excited. She was going to see her brother and their dog, ToJo, again.

The next afternoon they were about ready, car gassed up, bags packed and a blanket in the back seat for ToJo. Win came by to wish them well. Steve and Stell were talking to him when Liz came outside with an odd smile, which was vying with the stunned expression on her face.

"OK," said Steve. "What's up? I hope you never play

poker, Lizzie. You wouldn't stand a chance."

"I'm glad you are all here. I do have an announcement to make. God, I don't know how to tell you. So I'll just tell you...I'm having TWINS!"

Stella screamed and ran to hug her. "Awesome! Totally, totally awesome!

Steve came over and hugged her. "Congratulations Mama! You don't do anything halfway, do you?" he said smiling.

Win laughed. "Your monetary value just went up! You sure you don't understand how money works? Damn, Lizzie, you're going to rake it in. This was very clever of you. It will drive those Dandlers up the walls."

"Stop that Uncle Win! These sweet, innocent babies don't care a thing about money. Dr. Hu also said he did not see any little boy appendages floating around. It could mean I'm having twin girls!"

"Yeah!" Stella was ecstatic! "Now you are talking totally cool! I mean totally! Now we'll get two little pink ruffled swimsuits, two pink strollers, two pink tutus and four pink ballet slippers!"

Steve spoke up. "How did the doctor say you were, Liz? Did he think you and the twins were healthy?"

"Yes, but he said I should start showing very soon. Why am I so excited, I should be apprehensive...I'm still not completely comfortable with all this uncertainty. This is going to change my life completely. How about you Stell? Are you up for this?"

"Are you kidding me? When I saw you sitting there on the side of the road I said to myself, Stella, you pick up that lady, she's going to have twins!"

Liz hugged Stell.

"Are we still on for the trip?" Steve asked.

"The doctor said I was fine for the trip, just don't carry the luggage."

"We will take care of you and stop whenever you want." Stella responded.

Steve looked at Stella. "You sure you don't want to paint Liz's new SUV pink before we leave?"

"Can we?" Stella jokingly asked.

Uncle Win stood up, wished all a good trip and turned to leave. He took a few steps and turned around. "I don't know Steve, that Volvo might look rather cool pink!" And laughing, he walked off.

Stella ran off to her room to study for her driver's test. Steve stayed to help Liz with the dishes. "How do you really feel about two little girls, Liz? It going to be a life-changing event, that's for sure."

"I hope they are girls. If they were boys, I'm guessing the Dandlers would be a problem, but girls...I don't think they really care about girls. I feel like they are safer, being girls."

Liz looked at Steven. "How do you feel about twin girls?" she asked softly.

"You mean besides the fact they'll have a beautiful mother? Anything you do is fine with me. I love little girls... and I love big girls. So far our funny, made-up family is getting along very well. We'll just have to see how it goes. You're adding one more to the bunch tomorrow. It's a good thing you bought that SUV last week; you need it already. We should leave early tomorrow morning so you better get your sleep." He leaned over and gave her a kiss on the cheek. "See you tomorrow, Mommy."

111

27

One of the world's most spectacular events is a sunrise. It happens everyday but most people sleep right through it. A sunset is something people share...they toast it with margaritas, ring bells for the Angelus, play Taps, take sunset sails. A sunrise, on the other hand, is often a solitary event...viewed with awe and a glorious sense of promise!

Driving up the Overseas Highway at dawn, you feel as though you're heading straight for the sun itself, a beautiful experience but hard on the eyes. The sun, when it rises, is huge, bright orange, and casts its spotlight on everything, including the water, which reflects its brilliance and doubles the blinding effect.

Steve was driving. Liz was cuddled up in the front seat with a soft blanket and a pillow. She kept peeping at the sunrise but looked mostly at the purple and coral streaks in the Southern sky. Stella was asleep in the back seat with her pillow.

If I wasn't here, I wonder who would be driving. Thought Steve, amused. But it had been his idea to leave at the crack of dawn...fewer boat trailers and tourist on the bridges this time of day.

He loved early morning sunrises. Ever since he was a kid it had been his favorite thinking time. Allison had often teased him about it. "Seen one, seen them all", she used to say, as she had turned over and gone back to sleep. Steve did not agree.

To him, each one was different and each had its own spiritual renewal.

They had agreed to shoot straight up I-75 to Atlanta and veer northeast to Gwinnett County. It would take them two days to get there. Stella had called Mrs. Peterson to let her know their final plans. She was anxious to get there and get Kirk before their dad found out about him. Small towns held few secrets for long and Stella wanted to swoop him up and start back home as soon as they could.

Liz had not given being pregnant with one child much attention but with two babies growing inside of her, she felt more fragile, more responsible. Taking it easy was not her usual modus operandi but for the next six months she was going to try. What would she do without Stella?

The drive up went very fast. Traveling the freeways with three drivers, few stops and only one night at a motel got you where you were going. Stella was getting nervous when her cell phone rang. It was Mrs. Peterson again, this time saying she, Kirk and ToJo were on their way to Stone Mountain, Georgia and would be staying at the Holiday Inn there. She, too, was getting nervous about Kirk's dad finding him. What he didn't know wouldn't hurt them. And when he did figure out what was happening with his son, if he did, would he care? By then it would be too late.

Stella was relieved to know Kirk was safe and grateful that Liz and Steve were with her. Would Mrs. Peterson like them? Would ToJo remember her? And her baby brother...now ten...she had not seen him in over a year. After turning off the freeway for Stone Mountain, they pulled up to the Holiday Inn. Stella jumped out of the car and ran into the motel before the car had parked. She searched the lobby but did not see them. The lady behind the check-in desk called over to her, "Are you the sister looking for the little boy? Check over in the game room."

Beyond the lobby was a large room with chairs, tables and games. Stella yelled, "Kirk!" A young boy turned his head and yelled! "Stell!" They were hugging and crying in the middle of the room before Kirk remembered tough guys didn't do that kinda thing. "Aw, shit, Stell, whadija have to slobber all over me for!" Stella started to laugh and went to hug Mrs. Peterson. "Thank you so much, Mrs. Peterson, you are a life saver! I can't tell you how much I am indebted to you."

"Oh, my goodness. Stella! You look wonderful. I can't believe it's you." Mrs. Peterson was so excited. "Oh, I can't wait to hear all about you. But first let me go get ToJo. Don't want to leave him out of this reunion!"

"ToJo! It's me! I told you I'd come back for you and Kirk." Rolling on the floor, with ToJo licking her face, Stella was laughing trying to sit up. ToJo had not forgotten her.

Stella introduced her teacher and brother to Liz and Steve, who had big smiles at all the goings on. Although Stella had never mentioned it, her teacher was a very attractive, African-American woman with mocha skin and hazel eyes. Liz filled Mrs. Peterson in on how she and Stella met and how they were now living together as a family. Her teacher was very pleased about Stella continuing her education and having the opportunity to go to college. She also thought Liz was wonderful to take Kirk to live with them. Liz laughed, "I still have amnesia and I need Stell as much as she needs me...and we are happy to have Kirk. I was an only child and always wanted a big family...now with the twins coming...and Stell and Kirk...I've got one."

"Stella is such a bright girl. She needed to get away but how was she to do it?" Mrs. Peterson was talking to Liz. "She worked all the time to get a little money, and her father would take it from her. I ended up keeping her money in an old purse at my house. We called it her bank. I showed her where I kept the house key and the purse. If she ever needed to leave fast and I wasn't home, she could get her money. She is very mature for her age, but she had to be."

"Thanks, Mrs. Peterson for all you've done." Stella came back into the room. "You, Kirk and ToJo were the only things I missed after I left. Maybe you could come and visit us in Key West. She could stay in the big house, couldn't she Liz?"

"Of course. You just let us know when and we'll be ready,

Mrs. Peterson. I really appreciate all you have done for Stell and Kirk. We'd love to have you visit us in Key West. Just never mention to anyone where we are living, we don't want a visit from you-know-who!"

"Don't you worry about that," replied Mrs. Peterson. "I realize if he finds out where they are, he'll go get them just to exert his control over the situation. He doesn't want the responsibility but he's a control freak. I truly think he is a dangerous man to be around. When Stella reaches eighteen, she'll be old enough to be legally be on her own and responsible for Kirk. One of the reasons I wanted to meet here was so no one would see a Florida licensed car in my driveway."

Steven stood up and told the women he and the kids would be outside playing with the dog. He needed to stretch his legs after being in the car for two days. He also wanted to get to know Kirk. He could see that any long-range interest he might have in Elizabeth would include children. It was a good thing he liked kids. He always felt he was missing out, being an only child. After the explosion in the Sudan, being a father was not something he could count on. He found it remarkable that Liz seemed to attract children without even trying.

28

Being alone with Grace (she had asked Liz to call her by her first name) gave Liz a chance to find out more about Stella. Mrs. Peterson was very supportive of Stella. She had helped where she could, but Stella's volatile father had made it very difficult. He took any assistance for his daughter as a personal insinuation he was not good enough.

The two of them had finally realized any help at all had to be in secret. They had devised all kinds of schemes for fake school fees. When Stella would ask her father for money for required 'gym shoes' or 'library fees' he would yell that was not his problem. She'd have to earn it herself. She would then get a summer job, or tutor students, with all her money going into her 'bank' in the back of Mrs. Peterson's closet.

Grace Peterson had been a widow for about five years and was retiring next year. Her husband had been vice-president of the fabric mill. Stella had been one of her best students and she was thrilled that good things were happening for her and planned to keep in touch. She liked the idea of traveling to Key West. She wanted to do new things after she retired.

Back in the car and heading south, ToJo was excited, Stell was trying to get the dog to calm down and Kirk never quit talking. He had a lot he wanted to tell Stella about and it was all pouring out at once! He had brought very little with him, underwear, a cracked photo of their mother, a toy for ToJo, a faded pair of purple sox with big holes and a worn out toothbrush. With dark hair like Stella's and loads of energy, Kirk seemed to be a normal ten-year-old boy. His grin was engaging...his language and manners were a mess. Stella realized how much work they had ahead of them. He had not gone without casual love at his uncle's, but he had not had Mrs. Peterson to correct his grammar or choice of expletives. Stell just laughed. She felt complete now he was with her. Everything else was, at present, unimportant.

They had decided to take the back roads home. More bathroom stops for ToJo, Kirk and Liz, and more interesting sights and places for lunch. Liz liked to ride through a small town and find an interesting place to dine. She loved outdoor tables with umbrellas. She said fresh air and ambiance always made ordinary food taste delicious. Liz was fun to be around... seeing the bright side of things, making funny comments and always up...unless she was sleeping.

Stella and Steve shared the driving. Liz spent most of her travel time sleeping. Sometimes she shared the back seat with Kirk, he curled up in one corner, she in the other, ToJo in the back on the luggage. Steve told Stella that it was normal for pregnant women to sleep a lot. Stell realized she had never known Liz when she was not pregnant.

Steve laughed. " You know, we appear to be a typical family unit...a father, an expectant mother of twins, a teenaged daughter, grandfather Win and uncles Earl and Phillip. No one is related and no one planned it. Now we even have a little brother and a dog. Only in Key West would this be considered normal."

"It's amazing! I love being part of it all. I just can't wait for the twins. We'll have to think up some totally cool names. I hope they are as pretty as Liz. I think she is beautiful."

"Me too", sighed Steve. "Me too."

It took three days to get home. Long luncheons, potty breaks, plantation tours and other sights took time but made the trip fun. Stella and Kirk, who had never been anywhere, wanted to see it all...were interested in everything. But they were all anxious to get back. It might be new for Kirk but the rest felt like Key West was now home.

Stella promised that ToJo being in residence would mean the end to the iguana visits. Secretly, she wasn't so sure. She was afraid ToJo would take one look at that ugly thing and hide.

They were approaching Key West near sunset. The sky was flying magenta, orange and purple banners. Palm trees created black silhouettes against the flaming sunset and seabirds were returning to their rookeries. Driving home, they were heading into the setting sun. Steve had taken over from Stella just before Key Largo. She was in the back seat explaining it all to Kirk. Liz was sitting in the front seat smiling

"Those babies telling jokes?" Steve asked.

Liz laughed, "No, I'm just happy. I'm happy with the sky, my babies are happy, Stell's happy to have her brother and ToJo. You seem relaxed and sort of happy. I just feel happy!"

Steve smiled to himself. He was close to happy. Not there just yet but even the possibility of happiness was new for him. He saw the future, now, more positively. Maybe he could still do something with his life. Maybe hope was happiness or happiness was hope or caring about other people and their future was progress, whatever, he was getting better. He knew it. That was definitely something to be happy about.

29

It was good to be home. The weather was getting warmer but all you needed to do was find a bit of shade and a breeze. Liz and Stella were both swimming every morning with Steve. They usually waited until he had done his laps to go in the pool. Liz swam laps but much slower. They went to the beach a lot. This was paradise for Stella and Kirk. Liz sat under an umbrella with a book and a beverage. Steve often played lifeguard.

Kirk was trying very hard to learn to swim but did not take advice easily. He preferred his own method, pounding the water yelling, "I can do it." He and Stella were always arguring about it but Steve just laughed. "At least he can't drown in this shallow water, and he'll come around, Stella, don't worry about him...he's ten!"

Stella was learning a lot about the different strokes from Steve. She had thought swimming was just that, swimming. Now she was getting her master's in the butterfly stroke, the frog kick, the Australian crawl, the scissors kick, etc, etc. Who knew?

It seemed the more she learned the more there was to learn. This, she was finding, was true in a lot of things. The higher you climbed up the mountain, the more mountains you could see that needed climbing. If you just stayed in the valley, you were master of all you surveyed. Stella knew she was a mountain climber. No doubt about it! She relished a challenge!

Uncle Win had told Liz to just relax while he investigated her legal situation. It seemed all those wills were getting on top of each other. If she had a boy, all hell would break loose. The child would inherit all that Dandler money and Liz would always have Johnny's family involved in his lifestyle and education. Win wanted to get all his ducks aligned before they found out where she was.

Liz did not want or need all that money. It came with too high a price. Win wanted her to get her husband's $3,000,000 from the older Mr. Dandler and also $3,000,000 each for the twins. She had received hers before Johnny died. Now it was up to him and his Atlanta attorney to represent Elizabeth in this family estate mess.

"Lizzie," Uncle Win said one evening. "The wheels of justice are greased with molasses. It might take years before all is resolved. You are five/six months away from finding out if you are having a boy and that is critical to the estate's case. Sonograms are not going to count. My advice is to just forget it while you can. Enjoy your new home. Enjoy your pregnancy. Relax while you can. I'll take care of the Atlanta situation."

"I'd like for Bethanne to visit," said Liz. "We could have fun together and she could tell me about my life. She might help me remember things. I wonder if she has children? How could I get in touch with her without giving my location away?"

"If you think she can keep your location secret, you can communicate through your Atlanta attorney."

"Great!" Said Liz. "I will write a letter to Bethanne right now. Tomorrow we can get a bike for Kirk and go to the beach. OK, Stell?"

"Awesome, Liz, Kirk will think it's Christmas. I'll get out the map of Key West and plan our safari through the back streets. It will be safer on the little lanes. Key West has got to get rid of some of the tourists...they clog the streets. What beach should we go to? Let's go to that beach with the volleyball and every thing. They had some totally cool dudes. Can we take ToJo?"

"Not there," answered Win. "But there is a dog beach next

122

to Louie's Backyard. It's tiny but he'll meet lots of buddies."

Liz decided to turn in. She had heard of eating for two when you were pregnant, but she felt she was sleeping for three. Over five months pregnant now, she was definitely starting to feel it and wearing large tee shirts and maternity shorts, she wasn't keeping a secret anymore. Her maternity bathing suits were comfortable, although she felt they made her look like a whale, but she was happy about her babies. Dr. Hu had sent her to an OB/GYN for her pregnancy and she liked her a lot. She was playing a waiting game in many ways. Take each day as it comes was now her motto.

Win left and ToJo made his nightly security tour of the garden. Kirk had the pooper-scooper job and was trying to train him to use the bushes. ToJo had not yet seen much point in that.

Stella, with Liz's help, had opened a saving account at the bank. She felt better if she had a bit of money that was hers alone. She was never going to be poor again if she could help it. Out of necessity, she had been in charge of her own life for many years but now it was different. Now it was out of choice and with good advice about what and how to do things. Stella was amazed at how different people could be.

She and Phillip had bonded over cooking and now Stella was helping him with his cookbook. She would write down the ingredients as he went along, the amounts, the procedure. He would get so carried away, waving arms and cursing that Stella told him he needed his own cooking show.

"You think I haven't thought of that?" Phil responded. "That's been my goal all along. I just need a producer. I have the cooking ability, the engaging personality and the looks. I think I should wear just jeans, an apron and a chef's hat. Call it the 'Bare-chested Chef' and we have a show! What do you think?"

"Wow, you have thought about it. I think that all would be great. I love the outfit. Totally! If I were a producer I'd grab it. And you're right...you do have the looks, and in a chef's apron, you would have both men and women tuning in just to catch those biceps as you whisk. I could be the 'Bare-chested Chef's' assistant...I'll just wear the apron!"

They were bent over laughing as Earl walked in. "What is so funny about cooking?" he asked.

They just kept on laughing. Earl would never get it.

30

Steven was now assisting Dr. Hu at his clinic three days a week. Craig Hu, a specialist in Family Practice, was trying to get Steven interested in medicine again. He felt all the time, effort and money spent getting a medical degree should not be wasted. Steven was still ambivalent about the whole subject, but a lot of Dr. Hu's patients were children and Steve always liked seeing children. Even under stress they were usually interested in their situation and surroundings. Of course, not all were angels but just conversing with them could change your attitude about life. It was amazing but some five-year-olds had it all figured out and freely explained their opinion on any subject.

He and Dr. Hu had decided helping in the clinic was good therapy for him, mentally and physically. His hand might never be able to perform an operation again but, although scarred, he was physically healed and working with children often made him laugh. They had many questions about what and why and often asked him about his own scars. What had he fallen off of and had he cried? He had made up some funny stories about his 'accident'. It was a good icebreaker...a bond, and usually got a smile.

Liz and Stella always wanted to hear about his day. He always saved the funny things for cocktails. The sad things he tried not to dwell on. Stella had read that animals were good for helping withdrawn children to open up and be more social.

"If you ever need an animal for a child to pat or talk to, ToJo would be really good." Stella offered. "He seems to sense when I need him and comes over to me. I think he would make a good healing dog." ToJo knew they were discussing him and gave a little 'woof'. He was intently watching Kirk paint snail shells different colors and then release the snails into the garden. Not exactly what Stella had planned for the paint set but one did not stand in the way of creativity.

"Good idea, Stell." Said Steve, " I've got one little boy, he's six, but he only whispers to his mother. Maybe he would talk to ToJo.

It's worth a try." Stella said.

"Just call me." She jumped up and ran in the direction of the pool. The totally cool, pool dude had arrived and Stella always had a million questions for him. Where did he go to school? Which beach was best? Where did the cool kids hang? Had he seen their iguana?

Liz laughed. "Maybe she should go into interrogation. She can get the scoop about anything. It's a gift."

Piling her blond hair up and catching it with a clip, Liz sat back and put her feet in another chair. She had on white shorts and a lime green, tank top with a casual necklace of chunky turquoise. Her skin glowed with tanned health and her eyes, picking up the colors, were unusual.

"How are you feeling, Liz? Anybody kicking yet?" Asked Steve. He was always pro-active about her having a healthy pregnancy, making sure she exercised and ate well.

"I feel great. I guess I'm lucky so far and I appreciate you being so interested. I know I look like a plump pillow and my pillow is going to get plumper but I'm very happy with my present situation."

"You look happy and more beautiful than ever." Said Steve. "I think it's very exciting. Win, Stell and I all feel like we're expanding our family. As Stell would say, it's awesome. I guess Kirk would say...why?"

Liz laughed. They were very careful when they were together. Both Steve and Liz were feeling a strong but subtle

126

attraction to each other, but did not feel the time was appropriate to express it. Each was still tied to the past and their lives were getting more complicated every day.

" I finally talked to Bethanne." Said Liz. "We talked and talked on the phone. She is going to make plans to come down. She and her husband, whom she swore to secrecy, are working on it so no one will be suspicious.

"Good. I think an old friend is just what you need. I'll take all of you out for dinner while she's here, so think about where you want to go."

"Stella's busy tonight with Phil and the cookbook." Said Liz. "Why don't we go out for dinner? Just us two and very casual."

"We can go to Salute's on the beach. Wear flats, it's very sandy...I'm not even sure if shoes are required. I love their white bean soup and garlic bread!"

Later that evening Liz and Steve were sitting at a table almost on the sand. A full moon was rising from the sea, gulls were wheeling and squealing overhead and a warm breeze was coming off the water. One of Key West's old, red brick forts was silhouetted in the moonrise. People all around greeted each other and yelled to others. Seemed every one knew each other. Steve said this was where those who lived on the island came. Battered old shorts and flip-flops were proper attire.

"I like this place." Said Liz. "It's very casual but the people seem a rather sophisticated group. Does that make sense?"

"It does. You see the man with the white hair and the torn tee shirt. He had another bestseller published last spring. The blond with the baby is Diane Sawyer's executive assistant here for a few months on maternity leave. The plump quy in the Hawaiian shirt is a big producer of Broadway shows."

Steve went on. " Key West is very easy to get to from New York. Lots of somebodys in the Big Apple come down and pretend to be nobodys here. But they all know who's who and what's what. That is the fun of it. These are not the super movie stars that the paparazzi follow. The general public may have heard of them but don't know them by sight. It's a more subtle celebrity."

"How in the world do you know all of this?"

"I've had many meals here with Win. He knows everyone and they know him. They use him if they need a Key West attorney. He used to practice in New York, many, many years ago. He, his wife and son used to come here on vacations but they lost their son, when he was around three, to a terrible childhood disease. After that, they moved down here permanently. They were good friends of your grandparents and knew both of your parents. You are, probably, as close to family as Win has since his wife passed away."

"If only my memory would come back. I'm glad you tell me things like this because I need to know." Liz paused. "I like being here with you. You are very comfortable to be with, you're smart and very sexy! I just thought you might want to know. Of course, it could just be the full moon..."

Steve laughed. "You could be trouble...I can see that! I'll go pay the bill and then we'll go sit over there on the sand and admire the moon. Just the two of us!"

Liz smiled sweetly, blinked her lashes and said, "I hate to remind you, Steveo, but if we go over there and sit on the sand there will be just the four of us!" Steve was shaking his head, grinning, as he walked away.

31

A few mornings later, Liz and Steve were having coffee on the terrace of the little house. Steve was teasing her about her baby bump. She was wondering how big she might get carrying two babies. Her black maternity tank suit was definitely more comfortable than her red suit. She had to think about new styles and loose tops. It was rather exciting, if you took a positive point of view.

Stella came running out with the phone. "I think it's Bethanne," she whispered.

"Hello," Liz said expectantly. "Oh, Bethanne! I'm so glad you called. I've been hoping you would. You can? Oh my God, I am so excited!"

Liz and Bethanne talked for twenty minutes while Stella hung on to every word. Any good new for Liz was good and Stell tried not to be jealous. Liz was laughing a lot. Finally she hung up.

"Guess what? She is coming in next week on the afternoon's plane. We'll pick her up at the airport around four. She and her husband are coming to Key West on vacation. That's her cover and it will be good for us to all be together, I guess. I don't exactly remember him."

"I can help with her husband if you want. I'll take him to play golf or something...maybe deep sea fishing," said Steve.

"Well, the four of us can go out for dinner. We can all sit

here and talk by the pool. I am really hoping this will be a key to open my past. She can help me buy some maternity outfits. Maybe we will all take the Conch Train as they need to see the sights. What about you, Stevo, have you ever taken the Conch Train? I haven't so we all need to go play tourist. Oh, this will be such fun!"

"Well, this tourist is off to the clinic." Said Steve "I can see you girls are going to be busy. By the way, Stell, I wanted to ask if you or Kirk could bring ToJo by the clinic this morning around ten. That shy little boy is coming in and perhaps if you just walk in with your dog we can casually see what happens. Maybe you could get him to sit on the porch with you and ToJo while he waited. We'll play it by ear, it will be a learning experience for us all."

Liz was off to ready the guest room for their first guest. Stell went to check with Phil about menus for the guests. ToJo just lay there. He knew they were talking about him. He better rest up for whatever.

At ten sharp, Stell, Kirk and ToJo walked into Dr. Hu's office. The little boy was sitting next to his mother. Stell waved to the receptionist while the boy and the dog eyed each other.

"Hi," said Stella to the boy. "I can see my dog likes you. His name is ToJo. Shake hands with the young man, ToJo." ToJo dutifully put his paw up to shake. The little boy shied back against his mother. Mother put her hand out and shook. "Look Adam, he's shaking my hand." Adam smiled shyly. "Let him shake your hand, Adam," said Stella. "He needs to make some new friends. We just moved here from Georgia and he's lonely. We're going to sit on the front steps. Will you and your mother come wait with us?"

Adam's mother picked right up on it and soon the four of them, and ToJo, were on the porch and Kirk was showing Adam how to pat ToJo. The boy started out rather tentatively, but was patting nonetheless. Kirk showed Adam how to throw a stick for ToJo to fetch. ToJo, completely understanding his role in this little game, returned the stick to Adam.

"Oh boy! Mom, did you see that? He likes me! He wants

me to play with him!"

By the time Steve came out, Adam and ToJo were playing together and had become hugging buddies. Steve sat down on the steps and Adam called out to him.

"Look Dr. Steve, ToJo likes to play with me! We're playing catch the stick. Wow! He is a really a super dog. That's what I'll call him, ' ToJo, the Super Dog!' Watch this, Mom." The stick went flying and ToJo went tearing off like he was at the Daytona Five Hundred.

"Amazing, just amazing." Said Steve, laughing and shaking his head. "What a difference. That child needs a dog." He turned to Adam's mom and asked if she could get a dog for Adam. She said she certainly would. "Look at him," she said. "I guess it helps him forget himself and not feel so shy." The boy's mother was laughing and calling out to her little boy and ToJo. Kirk was yelling, the dog was barking and Adam was laughing out loud.

Stella told Adam he could come by any time to see ToJo and maybe take him for a walk but if they would go to the animal shelter he could get a dog of his own to play with. ToJo, walking home with Kirk and Stella, knew he had accomplished something, even had a little strut. He knew he was good at this stick throwing stuff.

Kirk, on the other hand, was still trying to get a feel for this new place. He rode his new, blue bike up and down the lane looking for other kids. He had left a great gang up in Georgia...they even had a club house in an old refrigerator box under Georgie Elton's porch. They kept it covered with pieces of tarp, so the weather didn't destroy it, and had it furnished with important 'found' items...jars for bugs, odd pillows, a rusty saw for cutting windows, paper and pencils for writing secret messages and a party horn for a danger signal. He could see so many places here where he could build a clubhouse but he needed members.

On the front porch of one of the more dilapidated houses on the lane, he kept seeing a dark-haired boy who looked around his age but never waved back when Kirk would wave...although he'd been watching Kirk ride his bike around. This, thought

Kirk, needed checking into so he stopped at the house, parked his bike, and walked up to the steps.

"Hi, I'm Kirk and I just moved into that house over yonder. You live here?"

"Si."

"You speak English?"

"Si."

"Does si mean yes"?

"Si."

Kirk looked around the porch. The whole house had an unpainted look of silver-gray wood on all surfaces, the walls, porch floor, railings and screen door...leaves and vines spilled over the railing and climbed the posts holding up the porch roof. The boy just sat there in a chair with wheels. Kirk noticed one of his legs stopped right below the knee.

Not one to stand on ceremony, Kirk asked, "Hey, what happened to your leg?" He should get more then a "si" with that question.

"I was in accident," answered the boy, staring at Kirk. "Where you come from?"

"Georgia," answered Kirk. "What's your name?"

"Iggy", said the boy.

"What kinda name is that?" Asked Kirk.

"Iggy... for Ignacio Hipolito Diez y Morales."

"Ya sure got a big name for a little guy." Said Kirk "How old are ya?"

"I'm ten...you?"

"Just 'bout eleven," answered Kirk, reaching for the upper hand.

"What's with a name like Kirk?" asked Iggy.

"Don't ya watch Star Trek? I'm named for Captain Kirk! He was captain of the starship 'Enterprise'. It's an old TV show that has a lot of reruns."

"Yeah, but he ain't real." Iggy smiled. "I like your bike. Wish I could ride a bike." An old lady's voice came from the house calling to Iggy in Spanish. "Guess I gotter go now. You come back manana?"

"Sure." Kirk got up from the step he was sitting on. "I'll come back tomorrow and bring my dog. You'll like ToJo. He's cool. See ya."

Kirk got back on his bike and peddled to the little pink house. Now that, he thought, was interesting. How can you be in a gang if you only have one leg? He was going to have to think about this. Maybe Steve could help.

32

At four o'clock the following week, Liz was standing at
the single terminal gate of Key West International Airport. This
was a small airport, but she had just read a sign that declared
KWIA the first international airport in the country. Evidently,
at the beginning of passenger flight, a Pan Am Clipper flew from
Key West to Havana, Cuba, ninety miles away. Key West was full
of surprising, little known facts.

Liz had on a loose top and slacks held together with a
large rubber band. She did not want Bethanne to yell out when
she first saw her..."Oh crap! She's preggers!" If she remembered
Bethanne at all, she remembered she often yelled when she was
excited. Liz had this odd feeling that her past life was going to
walk through that entryway. Would Bethanne be the wedge to
open up her memory?

She told Stella she would go by herself to the airport. Liz
never went anywhere without Stella or Steve. This was kind of
scary. What if she did not recognize them? What if two perfect
strangers came over and hugged her. What would she do?

All of a sudden, there she was. Bethanne. She knew her!
"Oh my God, Bethanne! I recognize you!" She threw her arms
around her friend's neck. "Oh, Bethanne!" Liz started to cry and
laugh at the same time.

"Well, I guess she's glad we're here!" Bethanne was
laughing with Liz and hugging her. "You remember Jake, of

135

course."

"No, as a matter of fact, I don't but I'm so glad you both came."

"You don't remember Jake? After all the trouble we had getting him to ask me to marry him? You were right there. I asked you to be in my wedding but you couldn't. Remember?"

"I hate to tell you this but I don't remember my mother or Johnny. My past has been erased. I'm hoping you can help. You are the only person I remember. Let's get your luggage. We'll go home and have drinks on the terrace."

"Sounds great to me," said Jake.

They started down Roosevelt Boulevard. "Look at that beautiful water!" said Bethanne. "I've got a feeling, Jake, that she's left us and moved to paradise."

Liz laughed. "I do love it here. I can't remember anything about it but I used to live here with my mother and grandmother. The island is beautiful, laid back and full of history. I love my house and I have a pool under a sea grape tree that is sometimes visited by a large, green iguana."

"Oh crap, I hope he'll find another tree while we're here!"

Liz told them about Stella and Kirk, Steven and ToJo. "Sounds like you are making up a family as you go along," said Jake.

They loved the island and her house and were soon sitting on the terrace of the little house having an assortment of cooling cocktails. In Key West, five o'clock often comes early! Stella joined them and soon Steven came down from the big house. Stella was serving hors d'oeuvres she had put together with local fruits and veggies. Win dropped by to meet Bethanne.

"I had to meet you, Bethanne. When you are the only person Liz remembers, you must be special. We hope you can be a key of some kind but regardless, it is nice having you in Key West." Win could not stay for dinner and left through the garden.

Stella was going to walk her dog and check on Kirk who was spending a good portion of every day sitting on the porch of his new friend's house. She needed to go and visit his friend and meet his great-grandmother. She was happy Kirk had found

136

a friend on the lane.

At dusk, Liz, Steven, Bethanne and Jake walked to Michael's for dinner. Bethanne was elated when she found out Liz was having twins. She looked at Steven. "Tell me, Dr. Steve, how do you fit into this picture?"

Steve chuckled. "That is to be decided in the future but right now we are all trying to live in the present. Of course, the past keeps infringing upon our island idyll but we're working on that. The only sure thing is the babies will arrive around December. Right now we're taking each day as it comes." Steve replied smiling, looking at Liz. "'Live in the present' is our motto."

Steve and Jake left early the next morning to play golf. The girls went shopping. Liz bought a few new outfits, cute but expandable, but also kept questioning Bethanne. Who? When? What happened then? Bethanne was very patient and answered all her questions in detail. Liz was starting to slowly remember some things about her past life by just hearing about it. Not recalling her life with Johnny but her life in college and the ZTA house and her major of Interior Design. "I can't believe I'm an interior designer! Do you think I can recall any of my training? Oh man, this is crazy. I'm glad I wasn't a brain surgeon. What a waste!"

The waitress would take their drink and food orders and Liz would ask Bethanne, "Did I like beer?" "What foods did I really like?" "Did I drink much when I went out?" If Stella was around she hung on to every word. Sometimes she would just hoot. It could be funny...the look on Liz's face when Bethanne recalled choice events of her past. But it was helping. She was starting to recall old college boyfriends even, but not Johnny. There had to be a reason for that.

33

The rest of the week was a fun, touristy time. The Bentons had never been to the island, Steve had been gone for years, and Liz, of course, remembered none of it, so they were all interested in the history of Key West. Because of the reef seven miles out marking the Florida Straits, water around the island calmly lapped up on the beaches so they swam in calm, ocean waters, toured old forts, had lunch under whispering palms and celebrated the sunset down at Mallory Square. One evening they took in a play at the Tennessee Williams Theatre and another night the four attended an art show at the historic Old Armory.

Liz had been studying the old yearbooks and scrapbooks that Bethanne had brought with her. She was starting to feel like something might be coming back. She was hopeful. Jake flew back after a week, but Bethanne, sensing Liz was being helped by their constant conversations about their past, stayed another week.

Stella lent Bethanne her pink bike and she and Liz peddled all over the island. They talked over lunches under umbrellas, discussed old friends while sipping fruity libations, paused for cute shops and never ignored a shady bench. They talked and talked. Liz started to understand her situation better as she learned details of her past.

Bethanne told her that Johnny had been a great guy. She felt he had been overtaken by his family, as had Liz. The Dandlers were a strong and powerful force to counter. She reminded Liz how Johnny wanted to be a high school football coach when they got married. He never got the chance; and after his father died, his life wasn't his anymore.

A week later, Liz put Bethanne on the plane, came home and slept for hours. Liz looked happy but exhausted. She had not been getting her daily eighteen hours of sleep.

The next day, rested and feeling on top of things, Liz and Stella continued their argument about the color of the babies' room. Stell, of course, was in favor of pink. Liz on the other hand, did not want pink or blue. They finally decided on pale, pale aqua for the walls, white for trim and furniture, pale lime for accent color and a touch of little girl pink for Stella. These were going to be island babies, Stella was seeing to that. Kirk thought all this baby conversation was boring and was spending more time on Iggy's front porch.

Steve was over the next Saturday to help with the painting. Phillip had brought down a ladder and a drop cloth. There was as much discussion about what to eat while painting as there was about the process. Liz was measuring for a rug amid all the chaos in the small room when Earl walked in.

"Liz, someone is here to surprise you." He paused as he waited for Liz's reaction. Liz stood up. She had on khaki short shorts, a large white tee shirt, her curly hair twisted up and no make-up. She looked expectantly at the women in the tailored suit and sensible shoes and smiled. "Hello."

Each person in the room stopped what they were doing and turned toward the women. No one spoke. Finally Liz said. "May I help you?"

Earl looked baffled. "She said she was a relative, Liz. Don't you remember her?"

Liz looked at Stella and Steve as if for support. "No. I'm sorry, do I know you?"

"Don't be ridiculous, Elizabeth, of course you know me."

Steve spoke up. "Liz has amnesia and doesn't remember people from her past. I'm Dr. Steven Sandford and you are?"

"This is unconscionable, Elizabeth, of course you know

me. Mary! Johnny's sister! We have been looking all over for you. What are you doing here, of all places? Who are these people? Why did you leave Atlanta?"

Steve stepped in. "Phil, I think this calls for refreshments on the terrace. Stell, would you call Win and ask him to join us, please. Mary, if you'll accompany Phil outside we will be right there."

Liz was standing in the middle of the room like she was frozen. Steve went over and put his arms around her, she was trembling. He just held her for a few minutes. "They were going to find you at some point, Liz, but you have all of us to help you now. Don't worry about Mary. I don't think she even remembers meeting me in Atlanta. Win is on his way over. Stella is like a mama bear, and I won't leave your side. Come on, Sweetheart, lets go out to the terrace and have a mango cooler. Nobody can make you leave Key West if you choose not to leave. Just remember, Lizzie, with you and Mary, even by yourself...it's three to one!"

34

It was kind of funny in a way. Phil immediately went into catering mode, but Stella stood next to Liz. "Of course," Phil said to Mary Dandler Cox, "if you do not prefer the mango smash we can get you whatever you might like."

"Have a bit of our guacamole dip," said Stella. "It's from Liz's garden."

Mary had a bit of a 'who are you people?' look on her face as she sat down in one of the wrought iron chairs and folded her arms. "What is going on here?" she demanded, looking around as if she had never seen anything this strange in her life.

Liz and Steve came out in their painting clothes. Liz, tanned, blond tendrils spilling down from pinned up hair, looking casually beautiful and sexy...but then, so did Steve. They took side-by-side chairs at the table and Liz said to Mary, "I'm so sorry I didn't recognize you, Mary, but I have amnesia and I don't remember people and events in my past. I don't remember my mother, my grandmother, living in Key West or Johnny. It's such an odd feeling to forget all you knew but I'm trying to recall my past. I've just not had much success."

Mary looked at Liz. "I don't believe a word of it. You left us at a very critical time. After the funeral we needed you there to keep up interest in Johnny...take over his seat in the Senate. You know you must do this, for Johnny. You are a Dandler now. Everyone is asking about you...wanting to interview you. What in the world are you doing in this god-forsaken place, and who are these...people?"

"Well, hello everyone. Am I late to the party? You know what I like Phil, I'll have a double." Uncle Winnie had arrived. "And who is this pretty lady might I ask?"

"I am Mary Dandler Cox. I am here to see my sister-in-law. With whom am I speaking?"

"I am Winslow Van Rensselaer Morgenstern. But you may call me Uncle Winnie or just Win. I'm a life long friend of Lizzie's and have always handled the legal matters for her and her family." Win reached out for his drink. "Thanks Phil, you're a prince."

"I can not believe any of this farce!" said Mary with haughty anger. "What game are you playing, Liz...what are you after? The Dandler money? Well, you won't get any of it staying down here. The only way you will ever see a penny is to come back to Atlanta and do the job you should be doing. You have responsibilities to the Dandler family, important responsibilities. I'll have my attorney tell you what you can expect if you stay here and continue this silly charade."

"I'll be happy to discuss the situation with your attorney, Mary," said Win. "Chris Calhoun, I believe. Perhaps you haven't noticed, but Liz is pregnant. With twins if you can believe it!"

"That's what we were doing today, Mary, painting the nursery," said Liz.

Mary Dandler Cox sat in stunned silence. This did change the entire scenario. What if Elizabeth had a boy. Twins? That dammed Johnny never did anything right!

"We would love to have you stay with us, Mary," Liz said. "There's a lot of room at the big house."

"No thank you, Elizabeth, I am booked at the Casa Marina Hotel."

"Well, let us take you out for dinner, Mary," Win said. "We can go to Louie's. It's a short walk from the Casa Marina. I'll pick you up at six-thirty. You should experience a little of Key West while you're here. The food is excellent!" Mary, realizing the present situation was far different from what she had expected to find, agreed. She needed time to confer with her lawyer.

At six forty-five, Mary and Win walked onto the back deck of Louie's and joined Liz and Steve under the canopy of trees. The setting was a 'tourist poster' view of mauve and yellow painted skies over a calm, reflective ocean as twilight crept in. Phil sent hors d'oeuvres, compliments of the chef. Every effort was being made to make this a pleasant evening.

Mary asked, in a very pointed, eyebrow raised manner, who Steve was and what his relationship was to Liz. She was told they were both here to recover from different accidents. She seemed to find this, and most everything else, suspect. After she returned to Atlanta, she would confer with her attorney. It was worse than she had expected, and she wasn't sure how this problem should be handled. She was getting the feeling Elizabeth was not returning.

"Tell me, Elizabeth, just what are your plans? You do have responsibilities in Atlanta, as I am sure you understand. I know you will do the right thing. When can we expect you back?" Mary was a perfect example of a southern magnolia with petals of steel.

Liz looked at Steve and Win, took a deep breath, and said to Mary, "I'm not coming back, Mary. My life, as Johnny's wife, is over. My life as a Dandler is over. I can't even remember Johnny or my life in Atlanta. I'm living in my own home, here in Key West, and plan to raise my children here. I feel comfortable among people who knew me and my family, even if I don't remember them. I'm sorry about Johnny, very sorry, but that life is over for me...why don't you take over for him, Mary? You have the desire for it. I don't."

"You had no idea what you are giving up, Elizabeth. People would vote for you. You could be successful in Atlanta and all of Georgia. Even move up to Congress! Think about it!"

"I have thought about it, Mary, and I don't want it. I want a garden, children playing around me, and a husband who cares about those things too. You have just described the life you want, Mary. It's your dream, not mine."

35

The next evening they were all casually sitting around the terrace. Win had driven Mary to the airport and they had talked about the Dandler situation as he waited with her until she left. He felt he was getting a better picture of what the problems were that Liz would be facing. Mary's family had power and influence and the more he knew, the better prepared he could be.

Liz was up after an afternoon nap, Steve was back from the clinic and Stella and Kirk had returned from biking to town to pick up conch fritters from B O's Fish Wagon. The terrace was getting to be the place to which everyone gravitated and they all loved conch fritters. Stella, Liz and now Kirk would have a mango smash, Steve a beer, and Win fixed his own.

Win sat back in his chaise. "I think that went about as well as it could. Mary and I talked about what she would say about you, Liz, when she returned to Atlanta. We decided on the truth plus a little fiction. You had an accident. You have amnesia. You spent some time in New England recuperating. You are still having problems with your memory and have chosen to move back to your childhood home in Key West. She can say whatever she wants about the twins, but they are a fact of life."

"That's for sure," said Liz. "They are starting to let me know that they are there." She put her arms around her tummy and gave them a hug.

"But I think," Win went on, "there will be a battle over the estate. Mary seems to feel that any money needs to be tied to working the family business. Even if that means just being a part of the social life of Atlanta as you had been. We will find ourselves in court for sure. But don't worry about it. That's my job."

"Thanks, Uncle Winnie. It's wonderful having someone like you in the family."

"Hello all," said Earl, as he approached the terrace. "Phil said before he left you were going to get conch fritters, Stella. I hope there's one left? I brought my own glass of wine and wanted to apologize for waltzing in with Mary. I should have given you a bit of a warning, Liz. I forget that you don't remember people you knew. It must be a very odd feeling."

"Help yourself, Earl," Said Liz, gesturing to the fritters. "Don't worry about Mary. I think we came to an understanding over some things. And by the way, I've been wanting to ask you if you have ever been in the attic of the big house?"

"No. I tried one time but there is no key that I could find. I always picture it full of cobwebs and treasures."

"I'll call a locksmith and see about it. Before we start buying baby furniture I want to check up there and see what we have. It should be interesting at the very least."

"Do you have a good mice, scorpion and spider spray?" said Steve, laughing at Liz and Stella's reaction to his comment. "Maybe there'll be a ghost up there."

"Cool!" Kirk was suddenly interested in the conversation. "That would be awesome, to have a ghost! I'll come too. Maybe there will be treasure in an old trunk or something."

"A ghost...not in my house there's not. I'd see to that!" Said Earl with a glint of a smile. "This house, with full-size porches on both first and second story, built to extend around three sides of the house with beautiful balustrades, is an architectural gem. The attic is the third floor, and above that is the widow's walk. I've been dying to go up there. You know the view is going to be fabulous. I can't wait. I hope I'm invited to be a part of this."

"Of course, Earl, we'll have an attic party...old clothes,

148

dust masks, feather dusters, hand vacs." said Liz. "Tell me, Stella, is there a menu for attic soirées or ghostbuster soup"?

"I hope we'll have no food in the attic...bugs, you know." Said Earl

"Oh, come on, Earl, bugs don't eat much," said Stella mischieviously. "Perhaps we'll have a ghost lunch on the terrace? I'll check with Phil. He'll know what ghosts eat. Phil knows things like that. Right, Kirk?"

"Heck, Phil knows about everything, even pirates. He was telling me they used to come to this island to hide their treasure. It could be hidden anywhere. Maybe the ghost is a pirate ghost! Man, this is gonna be cool!"

Liz was starting to take more interest in the big house. At first, with all of her personal problems, she was overwhelmed with the new responsibility. Now she was feeling better about her life and future. Now she did not feel so alone.

The big house was a classic design with gracious proportions. Painted white with dark green shutters, it had been many things in its history: hospital, restaurant, family home. On an island, with little or no zoning in its past, most old structures had unusual past lives. Some were even notorious.

As Liz ambled off to bed that night she thought about getting someone from the Old Island Historical Society to come by and tell her about her house. Tonight, though, she just hoped when the time came, she could make it up to the widow's walk.

She was sort of relieved about being found by the Dandlers. Now she knew they could not hurt her. It was wonderful to feel safe and know you had friends who were there for you in every way. She felt very fortunate. This 'family' may not be related but they were reliable!

Kirk and Stella were telling Steve about the boy across the lane, Iggy. Stella had gone over to meet him and his great-grandmother. His grandmother lived in Cuba, and his parents, who had come to Key West before he was born, had been killed in the automobile accident that had injured Iggy. Kirk wanted Steve to see him and maybe help him.

"Most days he just sits there on the porch in that dumb,

old chair with stupid wheels," said Kirk. "His great-grandmother is too darn old to take him to a doctor, and he has nobody to help 'im. I think you could help 'em get a fake leg or a peg leg like real pirates. He speaks English, but not so good, but he could be my friend and we could have a real club if he could get off that stupid porch. His great grandmother doesn't want him to leave the porch because she's so old she can't go anywhere. Some truck comes by once a day and brings ' em food. I really, really, really think he needs our help."

"Sounds like he might," said Steven. "Let's go see him tomorrow and see if there is something we can do. I'd like to meet him...peg leg, huh...I'm sure we could do a bit better than that in this 21st century. But then, who knows? We'll wander over tomorrow...guess we know where to find him."

36

A few mornings later, a locksmith in cutoff jeans, muscle shirt and flip-flops met Liz and Stella at the front door of the big house and followed Stella up to the attic. Liz ascended the three tiers of steps slowly with dust masks in her hand in case they needed them. She expected a jumble of things, all mixed together, but surprisingly, all was in perfect order...dusty, but neat. The last person to leave the attic had been very meticulous. Maybe they knew it would be years before anyone else came. It was a strange, eerie feeling, like you were somewhere you weren't supposed to be.

Pausing in the doorway, Stella said, "This is amazing! Like a secret room left untouched! I wonder how long it has been since someone was in here?"

"I've got to sit down," panted Liz, as she found an old, dust-covered chair. She and Stella just looked around. The attic was a large room with dormer windows, peaked ceiling, and a beautiful, even when covered with dust, heart-of-pine floor. In the ceiling were scuttles for ventilation. Before air conditioning these would have been opened for heat to pass up and out of the house. The walls were horizontal boards of pine. It was a finished attic and probably used, at one time, as a room.

The women did not know where to start. Liz saw an old brown wicker baby carriage in a corner. She exclaimed, "Oh, look! A perambulator. Look at all that fancy wickerwork. Oh my

151

goodness, it's a work of art! We can definitely use that, Stell."

Earl and Phil had arrived and they, too, were just looking things over from a distance. Steve came up, looked around, and commented, "A page from history. Amazing!"

"The maid is here today," said Earl. "Why don't I ask her if she would just vacuum the floor and maybe the tops of things? Then we won't stir up as much dust when we move these odd bits around."

"Great idea, Earl!" said Liz.

"While she is doing that, let's see if we can get up to the widow's walk," said Steve. Those are the steps over there."

"Looks like a trap door at the top," said Phil. He and Steve tried to lift it. "I think it's locked. Who has the key?" Liz got up and reached the key up to Steve. All of the sudden sunlight flooded the room. Steve and Phil climbed out and helped Liz who was right behind them.

Key West in all its sunlit, colorful glory lay below. You could see from the Atlantic Ocean to the Gulf of Mexico. Church steeples, tall trees, cruise ships, other large houses with widow's walks or cupolas ...it was a cyclorama of the island city. It was awesome! This time everyone agreed with Stella. The view was totally awesome!

Liz went over to Steve and nestled close to him. He put his arm around her and asked, "What's the matter, Sweetheart?" Liz answered softly, "I remember this view! I was up here with my mother and grandmother...I waved to people on the street but they never looked up...it was windy and mother's scarf blew off her head and landed in a tree. We all laughed. I remember it! I remember what she looked like! Oh Steve...it's all coming back!" Tears were sliding down Liz's face.

"Maybe we should go back down and sit for a while. I don't want you to get dizzy up here with all those memories flooding in," said Steve.

"No, just hold me. I don't want to leave yet. The memories might go away!" So they stood there...Steve with both arms around Liz and Liz gazing off into the distance.

Everyone came up, exclaiming over the view, pointing out

152

landmarks. Stella looked over at Steve with a questioning look. "Her memory is coming back," he said softly. "She remembers being up here before."

Kirk was amazed to see the huge cruise ships! He was so excited Stella had to hold on to him. 'I really feel like I live on an island now!" said Kirk. "If I had a gang, we could build our club house up here and spy on everyone on the island. We could watch out for pirates from here! Wow, I need to get a spyglass!" Kirk's ten-year-old's imagination was already flying the 'Jolly Roger'.

Everyone went up - even Elaine, Earl's maid. This was a special event. Earl was absolutely enchanted. They decided to leave the door wide open while they were in the attic. The light that came in was wonderful, and people went up and down. Elaine had finished vacuuming when Liz and Steve came down. Liz was smiling as she sat back down in her chair.

"I remember I used to play up here," she said. "I had a girl friend across the street, Zola. She and I played dolls up here by the hour, especially on rainy days. I believe that brown and tan trunk holds clothes. We played dress-ups and wheeled our dolls around in that wicker baby carriage. There used to be a lot of wicker furniture up here. When we played house we moved it all around. I'm so thrilled to remember everything I see. Oh, my God, I feel like my life is flowing back inside of me!"

Stella was as thrilled as Liz. "This is just totally amazing!" said Stella. "Do you want to stay up here? Or maybe go lie down? How do you feel?" Stella was hovering.

"I feel fabulous! I love it up here. Let's start opening things. I feel my life is starting over and I have to catch up!"

37

It was a pleasant place with the door to the widow's walk open...light, sunny and now, rather clean. Earl was using his camera, he always saw himself as the official historian in residence. The baby carriage was taken downstairs by Phil to be cleaned later. Phil, Stella, Earl and Steven each carefully tackled a box or trunk or chest. Liz sat and watched, occasionally going over to look at something. Anything not presently usable was put back into its container. Steve found more old wicker, including an original floor lamp with a huge wicker shade. The furniture had all been covered with huge dust cloths.

Liz was thinking out loud. "This would make a perfect play room for the twins and their dolls and doll furniture, little kitchens, stuffed animals. We could put fun cushions on the wicker furniture and leave it up here. A big, fluffy rug on the floor would make it very comfortable."

"It is also a perfect place for trains tracks, car races, some legos. Don't you think Stell?" Steve asked.

"I don't think trains come in pink, Stevo. Although Thomas the Choo Choo is kind of cute."

"Trains are not cute, Stell. Trains are tough. Cute train is an oxymoron," Steve said.

Stell responded. "I don't know who is the oxy here but I sure know who is the moron! Steve laughed. Stella always had the quick comeback.

155

"Oh look! Photograph albums. Maybe I'll recognize some of these people." Liz sat down again with the albums in her lap.

Steve came over. "Let me shake them a bit before you put them in you lap, Liz, you never know in the tropics, they've been stored a long time." Steve shook the books and dusted them off a bit more. He smiled at Liz, "We don't want any little bugs biting our babies. Has all of your memory come back or just things about the house?"

"I'm not sure yet but I seem to think I remember times in Key West...what I did in this house...my friend Zola, I can picture her. I can see my mom and dad...and Granny...I'm just thrilled with that...and these pictures...I remember when and where they were taken. Oh God, I am so relived! The view from that widow's walk must have broken through a barrier of some sort!"

Earl was cataloging the old things that seemed to have historical value. There was a faded hatbox with three beautifully trimmed lady's hats, high-buttoned leather shoes, umbrellas, a fox stole with his tail caught in his mouth...all from another era. It was obviously from the late 1800's, Key West's most prosperous years .

Liz could remember playing with that fox stole. It had been highly sought after by little girls playing dress-ups. She told Earl her great-grandmother wore that when the family sailed to New York for shopping and sight seeing. Liz was remembering old stories.

There was a saffron-colored, fragile chiffon gown covered with amber bugle beads from the twenties and a silk top hat. Many pieces of elegant costume jewelry were in velvet boxes. Stella and Liz wanted to go through those and lots of books, including a set of old encyclopedias listing the seven planets around the sun, "The Palmer Writing Method", "Good Etiquette and Manners for the Gentleman".

Liz wondered if anyone wanted anything. Earl asked if he could have the silk top hat. It would be a big hit during Fantasy Fest. Liz was going to call the Historic Association to see if they wanted some of the items. There were two silver-headed canes that Steve said he and Win would like, and Liz and Stell

156

were going to take the jewelry and the saffron gown. There was an old silver sword that Kirk wanted, but it was too historic to become a plaything. He said he would think about it; he felt the old toys were for babies, not ten-year-old boys. They left the door unlocked so they could come back at leisure. Steve closed and locked the widow's walk, but left the key on a peg by the steps.

Earl came up to Elizabeth to ask her about his lease on the big house. It ran until December 31st. He wanted to know if she had plans to move in after the babies. After all that talk about a playroom in the attic, he was getting nervous.

Liz thought about it. "You know, Earl, I thought I was about a year away from moving. Stell and I were happy in our little house. When we moved in there it was just the two of us and I still think it would be easier, taking care of two babies, in a smaller space...but now Kirk is with us...and after the babies I'm going to need a nurse...so it's getting a little crowded over there. The babies will be in cribs but they will need changing tables, rockers and all that stuff, so one room will have to be theirs. They won't need a playroom for a while but the rest of us will be on top of each other. Don't feel rushed but perhaps you and Phil could start looking for someplace else. You take very good care of the house and I really appreciate it. I'm going to hate to see you leave."

Win came by that evening to hear about the attic finds and was very pleased with his silver fox-headed cane. The tray full of costume jewelry on the terrace table had Liz and Stella oohing and aahing over the beautiful Art-Deco pieces. When Liz told him she was remembering her time in Key West, Win was very relieved. They talked about her family for quite a while.

Steve grilled grouper filets, and Stella fixed a Caesar salad and hot garlic bread with mango sorbet for dessert. Liz thought it was a perfect ending to the day. She did not have long to go before her perfect serene evenings would change. The babies were kicking now and it felt funny. But in every way, it was very thrilling! Steve looked over at her and smiled; he looked wonderful, even in a chef's apron. Oh my, thought Liz, is it the babies kicking or Steve smiling at me that creates this little thrill in my tummy?

Kirk was having a serious conversation with Steve about his new friend, Iggy. The two of them were going to visit him tomorrow. Kirk just couldn't imagine a life spent sitting on the porch; he had big plans for Iggy. Whether Iggy realized it or not, his life was about to change!

38

As Uncle Winnie had promised, the Dandlers were suing to amend both wills of the Dandler men, father and son. They thought it important to educate and raise a male child as the father and grandfather had been raised. The sisters wanted the bulk of the money to go into a trust to be administered by the three of them. Elizabeth had received three million from Johnny's father, that, they felt was more than enough to satisfy any spousal inheritance. The twins, if girls, were to get $100,000 on their eighteenth birthday. If a boy were born, his settlement would depend on conditions of his upbringing.

Win and Liz talked it over. Nothing would be done before the birth of the children, and then Win had other ideas. These were his 'grandchildren', and he would see they got what was rightly theirs. Liz, although she wanted none of the Dandler money, was entitled to a wife's share of Johnny's estate.

"Lizzie," Win said, "you just sit back and don't worry about a thing but those babies and let me take care of the rest. That good old boy, Chris Calhoun, ain't seen nothing yet. Jesus, Joseph and Abraham! This gets my juices flowing! I can't wait!

Liz walked back from Win's office, down the lane to the little house, waving to Aunt Norma on her porch and Kirk, Steven and Iggy on Iggy's porch. Stella met her at the door of the little house in a frenzy. She had a date with the pool dude! What should she wear? She had to be cool. This was Stella's first date.

No one had asked her out in Georgia. She was too busy working. This was awesome! He would be here in three hours!

"Stell, sit down a minute. Calm down. He is only the pool dude and you already know him as a friend. Where is he taking you?"

"To the movies. He's using his mother's car. What should I wear? Tell me Liz!"

"You haven't asked me what to wear since I met you. What about the pink and lime green sundress and pink flats?"

"Oh come on...you have got to be kidding!" Yelled Stella. "Who wears pink and green to a movie? You just want everyone to laugh at me!"

Liz started to laugh. Stell was not laughing. This was the most important outfit she had ever worn.

"OK, let's see here. What did you notice about other girls when we went to the movies the other night...slacks, shorts or skirts? How short were the skirts? Did they wear tee shirts with the skirts? What kind of shoes? Well, Stell, you have all of those things in your closet. Let's go look."

One hour later a decision had been made. Stella wasn't acting like her usual confident self but was OK with their decision. Liz was exhausted. When Steven came by for the evening on the terrace, he thought the whole episode that Liz was relating was amusing...until Stella came out.

She said she would wait out front for her date. Steve said, no way! Her date would ring the bell, come in and chat a bit with them. It was the only polite thing to do. Stella said that was for cavemen! Steve said she had to be in by eleven. Stella yelled. "I'm not your daughter and I'll come in when I come in!"

Liz started to laugh. "Oh dear, we sound like a real family here. Uh, Stell, we, um, care about you so I expect you to, um, act accordingly. No rules, just common sense." The doorbell rang. Steve answered it. Pool Dude came in, spoke to Liz and Steve, said he and Stella were going to the movies and would be home around eleven thirty or so and they left.

"Well, I guess we handled that OK." Said Steve.

Liz was laughing so hard she had to sit down and hold

her sides. "Maybe if we practice on Stella we'll have it down pat in sixteen years...especially the caveman part."

"We? Are you asking the caveman to hang around for sixteen years?" said Steve with a long, sexy look over his shoulder.

Liz looked flustered but still was smiling. "I guess I'm taking this made up family thing too seriously, but it seems like a nice thought. But who knows when you are going to leave Key West? You look better and better each day, and I can tell you're feeling better. While I, on the other hand, just keep getting bigger and bigger...still can't remember the father of my babies."

"I'm sure of only two things," Liz went on. "Having twins and making my home here on the island where I feel happy and safe. I suppose that's my nesting instinct coming to the fore, but it's true. Whatever I find out, I will still stay here. Maybe it's because I was born here, but I've got sand in my shoes." She paused as she looked up at Steve and asked, "Do you think you might have sand in your shoes someday?"

Steve sat down next to her and took her hand. "I'll be here till after Christmas for sure. You don't think I'd leave you and these babies do you?" He paused, looking serious "I also think you and I have something special happening between us, but it's not the right time for us yet. The past I can't forget and the past you can't remember keep getting in our way. But there's no hurry; it will be a while before the twins are dating!"

Liz laughed and grabbed her side. "Uh! One of them is kicking the other. Oh, it feels so funny! Feel right here."

Steve, sitting next to Liz on the sofa, put a hand next to hers on her tummy. She put her head on his shoulder. "I guess this is as romantic as it gets," she said.

Steve chuckled, kissed her on the forehead, and said. "We can name one Faith and the other Hope." Sitting side-by-side, Liz's feet up on an ottoman, they both were silent, considering their oddly amorous predicament.

"And then there's Charity..." Steve shook his head, smiling to himself. "I went over to see Iggy today, and Kirk's right. That boy could be out and about with a little effort and money. His great-grandmother is in her nineties and only sits in the back of the house and watches Cuban soaps. She is too old to be caring for any child, must less a handicapped child but she is the only family member he has still living. Also, she speaks only Spanish. I've got to find an interpreter and convince her Iggy needs to go to a new doctor. Also find her some help; the house is a mess and she is too infirm to do anything about it. I don't know how he gets around in there with crutches, and I'm sure their food situation is haphazard."

"You care," said Liz softly. "Maybe that is what appeals to me about you. You care about people and try to do something to help them. I agree. Helping Iggy walk is an exciting adventure in the making. We'll all help. I like having good things to do with my inherited money. We'll start with Iggy."

Steve turned around to look at Liz. "Start with Iggy? You started with Stella and then Kirk and ToJo...you're way ahead of me." He laughed "Maybe that's what appeals so much to me about you...and the beautiful eyes, the sexy lips, the perfect figure...if I can remember that far back."

Liz hit him with a pillow.

39

Key West was having a lot of rain. That did not mean the island had rainy days just heavy showers off and on during the day. The sun would then emerge, sucking up all evidence of raindrops but leaving a warm, humid consistency to the air. It was near the end of hurricane season. Hot sticky afternoons, cooled by tropical downpours, were the usual forecasts. Rain sounded exotic when big fat, cool drops hit large flat, hot leaves. Liz loved the familiar plopping sounds. It brought back a lot of girlhood memories.

So far, they had been lucky with hurricanes this year. It was always a summer topic of conversation. Oddly enough, it was never thought uncharitable to wish a storm on somewhere else. Like a lottery system, luck had everything to do with it, not to mention highs and lows and troughs and steering systems.

Liz had been advised by her doctor to take it easy. She was now over seven months along and a morning dip in the pool was about the extent of her exercise regimen. The nursery was ready with two cribs and two rockers. Stella felt they might need to rock two babies at the same time. Stella had also managed to get a soft, pink bunny into each crib.

School had begun and Stella and Kirk were meeting young people their ages. They both joined clubs and teams and Liz and Steve often went to school events. Liz felt Steve went mostly to drive her and take her arm when walking. Liz was in the 'waddle like a duck' stage. She spent a lot of time in bed. She knew twins were often early and the longer she could carry the babies the better off they would be.

Iggy was being home-schooled again this year by a special-needs teacher. Steven had run into a conundrum with Iggy and his leg. His great-grandmother did not trust anyone and did not want him to leave the porch where she felt she could watch him. Steve was trying to get a group of Cubans that she might trust to talk to her, but so far she was not convinced. Kirk was not showing a lot of patience.

Dinner on the terrace one evening after school started was dominated by TV weather reports that had everyone's attention. It seemed hurricane Marta was heading their way, churning across the Atlantic, and projected to hit the keys. They discussed plans for the storm, mostly which house would be best to weather a hurricane. If they used the big house, more people would be together and they could take in Aunt Norma. That would be eight people and a dog. Kirk was to find out where Iggy and his great-grandmother usually went. It could be ten and a dog.

"Perhaps Liz should go to the hospital before the storm," said Steve. "Just in case things might start early."

"No way," said Liz. "I am not sitting in the hospital all by myself while you all have a hurricane party. I'm not due for over a month. I'll just sit tight. I'll be fine."

"I'll talk to Earl and Phil tomorrow morning," said Steve. "Phil will want to go to the grocery; the stores will be crowded. I'll talk to Win. You, Stell, can check to see if Aunt Norma wants to join us. She should not be alone. Liz, your job is to keep off your feet until the storm is over. I mean it! Don't lift a finger!"

If the hurricane hit, it was about a day and a half away. It was still gaining strength and could veer off up the coast of Florida and hit Jacksonville. They were all hoping - that is, everyone but Kirk. He was thrilled with the idea of seeing a real hurricane. He was watching the weather channel with exuberant glee.

There is a certain amount of excitement engendered by an oncoming storm. Hurricane flags are flown in front of the

164

Coast Guard Station...one red flag with a black square in the center for a gale, two flags for a hurricane! As the winds picked up, the sound of pounding nails resounded over the island. Everyone becomes friendlier as people take in neighbors whose storm situation is not as safe as theirs. Young men assisted older neighbors in boarding up their windows. People checked on those known to live alone. Social Services picked up older and handicapped people. They were going to take Iggy's great-grandmother to a shelter, but Iggy was coming with Kirk to the big house. They were bringing Monopoly, Clue and a chess set.

On an island, preparation is very important. It only took one bridge to go out of service and Key West lost its landline. So everyone planned for the possibility of being without water and electricity for a while. With over one hundred miles of a two-lane road and many, many bridges connecting the island to the mainland, Key Westers had learned to be adaptable. They bought canned food and crackers (safe without refrigeration), bottled water (in case the water main, coming down the keys got blown away), ice (to preserve food or chill wine), and briquettes for the bar-b-que grill so all the frozen meat in you freezer could be cooked as it thawed.

School was called off so students could help get ready. Stella was going to the store with Phil. She wanted to make sure he got normal food and not just gourmet items.

Earl and Steve were securing all the shutters and touring the house, deciding where to put Liz and Aunt Norma. Both needed to be on the first floor. Steven decided Liz should use his room. It would be on the leeward side of the house. A bed for Aunt Norma was set up in the corner of the dining room, away from windows. The rest would be upstairs, if they went to sleep at all.

Bands of rain and wind kept sweeping by between bursts of bright sunlight. Steve wanted Liz and Stella to move over before it got too windy. Once Liz was in the big house, she could sit in front of the TV with Aunt Norma and keep everyone posted with storm reports, as long as the electricity stayed on. Candles, matches and flashlights were placed around the house.

Porch furniture and ferns were brought in and stacked in the hallway. ToJo's bed was put in the closet under the steps.

As the storm got closer, it was reported the eye would pass over Boca Chica, about five miles from Key West. Good, thought Steve, that put their island on the least violent side of the storm. He was concerned about Liz. Sometimes the low pressure of a storm brought on premature labor. He checked his medical bag again, just to be sure. If Liz did go into labor, he would be ready.

There was a barometer in the hallway of the house. Every old house in Key West had a barometer. It's how the true islander knew where the storm was, regardless of what the TV weather people said. That barometer was dropping fast!

40

The wind was picking up noticeably. Hurricane winds circle in a counter-clockwise direction. You know where the eye is if you know which direction the wind is blowing. As the center of the storm moves, the wind direction changes accordingly. Of course if you get the eye of the storm, there will be a lull in the wind until the other side of the eye hits...going in exactly the opposite direction and at its highest speed.

Watching a hurricane grow in strength as it approaches is the part you never forget. You keep thinking it can't get worse but it does. You are horrified and exhilarated at the same time. Many people want to experience a hurricane but usually once is enough. Key Westers have seen all kinds. Some turn out to be worse than predicted; others not so bad. Some cause flooding with the sea coming over part of the island. Others take out trees and ruin houses but no flooding. When it comes to wind and water you realize Mother Nature rules.

Everyone was looking out of the few windows that were not shuttered. The men were collected on the windward side, swapping hurricane stories and watching for disaster. Liz sat, head back, in a big cozy chair near a window on the leeward side, admiring, from a distance, the wild, turbulent choreography of trees bending and swirling to the insistent rhythm of the wind. In a safe corner, Aunt Norma was calmly playing solitaire. In her ninety-five years, she had seen it all before. Stella was trying to calm ToJo. He was not handling the noise of the wind and occasional flash of lighting very well. Finally, Stella put him in the closet and closed the door. His bed was in there and maybe he would feel safer. Kirk and Iggy were patrolling the house, checking windows, staring out through cracks in the shutters, having a fabulous time. Children always love the excitement of hurricanes.

Phil was hard-boiling eggs. They were good to have around when the electricity went. Win and Earl kept wandering around like air-raid wardens waiting for the worst to happen. Steve was trying to get Liz to lie down. She was now sitting on the sofa so he got her a pillow and a blanket, put her feet up and insisted. After a while Liz fell asleep. It was late afternoon and the storm was still growing in intensity. The eye was to pass Boca Chica around midnight. Spanish bean soup was simmering on the stove for anyone who wanted to eat.

POW! A big explosion was heard outside and the electricity went off. Everyone reached for the flashlights. Even though it was not nighttime yet the sky was so heavy it seemed dark. There was a deep gloom inside the house. Outside, the noise of the wind was fierce which heightened the sensation of the impending unknown. Steve had asked everyone to talk quietly so Liz would keep on sleeping. When the lights went off, Aunt Norma went to bed. She'd find out tomorrow what happened.

The noise outside was sounding more intense as trees were swished back and forth, some pounding on the house, and hurricane force winds blew stronger. The men were all in the kitchen, some eating soup while it was still hot. Steve thought they really needed better hurricane protection for the kitchen windows. He would talk to Liz about it next week.

CRASH!!! Everybody yelled! Wild winds were suddenly whipping though the house! The huge, old tamarind tree had been up-rooted and crashed through the kitchen roof! Glass and branches were blowing everywhere, knocking things off the walls throughout the house!

"Out of the kitchen!" yelled Win! "Let's try to get this

168

door closed! We need to reinforce it! Where'd I put the hammer and nails?"

"We need some wood to nail over this door! It's not going to stay shut!" yelled Steve. The boys were thrilled at the wind blowing through the house.

"Oh God, my beautiful kitchen! I was going to do my cooking show there...all my pots and pans...all those beautiful cabinets!" Phil was freaking out. Stella was trying to calm him down but thinking that it was really Liz who should be upset. Stell hoped she had slept through all the excitement. Aunt Norma sure had. Win and Steve were hammering away, nailing the door shut. They were using old wooden bed slats to nail over the door, struggling to keep it shut against the gale force winds.

As they paused they heard a very weak voice calling from the living room. "Steve... Stella...Steve...Stell? Somebody?" Steve and Stella ran into the living room and there stood the saddest sight Stella had ever seen. Liz, with wet clothes, a very woebegone expression on her wan face and holding her huge tummy, said, in a low, odd voice, "I think...my water...broke!"

Surprisingly, Steve started to laugh. "Perfect timing, Lizzie, it was starting to get dull around here." He put his arms around her and held her for a few minuets until she groaned and had to bend over. Keeping his arms around her he looked at Stella. "OK Stell, I think these babies are calling us, and I'm really going to need your help. Let's get Liz to the bedroom."

As they passed the dining room Aunt Norma sat up. "Is the baby coming? Well, don't worry. I had seven without going to a hospital. It'll be OK. Things have to get worse before they get better, Elizabeth, but there's no other way. You'll be fine. Good luck!" With that Aunt Norma rolled over and went back to sleep. She had been there, done that too.

Liz was in pain and it was hard to walk. Steve put a lantern in the bathroom and told Stella to turn on a warm shower; there would be enough hot water left to rinse Liz off and help her into her nightshirt. Steve got the bed ready with a special sheet he had brought with him. At least he was prepared. He and Dr.

169

Hu had assembled a double birthing kit in case this very thing happened.

After Liz was settled in bed, tucked under the covers, Steve took her hand. "Liz, Honey, I've delivered lots of babies so try to relax and don't worry. We'll be fine. Trust me, Sweetheart, we'll work together and do the best we can for our babies."

Looking up at Steve, Liz started to say something and then winced and gasped as a pain overtook her. "I'm afraid and embarrassed and I'm glad you're here but I wish…"

"Lizzie Love…Don't give it another thought. Think positive, work with Stell on your breathing and I'll handle everything else. After all, birthing a baby is one of the great miracles of the world. I'm happy to be a part of this…two little miracles! Just think, soon you will be the mother of two little angels. And don't worry about the babies…babies are tough. We'll get them to the hospital as soon as possible. They'll make it!" Liz let out a groan. "Stell, you time the pains. I'll lay out what I'll need."

Steve had everything he needed except incubators. He went out and told the guys the situation and their jobs…Earl, in charge of the house…Phil, baby holder number one…Win, baby holder number two. Both were to get a chair and put it in the hallway outside the bedroom. They needed to wash well and each put on a clean, dress shirt, backwards. Earl was to find the unused dust masks to use as sterile masks.

The storm was now roaring! Things kept banging against the house, broken limbs, coconuts and mangos, other people's roofs or shutters. Their own shutters were keeping the windows from breaking but might blow away any minute. No one was listening as the storm reports from NOAH kept coming, the house was creaking, ToJo was barking and howling and Kirk and Iggy were trying to comfort him.

In the hot, shadowy bedroom, lit only by two lanterns, Stella kept wiping Liz's face with a wet cloth. Liz kept moaning and panting like she and Stella had learned at the Lamaze classes. Steve was counting the minutes. They were getting close! He had clean towels ready to wrap around each baby as it was born. He wanted to keep the babies warm which was why he had those two incubators sitting outside the bedroom door.

Liz was in real labor now. Stella was trying to help her breathe and the pains were getting closer and harder. Steve kept telling her she was doing fine, they were just about to arrive. Winds were howling and Liz was groaning as the first, tiny little baby was born!

"Great job Lizzie! Here is the first little girl! Looking perfect. OK...wiping off her face...wrapping her up. Here we go! Stell take this little angel to incubator number one. OK, Lizzie, looking good for the second one, you're doing great, one more shove, Sweetheart, it's just about...here we go...second baby on the way. Awesome Liz, it's another little...BOY!!!

"Liz! It a boy! You have a boy and a girl! And they are both perfect! OK, Stell, he goes to incubator number two. You did a fabulous job, Lizzie Love! A perfect job! You should be very proud!"

"Can I see them?" asked an exhausted Liz. Stella was wiping away tears and hugged Liz very gently. "It's all over, Sis, and you hit another home run! I'm glad one's a boy! It is totally, totally awesome! Think they'll take that second pink bunny back?"

41

Liz was lying back on pillows, holding both babies, smiling and kissing them. " I can't believe they're here! They're so little! What are we going to do until we get them to the hospital?" Liz asked? "Which one is the boy? I can't tell. They're both wrapped up like little papooses."

"I can't remember," said Steve. "They look alike. Win, which one were you holding?"

"I think...the one on the right...but I'm not sure. Hey Phil, which one were you holding?"

"I don't know...the little one."

"It doesn't matter," murmured Liz. She was exhausted and about to fall asleep holding them. Steve picked one baby up and gave it to Stella. "Here Stell, your new little brother or sister."

"Awesome!" Stella started cooing to the baby. "I mean you are the most totally cool baby in the whole world and I don't care which one you are. You are pink and blue bundles of joy! And everybody loves you. And..."

"What is it about females that allows them to pick up baby talk in a matter of seconds?" commented Win. "We men don't have that talent. We need to know whether to discuss baseball or Barbie dolls with those babies. We need to unwrap one of them!"

"We'll need to put them in diapers soon and we'll find

out then. Right now they're going commando," said Steve. "Any diaper suggestions? Phil? Earl? Any soft pillowcases we can use?"

WHAM! Something hit the side of the house! Glass was heard crashing! Win, Phil and Earl ran out of the room to check for damage. The wind was still roaring, and sheets of rain still slammed against the shuttered windows!

Liz lifted her head to ask. "Are the babies safe in here?"

"Yes, and we are too. You go to sleep, Lizzie, you need it. Stell and I will stay here and care for these little gatecrashers who were not invited to our hurricane party but came anyway. As soon as this storm dies down a bit, I'll call 911, get an ambulance to take them to Monroe County Hospital. We can keep them safe and warm until then."

Liz reached a hand out to Steve. "Thank you" she said tiredly. "And Stell, thank you for your help. I love you both." Liz's eyes were slowly closing.

The door opened, five or six pillowcases flew in, the door closed. "I guess they're busy," laughed Steve.

At daylight the hurricane damage could, at last, be seen. The wind was still a factor but was on the wane. Bands of rain showers with storm-driven gusts came and went. The kitchen looked a mess! Tree limbs were throughout the room, some still attached to the tree, some snapped off. The walls were papered in wet leaves, even the ceiling. They had to get the tree out before they could assess the damage. Liz was not concerned about her kitchen. She was worried about her babies.

In all the excitement, Stella had forgotten about ToJo. There was not a sound from the closet. She opened the door. There on the floor lay ToJo, sound asleep and wrapped up in Aunt Norma's blanket with Aunt Norma snoring softly on her pillow next to him. Stella left the door ajar. They seemed too content to bother. Kirk and Iggy had finally fallen asleep on the sofas. What a night of excitement for two little boys. Everybody had been too busy to tell them what to do and where to be so they had the house to themselves.

The EMTs would arrive with the ambulance as soon as

they got the OK to cross the small bridge between Key West and the hospital on Stock Island. Steve talked to doctors to make sure the babies were getting the best temporary care.

Liz was trying to nurse them but they didn't seem strong enough. Stell had found pink and blue gift wrapping ribbon and had wrapped appropriate colors around each papoose after each change and rewrapping...to Win's great relief.

Aunt Norma woke up and asked if it was all over. She told Stella it was so noisy with Liz yelling in one room, the dog barking in the closet, the house creaking and the hurricane pounding on the walls, she went into the closet to sleep. ToJo, knowing authority when he met it, and when a blanket was thrown over his head, went to sleep too. Now the two of them were best friends and having a late breakfast of cinnamon rolls on her bed in the dining room. Aunt Norma was nothing if not adaptable.

The people of the neighborhood, as soon as it was safe to go out, were checking all the damage and trying to clear away some of the debris. Lots of water was standing: lots of trees were down. Chain saws could be heard all over trying to clear the streets. Phil was out telling people they needed an ambulance and everyone was helping move debris out of the way.

Finally, late that afternoon, the ambulance arrived. To great applause from excited neighbors, the babies and Liz left with the EMTs. Steven followed in her car. Steve wanted Liz checked out and maybe checked in. Liz wanted to be with her babies. Steve was going to oversee it all. One thing about his life in Key West, he was much too busy to ponder the past. He felt needed and had certainly been invaluable during the hurricane!

Phil brought someone with a chainsaw into the kitchen to get rid of the tree limbs. It took patience and a lot of discussion but new damage was kept to a minimum and Phil was feeling a little better. Earl was working on the broken shutter and glass pane in an upstairs bedroom. The yard and pool were a mess.

42

The next few weeks were busy. Key West is one of the few places in the country that, if they want to keep people away, they can. Simply closing the last bridge to the island is all it takes. The police set up a roadblock on Stock Island, the last key before the island city, and only people with Key West addresses on their driver's licenses are allowed through.

Until utilities are restored and broken trees removed, the island is not safe for tourists. This hiatus gives hotels and restaurants time to recover and repair damage. Pools are cleaned, roofs repaired and windows replaced. Cell towers go back online and boats are carted off from odd spots where they washed up. Schools are put back together, trees blown over by the winds are winched back upright and braced. The water line from Florida City, one hundred miles away, is checked and repaired.

For some reason, 'Conchs' (what native Key Westers call themselves) love this time...no tourists, no mopeds, no traffic. People have parties and grill whatever was in the freezer that is now thawing from lack of power. A neighborhood party is when somebody fires up their grill. Everyone comes, bringing their own thawing steaks, their own libation, their lantern and a chair. It's amazing how happy and congenial neighbors are when the lights are out, fences are down, tiki torches are lit and people eat and drink together in back yards, sometimes meeting each other for the first time.

Stella loved it when Gumbo Limbo Lane had a party. Someone moved a chair out in the alley so Aunt Norma could sit and hold court. She was back in her violin house and ToJo was a frequent visitor. In fact, they were new BFF's. Iggy's great grandmother was home, but according to Aunt Norma, not doing to well.

Liz and Stella were back in the little house, but Liz was spending most of her time with the twins at the hospital. They were in the neonatal intensive care unit and doing well. Liz was very relieved. She was contemplating hiring a nurse. Stella would be in school all day and Liz could see this was going to be more than a one-person job.

The little house did not have much damage. The pool, on the other hand, was full of everything but water. Wind had blown a lot of the water out and in its place left thousands of large sea grape leaves, big branches and limbs, half of a telephone pole with attached wires and transformer, and an assortment of debris from around the neighborhood.

Stella was helping pool dude all she could. Jean shorts, bathing suit top, tennis shoes with sox and work gloves seemed to be the accepted pool clearing attire. Kirk was spending time over at Iggy's. His friend was having trouble walking around in all the debris with his crutches.

Steve was driving Liz to the hospital - she was not allowed to drive yet - when he brought up the subject of names. "What are you going to call them, Liz? They need names before they come home or the hospital will be discharging 'thing one' and 'thing two'."

Everyone wanted to know what to call the babies and had lots of suggestions. Win thought 'Jackpot Dandler' was appropriate for the boy. "I never realized that such a little tiny piece of equipment could be so valuable." He said. Steve had laughed. Liz had rolled her eyes.

"When I thought they were going to be girls," said Liz, "I was naming them Edith and Allison and calling them Edie and

Allie. Now I'm confused. Which name should I drop? Should the son be named after the father? Which would make him John Stuart Dandler III. I just can't decide and it's so important! I'm confused."

"Well, let's talk about it. First the girl, I appreciate you thinking about the name, Allison, she was a wonderful person but you didn't know her. So don't worry about that name. Start new or use names in your family. What were some other names you were considering?"

"My mother's name was Caroline and I always loved it but then there's Edith. She left me the house. I loved her but not her name as much. And middle names ...I just can't make a decision."

"I really like Caroline too," said Steve as he drove around Roosevelt Boulevard toward the hospital. City workers were out propping up some of the coconut palms that had blown over and part of the sea wall was in pieces. Most of the motel signs were gone or only half there. "The prettiest name for the girl, I think, would be Caroline Elizabeth. That has an important ring to it. She's going to need an important name to hold her own around 'Jackpot'."

"Stop that!" Liz laughed. "I guess that will always be Win's name for him. I really don't want to name him after his father. I'm trying to remove those influences from our lives. I do like Caroline Elizabeth though. I was so hung up on Edith and Allison I couldn't think of anything else."

"If you don't like 'Trey' think of a name you do like for your son, strong and traditional, like Caroline Elizabeth."

"Well, I like William but not Billy. I like Robert but not Bobby. I don't mind Tommy. I could name him Thomas...Thomas Steven Dandler! That has a strong sound, don't you think?"

"Are you joking? You just met me. You can think of a better middle name than that."

"Well, look at it this way. If it had not been for Steven there might be no Caroline or Thomas, maybe not even a Liz and besides that, I like the name Steven. Thomas Steven...I like it! It has muscles!"

179

While at the hospital, Steve checked in with a prosthetic specialist who came in from Miami once a week. They discussed Iggy's problem and what to do next. It seemed everything waited on the great-grandmother, Mrs. Morales, to give her permission. Aunt Norma said she was very old-fashioned and did not believe in anything new since José Martí. Although she badly needed to move into a nursing home, convincing her of that was impossible; many people had tried.

Mrs. Morales had lived in that same house for over seventy years, coming as a bride from Cuba. Her husband had been a reader in one of the cigar factories, a man who sat up on a dais on the factory floor and while hundreds of cigar makers rolled tobacco, he read to them: newspapers, novels, political speeches. This was an important post in the old cigar industry, as it educated and entertained at the same time.

Steve realized he was in the middle of an ongoing child welfare situation that seemed to have no solution. Iggy did more than just sit on the front porch; he took care of his great-grandmother, and although he was a quiet child, he could do whatever was needed on crutches. As soon as he had a prosthesis, Steve knew he would just take off and catch up with his age group fast. Steve was getting as impatient as Kirk. Iggy, in contrast, seemed an old soul when it came to patience.

43

Caroline and Tommy were now a month old. Every day they grew and got stronger. On their one-month birthday, December sixth, their intended birth date, Liz, Stella and Steven brought them home. The nurses had dressed them in red Santa stockings and red Santa caps. Liz and Stella thought it was adorable. Steve just laughed. "Don't take any pictures...Thomas will never forgive you when he grows up," he said.

Putting two infant seats in the back seat left a tight squeeze for Stell to sit between them. How two small, utterly defenseless babies could have so much control over people's lives was amazing...and rules...babies now came with rules! It took all three of them to figure out how to strap the little Christmas elves into their car seats correctly.

Liz had hired a neo-natal nurse for the first few weeks at home. Christmas was coming but nobody, except Kirk seemed excited about it. Life was, at that point, all about the twins. They seemed more alert and Stella insisted they laughed. Everybody took turns holding them, and cooing or discussing lasts nights homeruns, depending on who held and which one was held. It had to be confusing for the babies. After Win had spent ten minutes discussing baseball with Caroline, he decided they needed a baby code of some kind.

The next day, he solved the problem by arriving with two tiny bracelets. A gold one engraved 'Caroline' and a silver one engraved 'Thomas'. He had given a lot of thought to 'Jackpot' but propriety (and knowing Liz's reaction), had prevailed. Steven kept the twins under close medical scrutiny, checking their weight and vital signs every day. Liz thought he looked rather sexy holding a baby.

Christmas trees went up in both houses. Earl's was perfect, traditional and beautiful. The wreath he made for the front door was a combination of orange/red pyracantha berries and naturally gold and red sea grape leaves. Wreaths in Key West were always creative. With no spruce or pine, other natural elements were used. Silver sprayed papaya leaves looked like giant snowflakes. Vines and small coconut bunches sprayed gold looked elegant wrapped in a circle. Often the designers of the fabulous windows in New York were doing a simple, natural wreath on their Key West door. Creativity flourished on the island at Christmas.

Stella and Kirk did their tree in the little house. With the babies sitting in their infant seats, looking wide-eyed in wonder at all the lights, they did the tree just for them. It was full of stuffed animals, colored lights and bright pink and blue balls. Kirk had his own ideas for Christmas ornaments, hanging rubber iguanas by their tails all over the tree. Caroline and Tommy seemed to be pleased.

Liz was still very busy. Nursing and pumping, bathing and changing twins, recording every little change on the baby chart, she was getting very tired. Thank goodness she had hired the nurse.

The pool was finally back in operation. In the evening, Liz, Stell and Steve, and often Win, sat on the terrace. Of course, now, along with holding a cocktail, you held a baby, who was often pooping, burping, crying or spitting up all over their adorable selves. It was funny how each adult responded to this change in the dynamics of an evening on the terrace. But it was fun and Win and Stella always found humor in the interaction. Even Earl and Phil came for a bit of baby holding. Earl always wanted the baby that was asleep.

Playing with ToJo was, to Kirk, much more interesting

than babies. Iggy had finally gotten permission to come over to Kirk's house, and he often stayed for dinner (usually taking a plate of food home to his 'Granny'). Phil called these afternoons 'Bambino Soirées'.

"The kitchen seems to be coming along, Phil," said Liz. "That contractor you found is good, and I love the changes we're making. It's going to be 'state of the art' but still not look too modern. The garden view from those new windows is fabulous. And how about the cookbook? Is it still coming along?"

"As a matter of fact, Liz, I wanted to talk to you about that," answered Phil with a grin. "There's a chance I could do a cooking show and cookbook release at the same time. If this works out, I wanted to ask if I could use your kitchen for the first few shows. A kitchen will be built at the studio if the show is successful. Stell and I already have our outfits planned." At this Phil and Stella broke up laughing.

"It's an inside joke," said Stell. "I can only tell people who smell like baby lotion, right, you little darling?" Stella was snuggling with Caroline. "Maybe we can find a cute little pink apron for you."

"That would be fine with me, Phil." Said Liz. "Some excitement that has nothing to do with babies is what we need around here. What will you call the show?"

"We're thinking of 'The Bare-Chested Chef' at present. Feel free to make suggestions anyone; it's still a work in progress but I am very excited about it." Phil answered smiling. He was very hopeful this could be the start of a glamorous new career.

"The garden will be presentable soon," said Liz. "It's recovering well but some things take time. Losing that huge, tamarind tree was a shame but I guess it was very old. Now that it is gone, I really miss the shade it gave to the kitchen and garden. James, who has worked in this garden since my grandmother lived here, says he's never seen it so sunny. I'm glad we still have shade on this terrace."

Stell and Phil were making dinner at the little house again tonight. The new kitchen was not quite usable yet in the big house. Stella got up and handed off to Win. "Here she is

Grandpa, your favorite granddaughter who wants to hear about princesses and fairy godmothers. Do not talk about baseball!" With that Stell went in the house.

Win looked down at the sweet, little face with big, trusting eyes and said, "There once was a beautiful princess who had a long, blond braid. She loved to play baseball with the handsome prince, so she would take this long blond braid..."

44

Every day Steve ran a few miles around the city just at daybreak. He loved running through the cemetery, a fascinating place in the early light. Key West streets were not crowded and few people were out at this time of the morning.

Before he left the clinic in Baltimore, doctors had told him the more he exercised the more of his abilities he would regain. It was now up to him and running gave him time to think. When he ran to the White Street Pier he got to see the sunrise. It was a long run from the house but well worth it. The run was for his physical well-being. The sunrise was for his soul.

Meeting Elizabeth had confused him. He had been fully prepared to mourn Allison for the rest of his life. It seemed only right. But now he was questioning that future. Would he want Allison to stay true to him if he had been the one to die? He wanted to be a positive presence in the world, not just take up space. What was the best way to accomplish that? Was falling in love with Elizabeth trivializing his love for Allison? He needed more sunrise runs.

The one thing he was sure of was this was not the right time for either one of them. They both had former loves they had to recover from and Liz, right now, was too busy to think straight. Bringing two premature babies up to their normal weight and abilities was a full-time job. He felt she might be feeling something for him but was too busy to do anything about it…she needed more time. But she sure was beautiful and, in his view, very subtly sexy!

Christmas arrived. Every person on Gumbo Limbo Lane had a gift for the twins. Some were homemade, like booties in pink and blue, or elegant, like silver rattles with engraved initials. Velvet stockings with hand-embroidered Christmas themes were beautiful, but Key West homes were not built with fireplaces; it was never cold enough to need a fire. That was another creative Christmas decision, where to hang the stockings?

Win, Earl, Phil and Steven came on Christmas morning to share Santa with Caroline and Thomas and the others in the little house. The twins slept through the whole present opening affair. Now they slept! Liz had been up with them all night. Now they slept through paper crackling, laughter at funny gifts and breakfast on the terrace. Kirk and Iggy were of an age where they did not believe in Santa but hated to give up the myth for fear of not getting as many Christmas gifts. Both seemed pleased with what he brought them and kept loudly thanking Santa.

Steve announced that he and Stella were going to look after the babies for the entire day, and Liz could sleep or whatever. The nurse was coming back tonight, and Steve was taking Liz to Louie's for Christmas dinner.

Liz, who loved her babies more then life itself, was thrilled at the thought of getting away from them. It was a present only an exhausted mother could truly appreciate. She slept till two in the afternoon, then was up to nurse the babies. They had been taking bottles all day and Liz needed to nurse them. She was really looking forward to the evening. Steve had not seen her looking good for months, and she wanted to knock his socks off. Knowing she still needed to lose a few pounds, she would just do the best she could… she had to have something that still fit.

When the nurse arrived, Steve left to get ready for the evening. Stella came into Liz's bedroom to help her look glamorous. They worked on her makeup and hair and nails. "Liz, you need a spa vacation, whatever that is. Right after the New Year we'll get you a trainer to put you back together. Totally!"

"Thanks a lot, Sis. Do I really look that bad?"

Stella laughed. "Liz, you couldn't look bad even on the worst day of your life. And I think I was there. It's amazing! You always manage to pull it together even when you're not trying."

Stell looked out the window. "Oh my God!" She whispered. 'Steve is coming through the garden! Look at him, Liz! He's awesome! He looks like an ad for GQ. He has on a jacket...no tie...loafers...no socks. I think you and he might attract a little attention tonight. He is one cool Dude! He's better looking than Dr. McDreamy! Totally!"

Liz turned to look in the mirror again. She had on a loose, strappy sheath of green silk and emerald earrings and bracelet... high-heeled sandals, of course, and her blond hair was down in softly curling wisps. She figured she had done the best she could.

Stella went out first. She wanted to get the full effect when Liz came out of the bedroom...and it was worth it.

Steve looked dumbstruck. "Wow! You look absolutely beautiful! I mean it! Are you sure you are the one that had the twins?"

"Tonight I want to pretend that I'm not and just worry about what I'm ordering from the menu. This is a wonderful Christmas present! Thank you both."

"Wait a minute...I want to take your picture...don't leave..." Stella was rushing around looking for the camera. Steve laughed, "Where do you think we're going, Stell, to the prom?" Then he looked down at Liz and said, "Maybe this is our prom night...you and me...all dressed up...I should have brought you a corsage."

45

Steve had asked Phil to reserve the best table on the terrace at Louie's. They were seated at a table for two on the porch overlooking the deck bar and the darkening ocean. White tablecloths and candles added to the ambiance, stars twinkled, the sea breeze was cool and tiny fairy lights lit the trees. Liz had carried a soft stole of green and apricot paisley. She put it around her shoulders.

"Those colors make your eyes look green," said Steven smiling. "You really are beautiful! Merry Christmas, Elizabeth!" He lifted his glass.

"Maybe it's the candlelight," said Liz, softly. "You look pretty good yourself. Merry Christmas, Steven!" She touched her glass to his. Liz had another six months before she could have a glass of wine, but sparkling water in a wine glass was very close.

They talked about the day, the gifts, and island life in general. They ordered the baked yellow tail with tropical salsa. Liz was enjoying her first night out without care. She felt happy... temporarily carefree...she just glowed.

Steve sat there, gazing at this beautiful woman. "We've got to talk about us, Liz. I think we have something very fragile but intense happening between us...and neither one of us knows what to do about it. My problem is, I don't feel quite free yet. I feel an obligation to Allison that is still unresolved. The babies have helped me put it in perspective...we are born and we die. That is how it all works. Babies are born when you aren't ready and people die when you're not ready," Steve continued. "I need to know that I've done the most I can for the memory of Allison. I want to feel she had a great life and died doing what she wanted to do. I want to truly feel that nothing I could have done would have changed what happened. That would finally be closure for me."

Steve smiled at Liz. "Because of you, I now know I can have a life again, here in Key West and it would be a good life. I know I can fall in love again and have a family...but... I'm just not quite there yet."

Liz leaned forward and put her hand over Steve's. She looked at their hands together on the white cloth and said softly, "You are right about us not being quite ready. But I do have feelings for you that are not going to go away. I've got to find out about Johnny and me and our relationship. I don't want to wake up one day and remember I was madly in love with him and suddenly feel the sorrow that you have felt. It's a great mystery to me...like a dark closet with a door I'm afraid to open. What I do know though is," Liz looked up at Steve and whispered... "I'm falling in love with you and it scares me."

Steve grinned as he said, "It's like falling off a cliff and not knowing where you're going to land but feeling so happy about it. I guess love is that way...we're going to work this all out, Lizzie. I promise! We can't let this get away from us."

Steve looked out over the dark water...back down at their entwined hands...he paused, then said, "I've been in touch with Doctors Without Borders and I'm going back with them for another six months, finishing our obligation so to speak. It won't be back to the Sudan though. I think, maybe, to a clinic in Colombia."

Liz sat looking at Steve as tears started to glisten in her eyes. She, too, glanced down at their hands again...entwined together...his strong and tanned, hers pale and graceful... "I don't want you to go," she said softly. "I'll miss you so much. We will all miss you. But I can understand it...I want you to stay safe though. I want you to come back to us in six months."

"After working with Dr. Hu, I feel like I can still stay in the medical field. Before I wanted to quit being a doctor. I was at a loss," said Steve. "Now, I think I would enjoy going into family practice here in Key West. Every place needs family doctors, and I like dealing with the whole family. What do you think, Lizzie Love? Will you wait for me?"

Elizabeth sat looking across the table at this man who had become so important to her. She patted her eyes with her napkin and smiled. "If you are willing to come back to a fat lady with two babies, a teen-ager and a ten-year-old, Jane's willing to wait for Tarzan to return from the jungle."

They sat there holding hands and looking at each other. The waiter came with an unordered serving of guava duff with butter cream sauce and two forks. Phil was managing their evening from the kitchen.

"When do you leave?" asked Liz.

There was a long pause. "I leave in three days, Lizzie."

She looked at Steven, stunned, and then out over the indigo water; deep magenta was fading to navy in the late evening sky. A tear slid down her cheek as she looked back. "I hate to say this, but I think you are right about timing," said Liz. "The right people met at the wrong time. We've had an extremely eventful and wonderful time together. You have helped me so much, I don't know how I'm going to get along without you."

Liz looked down at their hands again, now locked tightly together, like neither wanted to let go. "But you're right. Six months should be long enough to get ourselves together. I don't want you to go but, being who you are, I know you must. Don't forget us though. Just think...the babies might be sitting up by then." Liz smiled through her tears.

Steven laughed. "We might be ready for a real romantic relationship by then. Maybe in six months we can move beyond handholding!" He brought her hand to his lips and kissed her fingers.

"I don't know, Tarzan. In six months I might have forgotten what romance is all about."

"Aw, Janie Love," Steve nipped the end of her little finger, "you never forget the good stuff!"

46

Three days later, after a send-off dinner the night before, prepared by Phil and Stella, Win drove Steve to the airport. "Be careful, Steven, there is a lot here that's going to be waiting for your return. I think you are doing what you need to do but there is a family here that needs you too! They all love you."

"I'll be back, Win, don't worry. I promised Liz, I'd be back. I love them all, Lizzie, the babies, the pirates, Key West, ToJo, the lane, the pool. I feel like I'm leaving paradise but I need to do this. I'll be back in six months. Count on it!"

The plane flew off into the bright morning sky. Win drove back around the boulevard and the beaches. Paradise was famous for having a few serpents, and he had received one in the mail this morning. The Dandlers were suing Liz for marital desertion before Johnny's death. If they could prove this they would not have to pay her a large portion of his estate.

He had said nothing to Liz or Steven this morning. He had called his Atlanta attorney and they decided to hire a private detective to find out the real story of Johnny's death. The details had never been very explicit. Johnny was found in a parked car after having suffered a fatal heart attack. The where, why, what and when were a little loose. Win had an idea that a who was involved.

Mary Dandler Cox and her sisters had hired a big time New York attorney to assist Chris Calhoun with their financial claim. They had come out swinging. There was now a male heir. The game had changed.

He also had to find out what they had on Elizabeth. Was it made up or real? When did she really leave Atlanta? He had to gather the dates of all major events and see how they all fell together. He did not think this was a murder but something was not as it seemed. He'd wait for the PI's report before worrying Liz for details. That little Thomas Steven might be tiny and helpless, but old Winslow Van Rensselaer Morganstern had Jackpot's back.

Liz was so busy with the twins she really didn't miss Steve until late afternoon when he usually popped in. Caro and Tommy were out of danger now but still needed extra care and record keeping. They were gaining weight. That was the main goal; get them to a normal weight for their age. Liz let the neo-natal nurse go and hired a full time, live-in nanny.

Stella was wonderful with the twins; you could tell she really loved them but Liz made her realize that the twins were not her responsibility. Stell was in high school, and after school activities were part of that. Her background had matured her, and she was taking leadership positions in many clubs and organizations.

Stell and Phil had spent hours over Christmas vacation getting the beautiful wicker baby carriage all clean, polished and repaired. This was where the babies slept, side by side, when they were napping on the terrace. Liz always covered the buggy with a mosquito net, just in case. ToJo would sit beside the carriage as long as the twins were in it; 'Iguana Guard' was his job title. You got the feeling ToJo preferred to be with Kirk but felt a responsibility for the babies.

But Liz did miss Steve. Just knowing he was not around made the day less exciting. She worried about him but he promised her he was not being sent to a war zone. War zones, though, could change in a matter of minutes. He was going to an established clinic in a jungle village in Colombia, and they were going to E-mail every day.

Elizabeth knew that Steven was a good man. She had

194

married a good man once. At least, she figured, she would not have married Johnny if he were not a good man. What had happened? Had he really been so weak he let his family rule his life? Steven had admitted he had heard Johnny was a swinger. Had she known? Why had she let them tell her what to do? Bethanne had said those pictures of her in the paper looked nothing like she looked when Johnny met her. Had he wanted her to change?

She was now remembering most of her Key West years and some of her college years. Why were the Atlanta years so elusive? Was there something in Atlanta she did not want to remember?

She was glad she had met Steven after her amnesia; at least there was nothing mysterious about him she couldn't recall. She was sure he was strong enough to fight for her if needed. He was strong enough to recognize his own problems and leave for six months to settle them and strong enough to take on twins, a teenager and a ten-year-old, none of them his. Yes, if they were to marry when he came back, she would always be able to count on him.

With the twins all bathed and fed, Liz decided to take them for a walk. The nursery was a bit of a mess but she wanted to get out with her babies and feel the soft island air, see island sights, hear island sounds. This was going to be the start of her get-back-in-shape program. She walked, they napped.

She was walking up Southard Street, admiring the flowers spilling over walls and poking between cracks in the sidewalk when suddenly Kirk pulled up on his bike. "Liz, you better come back...I think something happened to Iggy's granny! The ambulance is at her house and Iggy is crying."

"Oh my God! I'm coming," said Liz, turning the carriage around and walking as fast as she could over the uneven sidewalk. Caro and Tommy, bumping about in their tiny space, never gave a peep. When they decided it was time to sleep, they slept!

When Liz got to the old unpainted house there were lots of people from the lane standing around, and the EMTs were still inside. A neighbor watched the babies while Liz went into the house. Mrs. Morales was still lying on the floor of the back room, TV still on and Iggy, sitting next to her, crying softly. The EMTs thought she had suffered a stroke or a heart attack, but whatever it was, she had not made it, and they were debating what to do.

"Iggy, sweetheart, you'll come home with us. Let's let these people take your granny where she needs to go and we'll all have a family meeting, including you, and we will decide what to do." Liz looked up at the EMTs, "He's my son's best friend, and he has stayed with us often so he knows us." Liz gave them her name and address and with her arm around Iggy, led him to the door. As the neighbors stood with questions in their eyes, Liz said, "Mrs. Morales has passed away, she was 94, and Iggy is going to be staying with us. We'll let you all know about details later."

Liz and Iggy walked over to the baby carriage, and with Kirk pushing and Iggy, on his crutches, trying not to cry, they walked home to the little pink house.

47

Stella had just returned from a school meeting and was now trying to comfort Iggy. Kirk was sitting next to him for moral support. Liz called Win and he came right over to discuss the legalities. They did not want Iggy taken away by child services before they could get the paperwork in. Phil called saying he would send supper over in about an hour. Liz was wondering where to put Iggy. When he spent the night, he and Kirk slept in sleeping bags on the floor.

Liz could see the writing on the wall. Iggy had no other place to go. Well, she thought, there's always room for one more. We'll work out the details later. First she had needed a bigger car, now she needed a bigger house! Wait till Steve hears about this.

The following day Aunt Norma came over. She told Liz that as far as she knew there were no relatives around to do the funeral or take Iggy in. Liz suspected as much, and when the funeral director called her, she knew she was in charge.

Iggy and Liz had a long talk. They decided to ask the Catholic priest to hold a service at the small chapel at St Mary's Star of the Sea Catholic Church, even though Mrs. Morales never could get to church, and bury her next to her husband in the Morales family plot in the old cemetery.

Three days later, all the people on Gumbo Limbo Lane attended the funeral of one of their oldest neighbors. Iggy stood, tall on his crutches, in a new dark suit and tie, the last living member of the Morales family. He then came home to live with the expanding group in the little pink house.

The New Year brought a lot of interest in Liz's big house. Earl and Phil had a large New Year's Eve party. It was very festive, and all kinds of people were there. Liz and Stella got all dressed up and walked across the garden, lit with the soft light of Japanese lanterns and mood music, to the big house. Stella said most of her friends were working the parties around town. Teenagers could make a lot of money in a resort town, parking cars, pouring drinks, passing hors d'oeuvres. Stella decided she wanted to go to Phil's party. They had become good friends, bonding over food and the critical event of the twin's birth. Mia, the new nanny, stayed at the little house with Kirk, Iggy and the twins.

The house received unusual attention that night. People from the Old Island Restoration Foundation wanted the house for their historical house tour in the spring. Phil and his group, backing the cooking show, were thrilled with the new kitchen and wanted to schedule a preview to be filmed as soon as possible.

After the party, Liz talked it over with Earl and Phil. Each was to be in charge of his own event with any damages to be taken care of by each one's respective group. They were to coordinate their schedules with each other and let her know when. It was interesting, but she did not have the time to handle any details.

The babies, although doing well, were still 24/7. They were more responsive now and alert looking...more fun to talk to and play with. They were getting little personalities that were distinctive and starting to notice things. Liz thought they were the most beautiful babies in the whole world. Stella thought they were the coolest, totally. Kirk and Iggy did not quite understand their popularity in the neighborhood but were protective and gentle when playing with them.

The new nanny was working out well. Mia Elleson was a young Swedish girl who had come to Key West to live with her aunt, who managed Liz's favorite dress shop, 'Commotion'. Caring for the twins, she said, kept her laughing because they were so adorable. She was a little older then Stella but they soon became friends. Taking the twins for a walk in the refurbished wicker baby carriage, while discussing boys, was their favorite thing to do. Liz felt fortunate to be able to afford Mia. Even though Johnny wasn't around to be a father to his children, she felt he was helping by making life easier for them all.

She often thought about Johnny. Why could she not remember him? Would she ever? Would Caroline or Thomas look like Johnny? Steven was truly their father in every sense of the word, except one. He had certainly been there since the beginning, and you could tell he had a soft spot for the twins. He loved working with children in Dr. Hu's practice. He would make a good family doctor. He would make a good Daddy!

Liz's plan was that six months was long enough to nurse twins. It consumed her days and nights and she was getting exhausted. In six months she wanted healthy twins, a slim body, no leaks at inappropriate moments and her old self back. She was totally committed to the twins, but she felt she was losing herself. She had to learn to strike a happy medium.

At their six-week check-up, Caroline and Thomas received a good report. Liz was relieved. Her pediatrician was very positive about their growth progress. One thing was for sure. They both got lots of love. Win liked to come over and hold 'Jackpot'. He'd talk to him about investing his inheritance, and baseball, and the joys of a good cigar. Little Thomas would look up at him with such soulful eyes...like he was hanging on to every word. Of course, the baby would then proceed to spit up all over Win's suit pants. "Good thing you got big bucks, boy, 'cause you gonna owe me a fortune in dry cleaning!" Win would laugh.

They had all been amused when Win had given the twins silver and gold bracelets. Now they realized the bracelets were godsends. Everyone knew at a glance which one was the princess and which one was the All-American baseball player. If you were burping or feeding or rocking or walking, at least you could keep up without checking the diaper. Earl liked to coo to the babies while someone else was holding them. Phil would hold out his arms and hold either or both. He said he was the first person to hold Caroline and referred to himself as 'the old incubator'. He was very proud of 'his' babies.

Mia was now part of the late afternoon 'bambino soirée'. Her English was perfect. She said they were taught English all through Swedish schools because who else, beside the Swedes, spoke Swedish? She was tall, very blond and quite gorgeous. Liz figured she would not be there long but she was great with the twins. Everyone loved the sweet little babies.

The late afternoon gathering was becoming an event. All the people who worked on Phil's kitchen shoot would arrive after filming and participate. All had to hold babies. Phil said it was the rule. This had hysterical results in many cases. Caro and Tommy just did not care about all the social niceties.

One of the cameramen, Mick Oropeza, looked past the babies and fell in love with the beautiful Mia! He wanted to put her in a cooking sequence. Phil wasn't too sure about that. After all, he was the star and who could compete with Mia if she was on camera? They left in heated discussion.

Mia laughed. "Nobody asked me. Maybe I don't want to be in that silly show. After all, we Swedes go in for dark, gloomy, deep dramas. I think I'll wait for Mick to do an edgy, fringe movie. But right now I'm busy." She was walking and patting Caro, of the golden bracelet. Mia had more important things to do than a little TV show.

Soon after Iggy had come to live with them, Liz took him to see 'the peg leg man', Kirk and Iggy's name for the doctor with which Steve had discussed Iggy's case. Next week he would bring down a prosthesis that had been molded to fit his leg and the boys were excited. "Don't expect too much," warned Liz. "These things take time and practice and getting used to walking." Kirk wanted to go to the hospital with them. He said if it were him, he'd get a real peg leg like a pirate. Stella said if he wanted to be a pirate, get an eye patch!

48

The kitchen shoot had wrapped up and everyone felt great about it. They had decided to call it 'The Galley Gourmet', not Phil's favorite. He liked something with a little suggestion of sizzle in it. He suggested, 'The Subtley Sexy Chef', but got no takers. Stella had a small role as prep chef. He figured Stell was cute enough to be fun but not so stunning as to take the attention away from him.

Stella understood him completely and thought he was a funny guy. They were both involved in planting an herb garden in pots on the back terrace of the big house. Liz and the family were definitely benefiting from Stella's cooking hobby. Every day was a mystery dinner and most were delicious. She would take the old Conch recipes and try to make them more health oriented. After all, no one fried fish anymore. She was helping Liz lose that baby weight and skinny Iggy to gain a few pounds.

One night Iggy said, "You know Stell, this is a lot better then Meals on Wheels." Stella hooted out loud, "That's what I'll name my cookbook...'Better Than Meals On Wheels'!" Everyone laughed...Iggy was coming around. Liz was taking him in for a fitting on his 'new leg' as he called it, tomorrow, and Kirk was getting out of school to go with him. They were excited because the nurse told them they could put designs from fabric on the fiberglass mold, and they had brought her a pirate flag. With the new tennis shoes, one he was wearing and one to go on the carbon-based foot, he was going to be one cool dude.

Liz and Stella had been discussing the overcrowded little house. The addition of Iggy had just been the straw Liz needed to act on the problem. She and Stell had to laugh remembering just a year ago, two of them had the whole house to themselves... now there were seven, and all ages! Liz had been putting off talking to Earl, but no longer.

Stella had been corresponding with Mrs. Peterson, and she was coming to visit during the Spring Tour of Homes. She was thrilled to be staying in one of the houses on tour. Liz had decided she could use Steve's room and bath. Stell wanted to do a little redecorating. Liz said it was OK but she needed to know what Stella had in mind.

"I don't think pink and lime is going to be appropriate for that room," Liz advised. "We'll be keeping the old furniture and Steve will be back in a few months. Why don't you try a Ralph Lauren look, white with touches of blue and white porcelain and fabric? After all I went through in that room, I think I have a say in this!" They both laughed.

"I remember there were blue and white porcelain urns in the attic. We could have lamps made from those and there were plates and platters too. I'll look for appropriate fabric. We can take the babies on an outing." Liz was getting excited. This was her interest and talent. All of the sudden, that room really needed redoing. Why had she not noticed before?

She talked with Earl. "I never touched that room because it was Steven's room. I just kept the door closed." Earl agreed it needed redoing before the tour. She asked if he had put out feelers about another house for him and Phil to move into. "After living in this house it is hard to find a comparable, but I think a house I like may be going up for rent soon. I'm keeping an eye on it," said Earl.

"I hate to bring this up, Earl, but we are going to have to use two of the upstairs bedrooms, one for Stella and the other for Kirk and Iggy. We are spilling out the windows in the little house! And, of course, the two littlest ones take up the most room."

"Well, I've been wondering when you would be coming with the good news," Earl laughed. "I'll see what I can do to speed up things. Let's go decide which two rooms you need. I hope we can work this so the tour can still take in upstairs?"

"Of course," replied Liz. "We can put Stella in my old room and she can keep it perfect till after the tour. The boys, on the other hand, we may just close that one door for the tour."

Liz could not believe how much she was looking forward to doing a little bit of design work. How long had it been? She had no idea. After lunch she and Stell left the babies with Mia and went up to the attic. There was a lot of blue and white stuff... even an old dark blue Chinese rug. A Chinese Chippendale mirror was leaning up against the wall covered in a faded purple blanket. This was so exciting to Liz. How had she forgotten she loved design and knew different design styles and periods?

Stell, on the other hand, could not understand why Liz was so enraptured with these old things. She did not need to use all this junk. She had enough money to buy new stuff. Stell decided this might be one of those live and learn situations. This was the first thing that had captured Liz's interest, besides the twins, since Steve left. Stella decided maybe she should stick to cooking and let Liz do the decorating.

Liz and Earl met about painters, rug cleaners, lamp restorers, and timetables. He was happy to help with the project. The house reflected on him. They had only about a month before the tour. That wasn't much time so they had to get right to it.

"Tell me, Earl, how much of the furniture in the house belongs to the house and how much is yours?"

There was a long pause. "Well, Elizabeth, I want to say it's all mine because I love it so and have cared for it like it was mine but in reality, it's all yours. When we moved in, your grandmother was not real well and she let me make all the decisions for the house. At first the furniture looked sad and neglected but over time we have revived it, polished it, and in some cases, recovered or repaired some pieces. She always paid for it but I made the decisions and saw to it. She was just pleased someone cared."

"I think you have earned this tour of homes, Earl. You should be very proud of your accomplishments. Maybe we can work out a small settlement when you leave. Do you have a favorite piece?"

"Oh yes!" Said Earl. "That fabulous mirror in the dining room! It is spectacular!"

"Well, we'll see what we can do. I've got to get back to my little angels. Let's get this done before the tour. That will keep us busy! Thanks Earl. I think Stell and the boys will move in this weekend."

Liz walked back through the garden, checking for new green shoots on some of the storm broken limbs and bushes. She was very excited about this project. She had forgotten she had been an interior designer. I wonder where my diploma is, she thought. Did I have 'stuff' too?

49

Eight-thirty the next morning, Iggy, Kirk and Liz sat in 'Dr. Peg Leg's' office. The boys were so nervous they sat up straight in their chairs and only spoke in whispers. When the nurse called them in, Iggy picked up his crutches and with a large dose of trepidation followed, then Kirk and Liz. Five minuets later, the doctor walked into the examining room carrying an object with a familiar looking tennis shoe on one end, a pirate flag on the other end and a round aluminum shaft connecting the two.

"Here she is boys, the pirate leg." Kirk let out a squeal of delight but Iggy just sat there and swallowed. He looked over at Liz, who had tears in her eyes and reached out to squeeze his hand. "Well, let's see how it fits, son. See if we put in the right coordinates and I have to tell you, it's the first pirate leg I've done. It should be tough!"

The next hour was spent with fitting and adjusting and trying it out and teaching how to take it off and put it on. This meant a new life for Iggy and he knew it. He kept taking deep breaths and smiling a little smile, sometimes grimacing at a pinch but saying little.

"How does it feel, young feller? It might feel odd for a while and be a bit sore but does it hurt?"

"No sir, it feels great! Muy bueno."

"You can wear it out of here but keep your crutches close until you get used to it. When you get tired, give it a rest. If you need to see me, I'll be back next week and we'll adjust it. If it feels OK, just keep practicing and I'll see you walk in here next month. I think you'll do very well, Iggy. You've got a good back-up crew."

Without help, Iggy slowly walked over to Liz, put his arms around her and whispered, "Thank you."

Later, they all sat around the terrace watching Iggy walk. Kirk was by his side and was used as a balance point when needed. There was a lot of laughter and good-natured kidding but you could see one determined boy out there. Iggy's life was changing in important ways and he was going to be ready. Life on the porch was over!

Win came by late that afternoon to check out the new leg. He told Iggy he was very impressed at his walking ability. He also asked Liz if she could meet with him the next morning. Atlanta again, thought Liz. Boy, she sure would like to get all that behind her.

The next morning, as a blue sky peeked out between billowy clouds and a fresh, salty breeze blew in from the gulf side, Liz walked over to Win's. Walking anywhere in Key West was always an adventure. The canopy of trees often sprinkled things on you...flower petals, ripe fruit, unripe fruit, berries, bird droppings, coconuts, and if a cold snap was passing, perhaps a cold-stunned iguana.

Coconut palms were the worst. If one curved out into the street, well, a yellow warning ring was painted around its trunk... what more could one ask? And why would you want to get rid of a perfectly good mahogany tree just because its trunk had grown over the sidewalk and into the street? Painting the curb yellow on both sides of the tree seemed to suffice. An old wicker loveseat, in peeling aqua paint, sitting on the curb waiting for the trash pick-up, could be considered someone else's treasure.

Win had coffee and guava tarts ready...he just loved his guava tarts. "Lots of things have been happening Liz, but there was no need to bother you till I got it all together," said Win. "Yesterday the last of their proposals fell into place. We now know where they stand so now we know how to proceed. Except for the three million dollars left to each of the family members, the estate was left totally to your husband. At his death, it was to be left to his oldest male heir, or in trust until said heir reached his majority. You are the trustee of the estate and also the wife of the deceased."

Win went on, "They want to overlook this and accuse you of leaving the marriage before Johnny's death. That is their case. You were out of the marriage before he died. Now this sounds odd and there must be something they are basing this on. Can you remember anything about that time? That night? Any little glimmer?"

"No," said Liz. "But I think whatever happened that night is the reason I can not recall Atlanta. Everything else has slowly come back, is still coming back, but not Atlanta. My mind has blanked that out and because of that, I dread remembering."

"It would certainly help your case if you could recall that night, before, after, anything. They can say whatever they like, and you can't refute it." Win sat back in his chair and looked at Liz. "Maybe we should do something to shock your mind into remembering. Maybe we should go to Atlanta. We have a PI working on the case, and he has found out that Johnny was having an affair with a women in the office named Alice White. Does that name ring a bell? This is her picture." Win handed over a photo and Liz looked and frowned and grimaced.

"Nothing, darn it! I'm sorry, Win, it's all a blank."

"Well, let me tell you what I think happened. This is just conjecture of course, no proof, but what if Johnny went to Alice White's condo and during a rather torrid evening, had a heart attack that killed him? Now, here he is in Alice's apartment and she does not want him found there, dead, involving her. What would she do? Who would she call? Someone else who wouldn't want him found there either. Right?"

"Oh God...she'd call me!"

"And if she called you...what did you do?"

Liz sat there very still... "I...don't...remember."

"Buck up, Lizzie. We can get through this. Now, think, without remembering, who do you think you might have called?"

207

They sat there in silence. Liz was pondering a whole new idea. Not what she did but what she might have done. She knew exactly what she might have done.

"I would have called Mary."

"Now, the big question, what did Mary do? He was not found in Alice's apartment but three blocks away in the driver's seat of his car. Alice White's bank account received a hefty deposit the next day. No reason was found for Johnny to be in the area. Why was he riding around at night? What, if any, was your role in this? Did you know about the affair? Were you planning to leave him because he was not a faithful husband? What does Mary have on you? And what is Mary hiding?"

"Oh my God, Win. What do we do?"

"We know that your home in Atlanta is vacant. What if we went in there and looked around, drove around with the PI, took Bethanne with us to help stir up memories? We could take a private jet up early in the morning and spend the day trying to dislodge some of the blocks that keep you from recalling what happened. We could be back by dark."

Liz chuckled to herself; what did men know? She knew she could not go all day without nursing a baby or two. "What if we took a private jet big enough for the babies and Mia also, spent the night in a motel and spent two days trying to find the answers," said Liz. "I'm tired of this unknown stuff. I want to find out once and for all and get it over with. Now I really want to know. Now I'm pissed!"

"Good for you Lizzie. We'll get 'um! Right where it hurts. We'll go after the money. Hot Diggerty, we'll get 'um or my name ain't Winslow Van Rensselaer Mogenstern!"

Liz smiled. "We'll get 'um because I might want to get married some day, and I've had it with all this Dandler baloney!"

50

The plan was set. It was amazing how much extra trouble two nursing babies made in a woman's life. Instead of a small plane with two people and one long day, it was now an army of babies, bottles, diapers, blankets, changes of clothing, infant seats, toys, one nanny, one attorney and a nursing mother. Of course, a larger plane was required and that needed two pilots. Liz felt like she was planning to rewage the Battle of Atlanta.

The Dandlers had come out with what they thought of as a knockout blow, but Liz and Win were going to counter. She was going to recall events if it killed her. This time she wasn't going to hide. If she could remember, she and Win could go on the attack. This was their first move...a stealth assault.

Three days later, around seven in the morning, a plane landed in Atlanta. It was met by two cars with drivers. One took away the twins, Mia, and a large assortment of stuff, to a near-by hotel with a nice pool and other amenities. Liz and Win climbed into the other car with Bethanne and the private detective. They were going to start at Liz's former house. She still had keys.

Nobody was around as they all went in the front door. It was a big house, and like others on the street fairly hidden from view by manicured shrubbery. Inside, the rooms were spotless. Someone was caring for the place. Liz walked all through the house. There were lots of photographs in silver frames of Johnny and Liz but none of other family members or friends. Liz went upstairs, through her large, walk-in closet...her bathroom... stood in the middle of the bedroom and stared at the bed... nothing. Back downstairs, she walked through the kitchen...the den...checked the book titles on the shelves in the family room... nothing came back. It was like she had never been there.

She was getting upset when she walked outside and spotted a large, old-fashioned, double-seated swing hanging from an oak tree in the back yard. She went over and sat down and grinned. "This was my swing. I would come out here and sit when I was upset about something." She sat pushing slowly back and forth with one foot. "Sometimes I felt I had to get out of that house!"

"Why Liz?" said Win softly. "Why did you want to get out of the house?"

"Because Johnny would get drunk and start slapping me for fun and laughing about it. Or Mary would come by and tell me what to do all the time. Sometimes his girlfriends would call to tell about Johnny messing around. They were usually mad because he had gotten a new girlfriend and they wanted to make trouble for him. But by then, it was old news. Many a night I carried out a pillow and blanket and slept in this swing. Being outside always made me feel better."

Liz looked around. "This yard was the only thing I liked about the property. The house was chosen for us by Mary and already furnished when we moved in. Johnny could never understand why that upset me so. I sat here the day of my grandmother's funeral. I couldn't go because Johnny was being honored that night for something and I had to be there next to him. It was all so fake. I was living a false life and I couldn't stand it! I felt trapped."

"That's terrible!" cried Bethanne. "Why didn't you tell me? I thought you had the perfect life. He seemed so nice."

"That was the hard part...no one would have believed me. He was a Dr. Jekyll/Mr. Hyde. When I married him, I thought he was so perfect. All that time we dated he seemed like a wonderful guy, lots of friends, very caring about me."

Liz got up and started back inside. They followed her to the den. She paused a minute and then went to the desk, opened the bottom left-hand drawer, turned the handle and lifted a false bottom.

"I don't know what these papers are about but he used to hide stuff in here. He thought I was too dumb to notice. I don't think Mary knows about this."

Win walked over and took the papers out of the drawer. It was Liz's house so the papers were hers to do as she pleased. He glanced at them. "I think these are real estate deals and diaries, maybe an attempt at blackmail. Looks like photos of a comprising nature. Some big checks. Should we take them with us Liz?"

"It's OK with me. I think it's starting to come back. Things that happened." She kept looking around and then went upstairs to her bedroom closet. Her clothes still hung in neat rows, shoes on racks, and lots of formal attire. She pushed aside a hatbox and there was a wall safe. She opened it. It was full of velvet boxes of various sizes.

"My God! It's still there." She opened a few...beautiful jewels of all kinds. "These are the Dandler Jewels and I wore them on special occasions. I don't even know if they are real. They could be as fake as my life with Johnny."

Liz started to cry. "How did my life take such an awful turn? No wonder I didn't want to remember. I must have been so stupid to get into this mess."

Bethanne went over to Liz and put her arms around her. "You aren't the only one to fall for his act, Liz; we all did. All those awards and honors...he must have been laughing the whole time."

Liz looked down at her blouse. "I need to get back to the babies for a while. Do we need anything else from here? We can come back. We'll leave the jewelry where it was. I sure don't want it."

"Let me check the mail," said George, the PI. "Are these from friends, Liz?"

"Take it all but the bills, George; I'll read them later."

211

51

They went back to the motel, fed the babies and had lunch. Liz was trying to remember things she wanted to remember, but recall wasn't flooding back like it did that day on the widow's walk. She felt it was out there but just beyond her grasp.

Win said, "We know you went to the funeral. Let's go to the cemetery and see if that reminds you of anything. If you have any suggestion, Bethanne, speak up. The oddest things seem to trigger her memories. I have observed, Liz, that usually you are outside when you remember something."

The PI drove them to the cemetery, to the special Dandler area marked with a marble obelisk, wrought iron fencing and a dozen dogwood trees. They got out of the car and Win motioned Bethanne and George to stay behind Liz, let her wander. Sunshine was shafting through the trees, birds and crickets supplied a background hum, and Liz, with no hesitation, headed straight for Johnny's grave. She walked around it, stopping and thinking, she stopped and looked beyond the gravesite and pointed.

"There was a woman over there dressed in white. After the service she came over to me and gave me a card. She looked like that picture of Alice White you showed me. What did I do with that card? She had on lots of make-up and a smirk instead of a smile. What could that have been about?"

"Did you have a purse with you?" asked Win. "If you put it in your purse maybe it is still in your closet at your house.

Who else do you remember here?"

"Not as many people came to the cemetery, I remember that. Mostly family and very close friends. Johnny had a little group of old college buddies that often partied together. The media was taking pictures. Maybe they have it all on film."

"I'll check that out." Said George.

"Evidently, I knew about Johnny's philandering before his funeral but I always felt like Mary did not know the extent of it. She had been a big help to her father and then her mother ,but Mary was very naive in many ways. She lived in a world of her own making...image was everything. I think she overlooked anything about her father and Johnny that did not fit in with the Dandler family reputation she worked so hard to preserve." Liz was staring off into the distance.

" By that time, my shock was over and I guess I was planning to leave Johnny...before he died. I don't think I told him about the Key West house. That was my ace in the hole...my safe place."

Liz sat on one of the marble benches with her arms folded, looking out over the trees, deep in thought. "I remember that after the funeral, I realized that this was my big chance to get away. Because Mary was always around, I packed at night and hid my luggage in the car. Mary was already talking about me taking over Johnny's seat in the State Senate and I knew I had to leave before she set things in motion. Already she had set up a meeting between Johnny's campaign manager and me, for ten the next day, to go over press releases. I left about six in the morning, packing only what I needed, the cashier's check, ten thousand in cash and that precious deed to the Key West house.

"I decided not to tell anyone I was leaving. I wanted to get to Key West and Uncle Winnie before anyone made a fuss about me being gone. I had no one in Atlanta whom I trusted, who could help me decide what I should do. Uncle Winnie could and I knew I could trust him. I took the back roads and about mid-morning a huge truck flew past me, pushing me into a ditch. That's where Stella found me."

Bethanne sat on a marble bench next to Liz. "Sounds like

it's all coming back Lizzie. Seeing these places is helping you remember all this crap your brain was trying to forget."

Win came up. "Let's go back to your house and check your purse, Liz. If Alice White gave you something, it may be important."

They returned to Elizabeth's former home and Liz went straight for her closet. The black leather purse was still hanging from a hook at the back. Liz looked inside. "It's still here," she said. She gave it to Uncle Winnie to open.

Win opened the envelope and shook his head. "I think she was going to blackmail you with this photograph, Liz; it's her and Johnny in bed together. The note says, "Don't forget I have this picture and the negative, I'll be in touch."

Liz walked over and glanced at the photo. "You know, I just don't give a damn what she does with that photograph. I don't live here any more and I just don't care. Maybe Mary should see that. She thinks he was such a saint."

"This adds to our case, Liz. Now we know when you left and why you left and have proof of both things. I think perhaps you're right, Mary should see this. She would be less inclined to go to court over the financial settlement if she knew we had unflattering proof about Johnny's secret life."

They returned to the motel and Liz was happy to see her babies. One great thing about babies, no matter what, they were always happy to see their mommy.

52

The next morning at the motel, Liz and Mia, in various sleeping garbs, were playing with the twins. They had put them in the middle of a big bed and Caro and Tommy were laughing and cooing. Babies tended to give life a focus.

George, the PI, had found photographs of the funeral. The cemetery pictures showed everyone, including the woman in white...even photos of her talking to Liz. The college buddies were grouped together with grim faces, all looking off in a different direction. Liz stood with Mary and two other women in black. It had been a somber but well-recorded affair.

Win decided it was time to call Mary. "Hello, Mary. It's Win Morgenstern. How are you? Good. I'm up here in Atlanta with Liz and wondered if we could meet with you today. Sure, I know the place...one-thirty...good...see you then, Mary." Win turned to Liz with a smile. "The Royal Piedmont Country Club... I'm sure she will be with her attorney. OK, Lizzie, let's dress for bear."

Mia was looking forward to having another wonderful day with the babies around the pool. Talk about an attention-getter. They had staked out a shady corner and held court. The pool dudes in attendance made a crib out of chaise longues for the twins, padding them and lining them with clean towels. They wanted Mia to stay while Caro and Tommy took their naps. The twins were starting a busy social life earlier than most.

Later, after a beautiful drive winding through pink dogwood trees and fuchsia azaleas, Liz and Win walked into the Royal Piedmont Country Club. It was, as Liz remembered, upscale, quiet, pretentious, with a beautiful view of the golf course. Mary and Chris Calhoun were seated at a window table. Chris stood as they walked up. There were greetings all around.

"Beautiful spot! Georgia hills and trees make a beautiful backdrop for golf," Win commented as they sat. "Do you play, Mary?"

"Of course not, but I often lunch here."

"I play golf, but I have an abysmal handicap," said Chris. "You look quite stunning today, Liz. How are the twins?

"Wonderful!" said Liz. She started to say more but was interrupted by Mary.

"Why did you want to meet with us today, Winslow? Are you having second thoughts, Elizabeth?" asked Mary.

Win answered, "As a matter of fact, we have come across information that is of a delicate nature. I thought you and Chris should be aware of it. Perhaps you already are."

"And what, pray tell, would that be?" asked Mary.

"I am sure you both knew that Johnny was not the most faithful of husbands," said Win.

"No, I was not aware of that, but no telling what Liz has been telling you," said Mary.

"Well, we have more than just Liz's interpretation of events. Unfortunately, we have photos and proof of a blackmail attempt. Have you heard from an Alice White, Mary? She might be attempting to blackmail you too."

"Let me answer this, Mary," Chris said, putting his hand over hers. "We do know of an Alice White. I believe she worked in Johnny's office."

"I refuse to listen to all of this gossip about someone not able to defend himself!" said a very annoyed Mary. "I think it's disgraceful."

"Mary," Liz said, "I'm sure you must have heard something about Johnny's many girlfriends. He often alluded to it...seemed proud of it. He and his circle of college friends talked and laughed about it all the time. It was like they were entitled to any women they wanted. You knew him best. Surely you knew that?"

"Men of Johnny's caliber do not have to live by the rules. They are above them," said Mary, as if this made perfect sense.

Win sat forward. "What we have here is an honest attempt on our part to settle this in an amicable fashion. We don't want to go to court and smear Johnny's lifestyle all over the South." Said Win. "But, we could easily prove a case against Johnny. We have materials that we did not know existed. They were supplied to us. Liz now remembers the horrific details of her marriage. These details were probably one of the reasons that extended her amnesia. Those 'good old boys' could be subpoenaed to testify against Johnny. That would open a can of worms! Television would run the tape of Alice, handing a note to Liz after the funeral. I've seen it. This is the photo that came with that blackmail note." Win passed the photo to Chris very subtly.

Chris looked at it and shook his head. "I assume this is a copy?"

"It is," said Win.

"May I keep it?"

"You may."

"So, what exactly is it that you are seeking?" asked Chris with a glance at Mary that said, "Please keep quite!"

"We want what is entitled to Mrs. Dandler, as John's widow, and her two children, one a boy, one a girl, under the wills of the two deceased Dandler men, and the Laws of Georgia. These are John and Elizabeth's children, to be raised by the mother wherever she sees fit. We ask nothing that is not right under the law. If we do not have to go to court, nothing will ever be said about Johnny's lifestyle. His children will know his outstanding college exploits, his popularity, his political achievements and his awards. If the aunts would like to visit their niece and nephew, arrangements will be made. Their home will be Key West."

Iced tea was being poured. Mary looked at Chris and asked to be taken home. Chris stood, as did Win.

"Goodbye, Mary," said Liz.

"Please stay for lunch," said Chris as he followed Mary out.

Win sat back down and ordered a double scotch on the rocks. Liz leaned back and drank her tea. "Well!" said Win, "I guess the whole can of balls is in their court now. It will be interesting to see which Mary values most...money or reputation."

"Thank you Uncle Winnie, I really appreciate it. Where would I be without you?"

"It's what grandfathers do, Lizzie girl, it's what grandfathers do. Let's go back to the motel. I've got to tell Jackpot all about it."

53

March had arrived on the island. Earl was very busy putting the final touches on the house and garden, getting ready for the tour. Steven's room was finished and looked elegantly simple. The blue and white scheme had been a good idea. Both Earl and Liz were expert in spotting the exact piece needed among the hodge-podge of stuff in antiques stores.

Kirk, Iggy and Stella had moved into upstairs bedrooms. The Pirate, as Iggy was now called, was doing fine with the steps. He couldn't wait for Steve to come home from Colombia to show off his fancy hardware.

Caroline and Thomas were about four and a half months old. This was an adorable age. They loved everybody and were taken everywhere. ToJo was their constant companion. Wherever the twins were put...propped up in baby seats... kicking on a quilt on the floor...in the new double stroller, ToJo was their sentry and playmate. Both babies loved to grab his fur. He would stay still till they let go. He sure wished they would learn another trick, like throwing something he could fetch.

Liz and Steve had been E-mailing each other since he left. She would report on the Key West saga, baby stories, Iggy's triumphs and the Atlanta trip. He would tell her about the people that came to the jungle clinic. Some stories were funny, some sad. He spent a good part of his day teaching about hygiene and

221

clean drinking water. The jungle was beautiful but dangerous in many ways. He had a special interest in the children. They were a happy lot till they fell ill. Many did not recover due to lifestyle.

Liz looked at her babies, lying on their tummies, chewing and drooling on toys and cooing at each other...happy, clean, full of milk and vitamins. She knew they all were very lucky. She was missing Steven more each day. Now that she knew she was free to fall in love, she was doing exactly that...and he wasn't even here. Would they ever get their timing right?

She had been fooled so badly with Johnny, but Steven was not even close to his kind. She knew this before she ever thought of falling in love. Steve was a real person. He was good, compassionate and honest...and very, very sexy! Three months to go before Tarzan returned. Liz could hardly wait.

Mrs. Peterson was coming for the House Tours. Stella was concerned that if she stayed in Steven's room during the tours it would be uncomfortable for her. Win offered his guest room. She could move back when the tours were over. Stella was planning every minute of her stay. Liz told her to relax and let things happen. Mrs. Peterson might like just to stroll around and look at the hundreds and hundreds of old houses that lined every street, maybe even walking ToJo.

Stella planned a big dinner for the first night. She and Phil had given this a lot of consideration. Win, Earl, Phil, Mia, Liz, Kirk, Iggy, Grace and Stell herself made nine people around the table. Stell was making place cards and figuring out an exotic centerpiece. She made room for two high chairs. Mrs. Peterson was to sit at the head of the table with Uncle Winnie at the end. She was as close to family as Stell and Kirk had, and Stell was making the most of it.

When her teacher got off the plane, Stella just about missed her. Wow, what a change! Where was that comfortable, dowdy Mrs. Peterson? Coming down the steps from the plane to the tarmac, with the ease of a twenty-year-old, was a thin, stylish looking, woman of color, wearing narrow black slacks, black tee shirt and khaki jacket with an animal print shoulder bag. Mrs. Peterson? Her hair was cut very short and set off by large gold earrings. Her appearance was striking.

Stell ran to hug her. "Oh, Mrs. Peterson, you look absolutely amazing. I cannot believe it! You look awesome, I mean totally."

"Thank you, Stella. You look pretty awesome yourself. You look happy!"

"I am and I can't wait for you to see the twins. They are so adorable. Kirk and I have a little baby sister and brother and also another brother who is Kirk's age. I am very happy. In fact, I can't believe it! Life is amazing."

They left the airport in the Mini Cooper with the top down, drove around the boulevard, past beaches lined with palm trees and past some of the prettiest homes on the island. Stell was now the teacher and was really getting into her role.

Liz wanted to get the babies all clean and dressed up for Stella's sake but it did not happen. When they walked in Tommy was screaming, Caro was having her diaper changed. The twins made their own schedules. They did not care what time the planes landed. ToJo, on the other hand, was very excited about his old friend. Stell had trouble getting him to calm down. They went out to sit on the shady terrace.

Earl came down to meet Stella's teacher. He told her in Key West, you waited to hear the afternoon plane fly over the island and then you left for the airport. You never had to call.

Stell introduced Mrs. Peterson. "Nice to meet you, Earl, but please call me Grace. You too, Stella. You are not my pupil any more. We are friends now and I'd really like you to call me Grace. I left that Mrs. Peterson back in north Georgia."

"That would be totally cool, Grace, if I can remember. You do look younger and more like a Grace now. I will totally try."

Grace said, "When I planned my trip to Key West, it made me take a look at myself. I had married an older man and assumed his age in how I looked and dressed. I was happy but when he died, I felt like I was still young. I'm only fifty-five. So I went on a diet, worked out at the school gym, got a new hairstyle and went shopping with a younger teacher. This is the new me."

223

"Awesome!" said Stell. "This island may be at the end of the road, but it is definitely the place for new beginnings."

54

Phil walked up to the terrace and met Grace. "I've heard so much about you I feel like we're old friends, but I've got to help with the special dinner Stella has planned." He and Stell had decided on a Cuban Dinner, a chorizos stuffed boliche roast, black beans and rice sprinkled with chopped onion, plantains fried slowly in olive oil, garlic bread and an avocado salad from their garden. For dessert, they were serving Key Lime pie. This was the quintessential Key West dinner. Phil was off tonight from Louie's and told Stell he would be in charge so she could visit with her teacher.

Mia came out with Caroline and Liz brought Tommy. Win came with a bottle of Cabernet Sauvignon and a bottle of Chardonnay. Everyone had arrived for Stella's big party. Stell was wearing her lime green and pink sundress with pink sandals. Kirk and Iggy had on clean clothes. It was a fun evening, a real party. Win was quite impressed with Grace. He had expected an old lady but this was no old lady. She was very knowledgeable, often funny and had an engaging personality. Stella was very proud of her.

Grace wanted to hear about everything Stella had been doing, her school, her cooking interest and the twin's stormy birth. A lot had happened to Stella and Kirk since they arrived in Key West, and all of it good. When the party was over Win walked Grace to his house, pulling her luggage. Tomorrow Stella

225

was showing Grace the island. He was thinking of tagging along.

The O.I.R.F. tour was over and a great success. Usually five houses were chosen for the tour, and after all the to-do was over, Grace moved into the guest room of the big house, breakfasting on the terrace of the little house every morning. She started swimming laps with Stell and Liz and was intrigued at the way ToJo guarded the twins. They were now getting plump and cuddly and thought their toes were the most delicious things in the world. If they rolled off the quilt, ToJo tried to push them back with his nose.

Liz always had a lot to E-mail Steve. His E-mails were not always pleasant. The guerillas had come through one night and attacked those they distrusted. There were some orphans in the village now. They were trying to place them with local families. They would give these families extra food to feed them. He was looking forward to his return to the island and setting up his own practice. He couldn't wait to see how the babies had grown. He could not wait to see his 'Jane'!

Stella was in school, but Grace decided to extend her visit. She was becoming very interested in Key West, maybe as a place to live. She would use Liz's bicycle and ride through the streets, discovering the bookstores and boutiques, finding museums and theaters but really just getting a feel for the island. Key West had its good points, and bad but it was undeniably an architectural gem.

A perfect place except for one important thing - it was very expensive to live in Key West. Housing was at a premium. Groceries and everything else had to travel the hundred-mile length of the mostly two-laned Overseas Highway to get to the island. That cost was added to everything in the city. Maybe she could get a job. Liz told her there was no hurry leaving the big house, as Steve would not be back till June. Earl enjoyed her conversation. She, too, liked antiques and historic old buildings.

She talked it over on the terrace that evening. Sipping her mango smash, she was holding Caroline, who wanted a sip. Caro also was twisting to hit ToJo on the head. Grace put her squirmy little bundle in the baby swing so she could talk.

226

Win said, "I think that would be a splendid idea. You have your masters in English Literature. Maybe you could teach at the Florida Keys Community College." He had a lot of suggestions. Stella was thrilled; she thought it would be totally awesome.

Liz also was encouraging. She thought it might give Win a bit of companionship. He seemed very interested in Grace. And Grace loved the casual attitude of the island. She could have a whole new life here. She would love to do something so different. She would think about this and figure a way to work it out.

Liz was starting to worry about Steve. He didn't say a lot about it, but Liz could feel the danger getting closer. He had said they were going to have to leave the village at some point soon. She wanted him to leave sooner than later. Her last E-mail to Tarzan had asked him to come home! Now that she had found him, she did not want to lose him. He had done his share for the world...she felt now it was their turn.

55

"Dear Jane, I think I may be on my way home. We are leaving sooner than expected. May not be able to E-mail for a while. Kiss the babies for me. I'll kiss you myself soon, I hope. Love, Tarzan"

Liz read the E-mail with elation and trepidation. She read it to Win. "Sounds to me like they are getting ready to leave but it might not be smooth," said Win. "I guess when you are dealing with guerrilla elements things can get tricky. But he does use the word 'soon'. Let's just expect him soon and try not to worry."

"Oh God, I just can't lose him now. But if I worry too much it will affect the babies. I'll try to stay calm, but I sure don't feel calm. Oh, Uncle Winnie, I've fallen in love."

Win laughed. "What a surprise, Lizzie girl, you must be the last to know. I think you are perfect for each other...and he'll get here. Don't you worry about that."

Liz walked back to her house. The babies were playing on the floor. ToJo was sitting on the side of the blanket. Liz lay between her babies and hugged them. They laughed and pulled her hair and slobbered all over her. "I think I'll stay right here till he comes." Liz laughed, "Just think, sweethearts, Daddy's coming home!"

Win offered Grace his guest room again. Steve's room had to be prepared for his homecoming. She accepted, but said she would be looking for an apartment. Grace had already notified a real estate firm in Gwinnett County to put her house on the market. She was getting serious about starting a new life. Maybe she should get all new furniture. She had been prepared for a quiet retirement, playing bridge and tutoring. It was like she had been hit by lighting. She wanted to yell, "I am woman, hear me roar!" She was going to have to watch it. She might get carried away with island fever. Maybe fifty-five was the new thirty.

The next day Liz had a spa day. Mia and Stell did her nails. Liz plucked her eyebrows, shaved her legs, washed her hair. "All because Tarzan is returning to their jungle," teased the girls. They loved the fact that Liz was all excited. But she was also very worried. When would she know? She and both girls constantly checked the computer for a message.

That afternoon they all went swimming, Liz, the babies in little float rings with seats, Stell, Mia and Grace. They played with Caro and Tommy and Stell told Grace about the iguana. ToJo paced the sides of the pool. He didn't like his babies in the pool where they were out of his protection.

Kirk and Iggy were off on their bikes. Iggy had a new bike and was working hard to add this to his list of accomplishments to show Steve. He was practicing in the lane, to the neighbors' delight. He was getting lots of thumbs-up.

Stella and Mia were planning a garden wedding. Grace asked, "Is it always like this here? Always something fascinating going on?"

"Those two have been planning a wedding for months. No one has been asked yet but it keeps them busy," laughed Liz. She had found the best approach to living with two babies, two teenaged girls, and two eleven-year-old boys was a very strong blasé attitude. She was trying to stay relaxed for the babies.

Liz liked Grace, she was around her mother's age, and was very practical, like her grandmother. They each had a baby in an animal-themed flotation device and were pushing them through the water. Caro's was a giraffe and Tommy's a zebra. Liz told her about her concerns. Grace said, "Honey, there is too much here for that man not to make it back. He'll be here and very soon. I just love this made-up family you all have. It's just perfect. I love the way Stella and Kirk fit in. I just love the way you took in Iggy...it's the whole island thing. It's made me happy again. I know it can make Steve happy again."

All of a sudden, ToJo made a woof sound and stood up staring into the seagrape tree. There was the iguana on the big limb. " Don't panic Grace, it's just the iguana. We'll take the babies out of the pool, but there is no danger. Iguanas don't eat people, they just look like they could." Liz waited until Grace was out of the pool with Caroline before she and Tommy got out. The iguana never came around unless new people were here. He either wanted to check them out or show off.

They were dressing the babies when Stella ran in. "Liz, I think you have E-mail from Tarzan!" Liz turned Tommy over to Stella and ran to the computer. It wasn't exactly E-mail from Tarzan but someone representing DWB told Liz to meet the morning plane. "Oh my God! What does that mean? Is he coming or is someone else coming to give me bad news? The morning plane comes in at ten. Let me call Win."

"It's probably him," said Win, over the phone. "If you want me to, I'll drive you to the airport tomorrow and wait with you. Don't worry, Lizzie girl, try to sleep tonight. It will be him for sure."

56

The morning plane was landing as Liz and Win walked into the airport. They stood waiting for the plane to unload. Others stood around but no one was as focused as Liz. She could see the plane through the window but not very well. The portable steps were wheeled out. The door opened, and out came all sorts of people, in various attires. Liz was holding her breath by this time. Oh, God, where was he? Had she missed seeing him get off? Was he not there?

Suddenly there appeared at the top of the steps a tall, tanned, bearded man, in cargo pants and black tee shirt holding a little blond child, whose arms were wrapped tightly around the man's neck. "Oh my God! It's him! It's him!" Tears were starting down Liz's face. People were looking around at her and smiling.

Liz was laughing and crying at the same time. "Oh, look at him, Win, he's here!" Win was looking over his glasses as he said, "Looks like he has someone with him."

Steve was walking across the tarmac, carrying an obviously terrified child in one arm with his backpack over the other. The child was dressed in a dirty tee shirt and diapers, no shoes. They walked through the gate. Liz ran up and put her arms around both of them and buried her face in Steve's shirt! She sniffled and kissed him. "You're back and I love you!"

Steve was hugging her back and grinning at her. "As you

233

can see, I didn't come back empty handed!"

Liz hugged them both again. She looked at the little boy, maybe around three, and said to him, "We have a big house and lots of love. There's always room for you." The little boy hugged Steve tighter and hid his face in Steve's neck.

"One of our problems, besides clean diapers, is he speaks and understands only German. I brought home the only German orphan in Colombia and," said Steve, as he looked down and kissed her again, "I love you, too!"

"Do you have any luggage?" Win asked.

"Are you kidding? I'm holding it all in my arms." Steve took a deep breath of the fresh ocean air and sighed, "Let's go home."

Win did not have car seats in his car but it would not have mattered. The little boy had a death grip on Steve. Win drove and Steve, the child and Liz sat in the back.

"I think his name is Johann Panholzer. I've been calling him Joey. He has not let go since we left the jungles. The rebels started attacking...shooting at anything. I think he saw his parents gunned down right in front of him. There was a mad dash to leave the area when a native woman came running up to me, thrusting him into my arms, yelling in Spanish, "Take him...take him...we can't keep him!" She left with other villagers in a truck. We were evacuating in trucks too, so all I could do was bring him along. To say he has become attached to me is an understatement. I'm the only thing familiar in his world and after seeing his parents shot...he is taking no chances. He doesn't cry, he just hangs on for dear life!"

"Poor little thing. I can see it might take a while but he's home now. We will all help him. What an awful thing to happen to such a sweet little boy." Liz gave both Steve and Joey a kiss. "I guess that's why I love you, Sweetheart. And you too, Joey."

As they piled out of the car, everyone was there to greet Steve. Liz told them to ignore little Joey for a while, let him get used to them and realize they were not a danger. Iggy walked up to Steve, put out his hand and said, "Welcome home, Steve!" Steve looked down, "Oh my God! Look at Jolly Roger here! You look great, Iggy! I can't believe it's you! After I sleep I want to hear all about it!" They sat on the terrace as Steve, exhausted, told Joey's story.

"His father, Georg, was a German engineer, his mother, Veronika, was a photojournalist doing a story on the village. They lived in a house, one of the few in the settlement, and kept Joey clean and well fed. The father was working on a small water purifying plant. I knew them well. They were a great family, part of the thousands of people around the world trying to help where help is needed. All too often they become targets for those who want no improvement. This is their little boy, Johann Panholzer. I call him Joey, but he only understands German. I think he is around three."

Mia spoke up, in German! "Would you like some milk, Joey? What about some crackers?"

Joey raised his head and looked back at Mia in awe. She was very blond, like his mother and spoke his language. Joey looked at Steve and he nodded to Joey and patted Mia on the arm. "She is OK, Joey. Milch ist gut! Ja?" Everyone sat still as the little boy made his decision. He looked at Mia, then at Steve and back at Mia. Mia whispered to him and smiled. Joey gave a tiny little smile and let go of Steve and reached for Mia. There was a collective sigh.

Steve sat back in his chair. "I haven't slept for two days. Joey naps but doesn't let go. He needs large diapers, clothes, a warm bath, food and someone to read him to sleep... like his mother did. Can I leave him with you all while I go up to my room, shower and sleep? I'm to tired to eat."

"Of course," said Liz. "We will take care of that darling boy. Don't worry about a thing. I'll walk up to the house with you."

As they walked out of sight of the little house, Steve stopped and hugged Liz. "I'm so dirty and smelly but I love you and I hope this little child doesn't derail the direction we were going. On the way out I had to trade my computer and my watch for his passage so I could not E-mail you about him. I asked someone to E-mail you the plane time." Steve touched his head to Liz's and gave a big sigh. "I love you, Liz, and I'm ready now. I'm free!"

Liz kissed him again. "Guess the timing is finally right for us at last. You go and shower and sleep as long as you want. Mia is a godsend and we'll make sure Joey doesn't miss you. Between the twins, ToJo, and all of us, we'll move him right into this family. We love him already. And I love you, Tarzan."

Steve chuckled, as tired as he was, he was happy. "Me, Tarzan, love you, Jane," he whispered.

57

When Liz walked back inside the house, Joey was sitting in one of the high chairs eating scrambled eggs off the tray with his fingers. His eyes were fastened on ToJo, who was sitting at attention giving Joey a 'who the heck are you?!' once over. ToJo finally decided to get things going. He reached up and licked Joey's toes. Amazingly, Joey laughed!

"He must have had a dog, Mia; ask him." After a few minutes of three-year-old German conversation, Mia nodded, "He did. His name was Blackie, I think."

Kirk and Iggy were leaning on the counter watching. "Whadayathink, Iggs. Looks more like a little girl to me...all those curls."

Iggy was considering..."Yeah, but you know what? He's been to war. He gets points for that."

Joey kept looking at the dog...he pointed at him and said, "Hund" or something like that. He and ToJo were having an intense staring contest. Joey leaned over and gave his new friend some of his eggs. This was usually a no-no, but tonight everyone just smiled. Suddenly ToJo gave a little woof and left the room. "The babies must be awake. Maybe they can play together," said Stella.

"Before Joey plays with anybody, he needs a bath," said Liz. " You check the twins, Stell, I'll fix Joey's bath. After his bath Mia, you can rock him to sleep. Poor little thing has to be exhausted. Where should he sleep?"

"Let's make a bed for him in our room, Mia," said Stell. "Then if he wakes up you can talk to him."

"He should be on the floor," said Liz. "He may fall out of a bed. I don't know what three-year-olds do. Use the yoga mats and quilts. While I bathe him, find him something to wear." Poor little thing, Liz was thinking, he's so tired he can barely keep his eyes open.

Mia did not have to rock him long. He went to sleep just as she started to sing an old German song she remembered. Curled up in her arms with his blond ringlets, he looked like an angel.

Late that afternoon people started to collect for the bambino soirée. Everyone wanted to meet Joey, the little blond, German boy from the Colombian jungles. Earl arrived with a whole bottle of Chardonnay, not just his usual glassful. Maybe he was going to share? Phil came with munchies, Win and Grace arrived in baby-holding clothes and Mia's aunt, Kristine, stopped by. She spoke German fluently.

As the babies woke up they were, as usual, fed, changed and dressed. First Tommy, then Caro and finally Mia arrived holding a bashful little boy who was holding a teddy bear. He sat in Mia's lap, looking around. The twins fascinated him. He slid off Mia's lap and walked over to the babies, who in turn studied him intently. " Bubchen?" He turned to Mia. "Ja, das Bubchen... baby," she answered. This went on for a while. Mia's aunt was also talking to Joey. He seemed satisfied, patted them on their faces and returned to Mia, stopped, went over to ToJo, "Hund," he said, patted him on his back and then came back to be held by Mia.

"That went pretty well, I think," said Win. "He at least has some of us labeled."

All of a sudden, Joey jumped off Mia's lap. "Vater" he cried excitedly and ran for Steve who was walking across the lawn. Steve leaned down and picked him up but instead of hanging on, Joey pointed to the babies. " Bubchen!" he said. Then he scrambled down from Steve and led him over to the babies.

238

"Bubchen," he said as he patted them on their faces again. He ran over to ToJo. "Hund!" Joey then patted ToJo again.

Steve ruffled Joey's hair. "You really are getting to know everybody aren't you. Good boy, Joey."

Everyone was looking at Steve. He looked wonderful now, rested and clean. His beard was neater and he was very tanned. He had on old white jeans, a navy blue tee shirt and flip-flops. He picked up one of the babies and sat down. "At last, I thought I'd never get to this point." He nuzzled Caro's neck. "How is my sweet little baby girl doing?" He smiled tiredly at Liz. She picked up Thomas and sat next to Steve on the wrought iron sofa. Joey, seeing this, ran over and got up on Steve's lap too. Sibling rivalry had begun.

Stell and Grace had bicycled to town that afternoon to get clothes and shoes for Joey. He loved the red flip-flops with fish on them so much he could hardly walk for looking at his feet. He had nothing and needed a little toothbrush, larger sized diapers, pajamas and regular clothes. They had to get the pool fence up right away. Stell called pool dude. He came right over to measure.

That night, Steve retired early. The men left and the women, Liz, Stella, Mia, Grace and Kristine, Mia's aunt, sat around discussing changes to be made. A three year old in the house would require some adjustments. All breakables and hurtables were put up high, the glass coffee table was covered with a quilt for safety, a youth bed and another high chair were needed. A list was made about things to see to right away... locks on gates, bicycle seat, car seat and etc., etc. Could her SUV hold three car seats in the back?

ToJo lay at Stella's feet. He, too, was thinking about the new situation. This new kid was different. He could chase your tail, bop you on the head with a toy, try to ride on your back and throw food at you from his high chair. This was kind of exciting...I wonder if he could play that throw-the-stick game?

58

Splashing was heard from the pool during breakfast the next morning. Liz was preparing scrambled eggs for Joey, who rose with the sun. When he saw Steve he starting yelling, "Vater", and wanted to go out. Liz picked him up and carried him to the pool. She was laughing. "I think Boy wants to swim with Tarzan!" Joey was jumping up and down in her arms, reaching for and yelling 'Vater'. Steve reached up and, with squeals of delight, Joey was plopped into the water.

Liz was still in her nightgown, a long, soft, white cotton, strappy thing. Steve grinned up at her. "This is what I was dreaming about in the jungle. Why don't you join us? Boy and Tarzan won't mind."

Liz sat down on the side of the pool laughing. "Don't you dare get me wet. I don't want a see-through nightie." Steve just laughed. It was sort of see-through without being wet!

"How do you feel this morning, about back to normal?" asked Liz.

"Not up to a morning run yet, but the pool feels great! And this added exercise I'm getting," Joey was trying to splash the water out of the pool, laughing and kicking, "will bring me back fast."

Stella ran out. "I'm off to school. Love seeing you in the pool again, Stevo. Bye- bye Joey, no no, don't splash me. I love you, Sweetie Pie! See you later. Bye Liz." And she was gone.

"I'll fix breakfast for you, Steve. Any particular thing you want that you couldn't get in the jungle?"

"Two eggs, over light, on toast would be wonderful!" Liz turned and walked back to the house. Steve just grinned as he enjoyed the view.

"Coming right up," said Liz.

"You got that right," sighed Steve.

After breakfast the pool fence people arrived. Steve called the YMCA and signed Joey up for swim lessons. He needed to be drown-proofed as soon as possible. Stella was now an expert. She could help him too.

It was mid-morning when Steve came back down carrying Joey. They had taken a walk, and now the little boy had gone to sleep. Steve put him in his bed.

Liz fixed coffee, and she and Steve sat on the terrace while the twins played in the playpen. "We have to talk about Joey, Liz, and find out if he has a family in Germany. We all left so quickly, no one really knows where he is, except me. I think his mother or father's families might be looking for him. I just want you to know that he may not be here for good. I don't want you to break your heart over it. If we can find his family, you know it will be for the best."

Steve continued, "I notified the main office in New York this morning, and they are checking it out. His father was with a German engineering firm but I don't know the name. His mother wrote for some French publication."

"I'm glad you brought him home with you...what an awful thing for a child to go through. It's good he's so young. He'll recover. I'm not sure he is even three. Was his father tall?"

"Yes, and so was his mother. Three was just a guess."

"No no, don't pull his hair, Caro," Liz jumped up to pull the twins apart. ToJo woofed. Liz picked up a crying Tommy. "We seem to have time for everybody but us. When is our turn coming? Earl thinks he might have a position in Savannah as curator of an historic house...a paid position. Phil wants to go to New York. The big house will be ours soon. We'll need more room for...you know."

"You're right, Liz," said Steve, as he picked up a fussing Caro. "We need to talk more about...you know." Steve was laughing as he bounced Caro around in his arms. "If we can arrange it, would you like to go to Louie's tonight for dinner? Just the two of us? Alone?" Steve leaned over and kissed Liz on the mouth. Then both babies wanted a kiss on the mouth. "They slobber more than you do," he said seriously.

Liz was laughing, "You think you are so funny...but if I can arrange it...I would go anywhere with you. I'll look into sitters; you handle the reservations."

"Call me when Joey wakes up," said Steve. "We'll walk ToJo. He likes that. ToJo is going to have to learn German."

They took the twins inside and put them in their high chairs. Steve left to walk up to the big house. Liz went to the window to watch him. Well, she smiled to herself, I guess that new nightie worked out as planned. It sure got his attention.

Mia was straightening the nursery when Liz walked in. "Morning Mia, Steve and I are going to Louie's tonight for dinner and I need a new dress. I'm going shopping right now, before I get involved and can't get away. Caro and Tommy are in their high chairs throwing Cheerios at ToJo."

"Don't worry about a thing," said Mia. "I'll give them their snack and put them down for their naps. Good luck...buy something sexy!"

Later that evening, at their favorite table at Louie's, under an orange flowering Geiger tree, Liz was definitely looking sexy. In a pale turquoise and green, one-shouldered dress of soft, floating, Indian cotton with touches of gold filigree caught in the threads, she was very beautiful and exotic looking. Dangling gold earrings and a wide gold bracelet were her only adornments. The little fairy lights in the trees gave her a shimmer when she moved.

Steve, in an off-white linen jacket over a dark blue linen shirt had a bit of a George Clooney look to him. Close cut dark beard, a deep tan and naughty blue eyes that looked amorous as he smiled at Liz. "You look exceptionally gorgeous tonight, Lizzie love...or have I mentioned that before?"

"You have, but feel free to return to the subject," said Liz with a sly little smile. They had already ordered dessert to share, 'Sinfully Wicked Dark Chocolate Mousse'. When it arrived, there on top of the dessert, was a Tarzan, molded out of marzipan icing, kneeling before a marzipan Jane. Tarzan was holding out a ring, a square cut emerald surrounded by diamonds, and Jane was reaching for it!

"Oh my God...it's Tarzan and Jane! Oh, I can't believe it!" Liz had both hands up to her cheeks...tears were starting. "Oh, it's so beautiful! You are so romantic, Tarzan, I'm speechless!"

Steve smiled. "What's the answer, Janie Love, are you going to accept my ring or should we send it back to the kitchen?" Liz reached for the ring, licked off the icing and gave it to Steve to put on her hand.

As Steve slipped the beautiful ring on Liz's finger he said softly, " Will you marry me, Elizabeth, I love you and I always will."

Liz, looked at her graceful hand with the ring being held in Steven's strong, rugged hands and whispered, "Yes, yes...I love you too, Steven", she looked at him..."and I have since the first time I saw you... in your Tarzan of the jungle suit! "

At this point there was a smattering of applause from the end of the deck. The entire kitchen staff, led by Phil, was softly clapping and smiling. Evidently, Tarzan and Jane mousses, sporting emerald rings, were rather rare.

59

The dinner seemed to work out real well! Liz woke up the next morning with an emerald ring on her finger and Steve whispering in her ear, "I knew you would look beautiful in the morning. But if we want to go skinny-dipping we have to beat the six-thirty German onslaught. It's six o'clock, and all the munchkins are still asleep."

The water was cool with the first rays of pink and mauve peeking through the trees. Liz still had a sleepy look. Steve swam a few laps, bare-bottom up but quickly lost interest and swam over to Liz. She giggled as he pulled her close. She felt like they were teenagers hiding from adults rather than adults hiding from the children.

After a while they heard Mia call out to Steve. Joey was awake. "Send him out. I'll get him." Joey came running and jumped into the water in front of Steve. Liz was putting on her swimsuit. She looked at Steve. "He'll never notice," said Steve. They played a while then Steve swam the splashing little boy over to Liz and slipped into his suit.

Soon, Stella came out dressed for school, carrying one of the twins. "He's kind of fussy. Maybe he needs a swim before breakfast. As she passed Tommy to Liz she noticed the ring. "Awesome!" Stell shouted. "Totally awesome! Y'all are engaged! How fabulous! This is amazing! I mean totally! I'm so excited for you! Let me see that ring! Oh wow! Yep, It's a keeper!"

Steve came over with Joey and put his arm about Liz. "So we have your approval then, Stell?"

"You two are my most favorite people in the whole world and I am totally thrilled! I'm going to school and putting it on the morning notices. Tarzan and Jane to mate! You don't have to worry about a thing, Liz, Mia and I already have everything planned. We even know who holds which baby. Oh, wait till I tell Mia!" Stell ran yelling back into the house.

Half a minute later, Mia ran out with Caro who was completely naked, to see the ring and ooh and aah over the whole romance thing. Caro was contentedly sucking on her toes and wetting at the same time, very unconcerned about the whole thing. Joey took notice, pointed and yelled, "Bubchen wee wee! Bubchen wee wee!"

Steve was rolling his eyes and laughing. Liz said, "Can't you just feel the romance in the air?"

Still holding a splashing Joey, Steve hugged Liz and Tommy. "Just looking at you is romance for me, Sweetheart."

Joey splashed Tommy. Tommy started to cry. Steve leaned down and kissed Liz. "We're together and all the rest is gravy."

Kirk had already left on his bike for school. Iggy was continuing with his tutor until the end of the year. He and Kirk were then going to ride to summer school together, and Iggy was going to Kirk's public school next fall.

Earl got the job in Savannah. He hated to leave Key West but this was too good to pass up. Phil was moving to New York. The cooking channel had picked up his show. It was now titled, 'Beefcake Cooking'. He was very happy about how it was turning out. He was trying to grow a beard like Steve's. He said, "Steve doesn't know it, but he has more than his share of sex appeal. Maybe a beard will give an edge to my personality." Stella hated to see him go. They had a lot of fun together.

The bambino soirées were going through another change. With Earl and Phil gone, and Joey running around eating the cocktail munchies and throwing sticks for ToJo, the relatively

246

calm atmosphere of sharing the day was over. Often those sticks, thrown in the general direction of the dog, hit a head or glass or baby. The twins moved around on their blanket, goo-gooing and gaa-gaaing as they munched on their toes or anything else they could get in their mouths but they, at present, stayed, generally, where they were put. Joey was discovering the new world. At three, everything is exciting and loud, and, in his case, German. Mia said sometimes he asked for his mommy but they were hoping he was too young to remember much of his past.

At the engagement (Liz and Steve), going away (Earl and Phil), welcome (to Grace) party, Liz knew the dynamics of the small group had changed. Stella was getting more independent and involved in school and a busy social life. Win and Grace announced they were going to drive up to Grace's home in Georgia to prepare for her move to Key West. They both seemed intrigued in their new friendship, often quoting Shakespeare at appropriate moments, or inappropriate moments.

Liz did not know when she, the babies and Mia were moving to the big house. She and Steve needed to talk and plan. It was all a matter of timing. It was turning into May, as good a month as any for a wedding.

As Win and Grace were leaving for the evening stroll back to his house, he said to Liz, "Can you come by at ten tomorrow? This afternoon I heard from the Dandlers. It's pretty good but if you are marrying Steve and want him to understand your finances, I'd bring him. If not, it's between you and me."

"I'll bring him. I don't like secrets. Too much like my first marriage. See you at ten, Uncle Winnie."

60

"I know you inherited some money, Liz, and I feel that is yours." Liz and Steve were walking over to Win's office for Liz's meeting about Johnny's will. "I think it's great. Stella, Kirk, the twins, and perhaps Joey and Iggy will be able to go to any university they can get into, and we can take a vacation now and then. It frees me up to do more charity work in my practice. I'm all for it. But I'm glad you asked me just the same. I agree, no secrets."

Fifteen minutes later they were sitting in Win's office.

"Holy Toledo!" yelled Steve, "You have to be kidding!"

"I can't believe this," said Liz, mouth and eyes wide open, hands on her head! "I never dreamed they had that kind of money! What happened? Johnny never referred to money. I knew we weren't poor, but seventy-five million? I don't believe it!"

Win sat back in his chair and explained. "Well, I guess they have been working on their sad family situation since that non-lunch at the country club. A European group has been offering to buy their company for a while, but they weren't selling. Now, after all was said and done, there was no one left to run the company that the sisters trusted. And no one in their family to support in politics, so they decided now was the time to retire from public life and accept the offer. They did so for approximately one hundred fifty million dollars. The company name, Worldwide International Financial Investment, will stay the same but the main headquarters will now be in Düsseldorf, Germany."

"Since it had all been left to Johnny and you were his wife, you get half. You could get more if you want to pursue a court case because of the male child but they hope you won't want the family name smeared in that way. They feel this is a fair settlement. The three sisters each receive about twenty-five million each. Of course, these are round numbers, before taxes and other costs and it will take a while to iron out details but, essentially, this is the gist of your inheritance from your husband."

Liz looked at Steve and just shook her head, her fist over her mouth. They both sat there for a minute or two, staring at each other, trying to comprehend this overwhelming, life-changing news. "You won't leave me because of this, will you?" Liz, still looking at Steve, spoke softly. "I don't know what to do?"

Steve leaned over and took Liz in his arms, "This will never come between us, I promise. It might give us problems but they'll be good problems. You can count on me, Lizzie, whatever comes, I'm in it for the forever part."

"I'll have to agree this gives you a lot of problems that otherwise you would not have," Win said. "You will need tax attorneys, accountants, secretaries, etc, etc. People will have to be hired to handle it for you, but at some point, you have to decide what you want to do with it. Knowing you two, a lot of good will flow from this unexpected windfall."

Win continued, "You don't have to do anything right now, Lizzie. It will all go into an account in your name. It can sit there a while, maybe years, while attorneys argue the details. I will answer them and agree to the deal; you go ahead with your wedding. I would recommend that you say nothing to anyone about this. It's safer that way."

Liz and Steve left Win's office in a daze. While walking home Steve said, "Let's go to Annabelle's up there on the corner and order coffee. We need to sit down."

"I am absolutely stunned," said Liz. "I thought my three

million was plenty of money. I'd never have to worry about another thing. Now this, and all the worry that goes with it, I don't know what to do. I was so happy without it."

"Don't panic, Sweetheart, we'll figure something out together...some kind of a foundation or something that disperses to worthy causes. Let's just relax and let it slowly seep in. We will move, get married, and take care of our babies and the rest of our growing crew. We will keep our life here because we love it here. Come on, Janie, Sweetheart, don't cry, it'll be OK. This is our life and we can live it however we want and as long as we are together, I'm happy."

"Me too," whispered Liz. She put her head on his broad shoulder and sighed. "Let's try not to let this rule our lives. We'll think about it later, after the wedding and the honeymoon." All the sudden Liz sat up, laughing slyly, "Maybe I should think about a pre-nup."

They both started to laugh. "I'm only marrying you for your money, you know,' said Steve. As they were laughing, the tension was easing. "I always heard you couldn't be too thin or too rich!" said Liz.

"Ah, but you have to be rich in all the right places," teased Steve as he and Liz got up and with their arms around each other, started walking home. They felt better. Why get upset? It was only money.

61

They were strolling, arm and arm, down Gumbo Limbo Lane and back to the little house. Liz was talking about when and how they should move over to the big house. What needed doing before they moved in. Who would go where. There were lots of beautiful bedrooms but they were rather formal in appearance, not exactly appropriate for babies, teen-aged girls and little boys.

Liz definitely had to change the master bedroom. She wanted a light airy feeling, more of a casual British Colonial look, with shutters and a romantic, four-poster bed, hung with sheer linen drapery. Steve just said any kind of room was fine with him, as long as she was in it.

Liz decided she would call a designer and have her come over and talk about it. She knew what she wanted but did not have time to find it on short notice. Stella needed to be consulted about her room, and the babies needed a nursery. As she was talking about little Joey's room, Steve's cell phone rang. He was surprised, as few people had his cell number.

"Yes, this is Dr. Steven Saunders...yes...yes I was...I do! I have that little boy right here with me in Key West! He is fine and happy...remembers very little about what happened. He is laughing right now playing with our dog." Steve was smiling as he talked. "We will be here, you just let us know when you will arrive. We'll pick you all up at the airport. Well, you are

253

very welcome...he is a wonderful little boy. How old is he? Oh, two and a half? Good... I think that is a great idea. We all look forward to seeing you soon.

"That was one of Joey's grandfathers. They have been searching the Internet and crossed with our information about the boy. All four grandparents will be here as soon as they can get here. I could hear them screaming in the background they were so excited to locate him. I know they are celebrating right now. This is great! That little boy needs to grow up with his family," said Steve.

He put his arm around Liz, "It's for the best, you know that, right Lizzie?"

"I guess we will still have a guest room in the big house," sighed Liz. "Maybe he can come back and visit us when he gets older. I just fell in love with that sweet little person who was so traumatized when he arrived. You were his lifeline and he wasn't letting go of you. I'll never forget it."

"They plan to stay for a week or two so he doesn't have another scary situation when he leaves. They want him to be comfortable with them when they all go back to Germany," said Steve.

"Sounds like a caring family," said Liz. "He's big for his age if he's only two and a half. Let's not say anything to him yet."

"And about the elephant-in-the-room," Steve said. "I'm sure it will be with us but lets not worry about it or discuss it seriously until we get past the Panholzers' visit, the move to the big house, the wedding and, of course, the honeymoon! A non-profit foundation or scholarship program or whatever we decide is the best thing to do with all that money will probably take a year or more just in planning. We'll have lots of time to get organized and find our way."

"I agree," said Liz. "The twins are trying to sit up now and are so funny. We don't want to miss any of that." Liz turned to Steve, put her arms around him and said, "We won't ever let this money thing come between us. We'll figure it out."

Steve hugged her back. "We will, Lizzie love, we will."

As they walked into the house a flying missile came at

Steve. "Pol, Vater, pol!" Steve laughed, "Guess he wants to go swimming."

"Both of you, wear swimsuits!" Liz teased.

Mia came holding Tommy. "I wanted to take them but I can't handle three non-swimmers in the pool. Joey needs a catcher in the water, all he wants to do is jump."

"Let's put on our suits and go jump, Joey," laughed Steve. Life was back to normal.

Later, after an exhausting time in the water, Joey was napping and Steve was lying on the floor with the twins climbing all over him. He was now in limbo again. Should he go back with Dr. Hu, three days a week? Should he be looking for a place for his clinic? Maybe he should do nothing yet, wait to see what a foundation was all about and how he was to be involved. It was probably the best plan...at least until after the honeymoon.

As Caroline stuck her fingers in his mouth and Tommy tried to pull out the hair on his chest, he realized that the money would change the course of his life and Liz's. Seventy-five million dollars needed a lot of attention. You could do a tremendous amount of good with that kind of money. Maybe this was what he was meant to do. He had seen the other side of philanthropy with Doctors Without Borders. Perhaps that experience gave him insight and knowledge that would be valuable in the rarefied field of non-profit foundations. Maybe, helping Liz with this huge responsibility was his answer. As surprising as the money was, it was a challenge that had to be met. He and Liz could do it together.

Kirk and Iggy made their usual noisy entrance...slammed screened door...loud voices and laughter. Noticing Steve on the floor with the 'peanuts', their name for the twins, they had to stop and comment on the ongoing baby-assault. "That one got me last week, right in the eye," commented Kirk. "They're dangerous!" Iggy laughed, " I think they are going to be really big trouble when they start crawling, good thing we're in the other house. They can't get us there!"

62

Liz and Stella walked through the big house with the interior designer, who, after lots of discussion of Liz's casual vision, quick sketches and color preferences, finally understood exactly what Liz wanted to do with the house. History was great in a museum, but this was to be a comfortable home for a young family and their friends. Nothing was to be brought over from the little house. It would stay, as it was, a perfect little gem.

In Key West, the façades of the old homes were required to remain as they were. If you wanted to paint your old house, the color had to be approved. But the inside could be modernized to your taste. With the new kitchen already in, the big house only needed a few furniture changes to start with. Later, Liz could envision a large, sun-room/family-room across the back of the house, opening to the terrace and garden. But there was lots of time for that later.

In the living room now, Liz wanted loose cushioned, comfy sofas in washable white linen with colorful throws, painting, pillows, palms and bright, striped, dhurrie rugs. The good antique pieces she was keeping and mixing with eclectic, amusing finds from local antique shops. Furniture she didn't need was to be donated to the O.I.R.F. or stored in the attic. The dining room furniture would stay, but the chair seats would be changed from a dark tapestry to a bright cotton in a curry yellow and white batik print from the island of Andros in the

Bahamas. Liz wanted an attractive but informal home where toys, scattered about on the floor, did not look out of place.

Upstairs the woodwork, doors and windows were to be painted white. Stella wanted lime green walls in her room. She had great plans, which included a comforter made of Key West Handprint Fabric. Liz laughed, "Go for it Stell. I think it's your signature color!" They decided they could do the upstairs painting and furnishing first, move in, and finish the downstairs later.

Liz and Steve were eager to get married and move to the big house so they could openly share the master bedroom. His official residence was still the guest room that Edie had given him in the main house. This sneaking about was getting tricky.

Many a night Joey would wake up, come into Liz's room and climb into bed between her and Steve. The little boy would softly say something about 'schlafen, or 'Bubchen', snuggle down under the covers between them, and contentedly go right to sleep, hugging his teddy bear. Sometimes he would be sobbing and repeating 'Mutti, Mutti'. They always made room for him. Later, as Steve left for his early morning run, he would leave the little boy curled up beside Liz, both sound asleep...Liz hugging Joey, Joey hugging his bear. They were going to miss him.

The frightened child that clung to Steve for dear life was gone. Except for the occasional bad dream, he was happy, playful and a loving little boy. He was definitely ToJo's BFF and was developing into a super stick thrower. Where it went was always such a surprise! A little arm that never tired of throwing had usurped Aunt Norma's favored BFF position.

Liz liked working with Carmen Delgado, the interior designer. The painters were now hard at work. Bedcovers were being ordered or made. Rugs, to warm up the beautiful heart-of-pine floors were being chosen. Liz was having all the oriental carpets rolled up and stored in the attic. Someone might want to use them later. Right now she was going for a fresh, youthful, happy look and eager to settle her family into the big house. High chairs, play pens, cribs, strollers, changing table...the twins seemed to have most of the furniture. Very soon they would be crawling and they would need guards on the stairs.

They had heard from the Panholzers. In three days, the four grandparents were arriving and had reservations at the Casa Marina Hotel. Hans Panholzer had suggested they go right to the hotel and then come over to Liz's house. This way they could slowly get to know the little boy and not overwhelm him with hugs and kisses at the airport. Joey had been an infant when they had last seen him. He would not know them, but they were counting on the fact that they all spoke German to help bridge their reintroduction to their grandson.

The grandparents, Heinrich and Eva Panholzer and Georg and Sophia Seifert, were friends in Garmisch, Germany. The four had been devastated when they learned their children, Georg and Veronika had been killed in Colombia. Adding to that shock was... no one knew anything about Johann...not a trace of him, dead or alive. Eva knew there had been a Doctors Without Borders clinic there and she had searched the Internet for information. The grandfathers were planning to travel to Colombia to search for the little boy. Now, finding him alive and well, on a little island in the United States, was so incredible they could hardly believe their good fortune!

Liz had invited them over for the bambino soirée and then for dinner on the terrace. Joey and ToJo were blasé to the importance of meeting grandparents and the new life it would bring. Steve knew Joey's future was in Germany with his family, but he was going to miss this little boy. He had fallen in love.

63

When the two sets of excited grandparents arrived at the little house, Joey and ToJo were at their favorite game of stick throwing, running, laughing and falling down in the garden. The four stood in the kitchen and watched out the window, tears streaming down faces, sobbing, laughing and crying with joy. They hugged and talked softly in German but never took their eyes off the little blond angel happily running circles in the grass.

Liz and Steve stood behind them. Heinrich Panholzer was a big man. He turned to Steve and enveloped him in a bear hug. "Danke," he said. "Danke schön! We are so very grateful to you for saving our grandson!" All four spoke English very well and all were hugging Liz and Steve saying "danke" and "thank you! "

"Go out and sit on the terrace and watch him," said Steve. "He puts on a very energetic performance. We'll be out in a minute."

The four grandparents were all sitting in chairs turned toward the garden and struggling with their emotions when Joey noticed he had an audience. He ran up to them and looked them over. He looked at Sophia Seifert a long time. "Mutter," he said, pointing to her. Then he turned around and ran back to ToJo with his stick. Joey's mother and Sophia had always been told they looked alike. Sophia sat still and sobbed. Martin, her husband, put his arm around her. "Let's not let him see us cry, if we can," said Martin, wiping his eyes with his handkerchief. The four just sat there quietly, wiping away tears and watching a two-and-a-half-year old blond angel play with a dog.

"Good thing they didn't bring him to meet us at the airport," sobbed Eva. "We would have all washed away."

"He is so big for his age," said Heinrich. "And smart too! Look how well he throws that stick!"

Joey ran back up to the terrace. "Hi, Joey," said Heinrich in German. Joey looked at him in surprise. "You want me to help you throw that stick?"

"Ja," answered Joey and off he ran to get the stick for his grandfather to throw. Now they were all laughing. Joey too. He really had an attentive audience, and they spoke his language.

Liz and Steve came out, each carrying a six-month-old twin. Joey came running back to show the new people his babies. "Bubchen!" he said, patting Caro on the head, "Bubchen!" He was now patting Tommy but missed his head and patted him in the eye. Tommy started to cry. Joey hugged and kissed him and, jabbering in German baby talk, ran to get his teddy bear, thrust it into Tommy's tummy and ran back to play with ToJo. The grandparents were entranced!

Liz was laughing at Joey's performance. "He is adorable and we have fallen in love with him. The babies are fascinated by his energy and he tries to be gentle but he is just so full of high spirits he can't slow down. Caro and Tommy love to watch him race around."

Mia came out and introduced herself in German. She and Stella laid down a quilt and lots of baby toys. They were all sitting down as Win and Grace came walking across the garden. Joey ran up to them, calling out "Vin, Vin," was picked up and carried back to the terrace. Drinks and hors d'oeuvres were served. The eclectic history of the bambino soirée was explained to the visitors amid laughter and Joey's love of jumping into the pool was amusing but there was also a sad feeling to the gathering.

Everyone was talking about Joey, but Heinrich and Martin wanted to hear about what had happened in the jungle. They walked with Steve and Win into the kitchen to fix another drink and Steve told them the details of the traumatic attack by the guerilla band on the jungle village and what he knew of the deaths of their children, how he became the instant guardian of a small, traumatized, German-speaking, orphaned boy and their dramatic escape and subsequent chancy passage through customs.

The women stayed on the terrace and talked about where the grandparents should take Joey for their first outing. Mia was to go with them the first day. The Aquarium was a good place to start. He would love seeing all the fish and turtles...or they could ride the Conch Train...the Casa Marina Hotel had a big pool and a nice beach.

When Joey walked ToJo around the block they could walk with them. But Joey took a nap every day after lunch. The first day he would come back to the little house, but after that, maybe, he would nap in their hotel room. He seemed to like being around Sophia. He was calling her 'Mutter'.

Stella was moving the wedding plans right along, and the Panholzers and the Seiferts got caught up in all the hoop-a-la. They wanted to be part of it because they felt Joey should be there for this important event in his hero's life.

Joey was still calling Steve 'Vater.' Steve said it was the first word he said after all the tragic events of that terrible day. "He had those little arms around me so tight and when he finally whispered, 'Vater,' we were at the Miami airport. Up until then he had not uttered a word or cried. I wasn't about to correct him. Of course, I was very busy trying to talk mothers with diaper bags out of a few disposable diapers. He was a sport about it all. I think he has come through it very well. Babies are highly adaptable. And he has been surrounded by love and family since he's been here." Steve indicated the group. "And of course, his best friend, ToJo."

About a week later they were all sitting around the terrace as the grandmothers were teaching Joey a German nursery song. The grandfathers looked at each other and Eva nodded to them. Herr Panholzer asked Steve if he could join him and Martin on the front porch of the little house. They wanted to talk to him about the little boy.

Heinrich Panholzer explained that the four of them had been discussing and arguing this for a week or so and wanted to get his feeling on an important decision. Sophia, who looked like Joey's mother, was in the first stages of Alzheimer's. She was all Martin could care for, and it would get worse.

The Panholzers had already moved into a retirement community that did not allow children as permanent residents. The only other family member who could take Joey was Heinrich's other son, who was divorced and in the military. They were sure they could find a home for him in Germany but wanted to get Steve and Liz's feelings about keeping him here as part of their family.

"After seeing him among all of you, we know he would be happy being part of your wonderful family, have a good upbringing and help finding his role in life. We, of course, would send support money and vacation here as long as we can, but our time is running out, and his is just beginning. We just want to do the right thing for him."

Steve sat still, eyes glistening, "Liz and I have both fallen in love with that precious little boy...I will talk to Liz but I think I can say, without a doubt, we would both feel fortunate to have Joey in our family. We don't need you to support him as, oddly enough, Liz has inherited a lot of money this week, but you could send pictures and stuff so he will know his heritage. We'll work out the rest but I am thrilled he's not leaving!"

Wow...what a week! Steve thought... seventy-five million dollars and a little angel!

64

Stella and Mia consulted with Liz about the wedding, but they wanted to do it all by themselves. It was their wedding gift to their favorite couple. Liz felt it might get a bit over the top, but the girls were so excited about the whole affair Liz could not say no. She told Steve about some of the plans. He just laughed, hoping they did not forget to include the bride and groom.

Invitations were handmade by Mia. She and her Aunt Kristina were also doing the flowers. Stella was making the wedding cake, with a tiny Tarzan and Jane on the top, but Louie's Backyard was catering and serving the food. Earl and Phil were coming down for the wedding, and Phil said he would help wherever needed. Earl was selecting the wines and champagne. Grace agreed to be the photographer, and Win was marrying them. It was definitely a family affair in the garden.

Stella and Mia had debated what flowers for the wedding bouquet. Liz wanted native Key West blossoms and greenery. So the girls bicycled around the island and found what they wanted. On the fence around the cemetery, growing wild, was the beautiful pink coral vine. Uncles Win's back yard had stephanotis vines with waxy, white flowers in abundance. A white orchid tree was blooming in Aunt Norma's yard. Sprays of pale tangerine-colored bougainvillea hung over Mr. Pinder's wall on Gumbo Limbo Lane. These locations were noted, but cutting and arranging were last-minute affairs.

The only thing Liz and Steve had requested was a small family wedding. There would be about twenty people total. Stell and Mia could handle that, and Liz gave them a small budget. With that they hired a steel band to play island music to softly waft through the trees. Round tables with white tablecloths were to be set up with floral arrangements on each. A sitter was hired so Mia would be free. White mosquito netting was to float down from the trees, and white orchids were secured to tree trunks. A small peaked white tent would serve as the wedding pavilion. This the girls were draping with loose white mosquito netting. They were adding romance to the beautiful garden. Kirk and Iggy were to make a last-minute tour of the garden in case ToJo had misplaced the bushes again.

The twins had new outfits, matching boy and girl confections that Liz and Stella had found and could not resist. Both were white silk with smocking and lace. Win was going to die when he saw what they had put Jackpot into. But this was not a barbeque. Joey's grandmothers had found him an adorable blue and white outfit, as if he cared. ToJo was to wear a big white bow.

They were all waiting to see what Aunt Norma would wear. She was an eclectic dresser. Some of her clothes dated back to the twenties. If she liked them, she kept them.

Liz had found her wedding gown, but no one had seen it. Stella, her Maid of Honor, was wearing a simple sheath in pale lime with tiny straps. Liz had approved. Stell was going to carry a cascade of pink coral vine mixed with a little pale tangerine bougainvillea and pale green asparagus fern.

Things were going very well with Joey, but his grandparents were leaving right after the wedding. They were spending a lot of time together, but Joey now slept at home where he would be staying after they left. Liz and Steve, who had been backing off, now were giving Joey a lot of attention. They were both thrilled he was staying.

The last night before the wedding, they had all been treated to dinner at the Casa Marina by Joey's grandparents. During the dinner, Joey had presented Steve with a finely crafted,

German watch. On the back had been engraved, simply, 'Danke, Joey'.

Grace and Win were talking about traveling and cruising the world together. They seemed to enjoy each other's company, and Italy was being considered for their first trip abroad. They were going to start out as traveling companions and take it from there.

Steve, after thinking it over, wanted a pre-nup, but Liz said it was unnecessary. If they ever broke up, she knew Steve would still use his share for philanthropy, and that was fine with her. When they got back from their honeymoon, Win was introducing them to people who knew about setting up a non-profit foundation. They would have to be careful it did not take over their family life. Win felt it was a perfect fit for Steve and his experience and medical background.

Of course the honeymoon was going to be short and secret. Grace was going to help Mia and Stella but three days was about it. Liz could not imagine three days without the twins! Three days with Steve and no babies? It was a mind-blowing concept!

65

The Wedding Day dawned bright and blue, cool breezes rustling the palms. Steve went off on his usual early morning run. Liz, the babies, Joey and Stella were in the pool kicking, splashing and laughing...and jumping. The start of another day but there was excitement hanging in the air. Liz couldn't wait for Steve to jump in the pool, his usual entry after removing his shoes and shirt. All of the sudden, there he was! Oh my God, thought Liz, he is so perfect.

Steve, now holding Joey, swam over to Liz, holding Caro, kissed the back of her neck, and whispered, "You take my breath away!" Liz turned and kissed him full on the mouth. He was hugging her when Caro started jabbering. She wanted a kiss too. Watching this, Tommy started pushing in Stell's arms for a kiss from Steve. Stella laughed, "I hope you aren't letting all this adoration go to your head, Stevo."

"Heck no, that's why you are around Stell...to keep me humble." He and Joey started chasing Stell and Tommy around the pool and splashing them. Tommy was laughing, Stell was screaming, Joey was jabbering in German and Caro wanted to get into the fray. Liz started over but then Caro didn't want her face wet. A typical day in paradise had begun.

Stella handed Tommy to Steve and got out of the pool. "Big day today, I've got to get moving! Got things to do! Cakes to bake! Flowers to pick! Brides to adorn!" And off she went.

Tommy and Joey, both in Steve's arms, had a brief shoving match but decided it wasn't worth it.

Steve and Liz lingered. "Tomorrow morning will be a little different, Lizzie Love. We won't be here!"

"Where will we be, Sweetheart?"

"Who knows, Lizzie Love, who knows? Just pack for the city."

Steve helped Liz dry off the babies and get them into dry clothes. "If you're not busy today, maybe we could meet up later, do something?" Steve said, with his arms around her, grinning

"Well, maybe, I'll see if anything interesting is going on," answered Liz with a teasing smile. Steve left and Liz got dressed. She had finished packing. Mia was feeding the babies and Joey their breakfast and Kirk and Iggy were still asleep. Liz was left with nothing to do. " Just relax," she told herself, " just relax."

Herr Panholzer came by to get Joey. They were going to dress him at the hotel later and come with him to the wedding. After the babies' naps, the sitter arrived to take Mia's place and took the babies for a walk. The hairdresser arrived to do Liz's hair. Stella and Mia were in and out. Liz walked out into the garden and there was such goings on that she came back in. Steve, in the big house, was probably holed up like she was, staying out of the way.

The babies were now starting to be dressed in everything but the top layer. It was a real challenge, dressing two babies who were both practicing enthusiastic crawling techniques. Stella came in and brought white stephanotis blossoms to put in Liz's hair. Mia and Stell took quick showers and got dressed. "I'll be back to help you into your gown. We don't want to mess up your hair." Stella was gone again. Timing was everything in a wedding.

Stella ran back in. Liz put on her gown with Stella's help. "Awesome, totally, totally awesome. You look like a movie star! Oh Liz, I'm so thrilled for you! You are gorgeous! You two will be absolutely amazing together! Stand right here. I'll be right back!" Stell ran to the terrace of the big house...checked and all was ready...ran back to the little house. Grace was photographing it all.

Music was starting. "OK, Liz! This is it! When I turn toward the tent pavilion with Dr. Hu, you come out. Steve will meet you there at that spot and you will both walk together up to Win. I love you, Liz!" And Stella walked out the door of the little house with her bouquet of flowers, in her lime green dress and shoes, looking like a completely unruffled, seventeen-year-old model. She was styling! She met Dr. Hu, Steve's best man, at the center of the garden, and they turned to walk toward the bridal pavilion.

Now Liz walked out of the little house and Steve walked out of the big house. Smiling at each other, they met, turned, and to the soft strains of island music, followed Stella's carefully arranged choreography toward the romantic white pavilion. Steve wore white slacks, white shirt and navy blazer with a sky-blue silk tie. With his close-cropped beard, dark hair, deep tan and blue eyes, he was, as Stella would say...amazing! He had come a long way from the haunted, sad, injured doctor who first came to the island house.

Liz had chosen a one-shouldered white silk, bias-cut gown that flared at the bottom into a graceful, chapel train. It was very simple and worn only with her pearl and emerald earrings and emerald engagement ring. She carried a bouquet of white stephanotis and sprays of Aunt Norma's white orchids. She looked enchanting. Stella was right. They made a very romantic couple!

Win looked over the assembled group. It was a small family wedding. Even though few people were related, it was a family nevertheless. Liz's family. In one way or another, she had brought them all together at the island house. Edie had promised Steve he would heal here in Key West, and it seemed true for them all. The group looked very happy and expectant as they sat, waiting for the wedding to begin.

Stella and Dr. Hu stood with the bride and groom. Seated on one side were Mia holding Caroline, Mia's aunt, Kristina, Aunt Norma, wearing a thirty-year-old peach colored frock with matching feather trimmed hat (a nod to the Queen?), Herr and

271

Frau Panholzer and Earl. On the other side were Grace, Mrs. Hu, Phil holding Tommy, Herr and Frau Seifert with Joey sitting in Sophia's lap. The babies were quiet, the shade was soft, the air was scented. Soft island music played in the background. All was perfect...too perfect!

WOOF! WOOF! barked ToJo loudly! The dog spun off like a tornado, running and barking toward the pool, streamers from his beautiful, white satin bow trailing in the breeze!

"GUANA!" yelled Joey, slipping from Sophia's lap and tearing off after ToJo. This kind of thing a little boy could understand! "GUANA! GUANA!"

Up jumped Martin! "Come back, Joey!" he yelled as he followed the little boy across the lawn.

Sophia was now up and running! "Nicht so schnell, Joey, nicht so schnell!"

Mia handed Caro to Kristine and went running after them. "Come back, Joey! No, no, ToJo. It's just the iguana! Come back!"

"Iguana? I want to finally see that thing!" Phil jumped up and took off across the garden with Tommy laughing in his arms! "Where? Where?"

In all the excitement, Caro looked up, uncertainly, at Kristine and started to squall.

Aunt Norma did not even turn around. She may have thought this was part of a new kind of ceremony.

Grace was laughing...only in Key West, she thought.

"I can't believe this," moaned Stella, "my perfect wedding... ruined!"

Liz hugged her. "It is a perfect wedding, Sis, I love it! I'd have it no other way! Who wants a wedding without an iguana?"

The four turned back to Win, who was smiling broadly. ToJo had performed a perfect bodyguard job... the iguana was gone. The dog was now primly sitting at Mia's feet with great aplomb. Joey was back in Frau Seifert's lap, looking like an angel, ready and waiting for the next athletic event. Phil and Tommy looked pleased as they sat...Tommy jigging up and down, ready to go again. Everyone was finally in place. Uncle Winnie asked, "Are we ready?" Everyone nodded. Liz, was smiling up at her

Tarzan, who, with an arm around her and holding her hand, was smiling down at his Jane…

Uncle Winnie took a deep breath. "Dearly beloved…"

66

New York! New York! Liz figured that's where they were going because once she had told Steve she had never been there and always wanted to go. He had planned it well. They stayed at the Plaza with a view of the park, had brunch at the Palm Court and a late lunch at the Boathouse. After a leisurely walk through the park, they went into the Metropolitan Museum of Art and wandered around for a few hours. Later they dressed for dinner and saw an opening night play.

The next day they did a little shopping for those they had left in Key West, had lunch at the Delegate's Dining Room at the UN, a drink at the Monkey Bar, famous for its murals, and a subway ride. Liz had never been on a subway so they took it down to Wall Street just for fun. Steven had planned it all, including reservations and Liz was just swept along on a magic carpet.

Every evening before they took the elevator up to their beautiful room, they had a nightcap in the Oak Bar at the Plaza. Liz and Steve would make a call to the little house, get the OK that none of the children had been kidnapped, come down with polio or broken any important bones, and return back to the world that was just for them. Most couples did not honeymoon and leave six children behind. But Liz and Steve made the most of their three days. After all, honeymoons are always wonderful, and maybe leaving six busy children made it even more so!

The last day they walked again in the park. Taking a carriage was discussed but Liz liked the peace of walking and stopping, sitting on the grass just relaxing with Steve, his arm around her. The shady spots were inviting; a little breeze occasionally swirled.

"This has been so wonderful, Sweetheart," Liz said, "everything so perfect. I'll always remember our honeymoon. And I wanted to tell you again what a good sport you were about all the pageantry of Stella's beautifully planned wedding. I love you for that."

"It was a little sweet, very romantic, and that iguana knew what he was doing, adding a bit of spice to the whole thing. He probably wondered why we were messing up his garden. Stell will never get over it."

They were laughing about Stella's reaction when Liz remembered one more place she wanted to see before they left. She had seen an advertisement of a Matisse show at MoMA, the Museum of Modern Art. To save time, Steve hailed a taxi. Liz was excited they were having a special showing of the Art of Matisse, her favorite artist.

It was their last night, and they walked from MoMA to Michael's Restaurant for an elegant dinner. This was a favorite place of publishers and media people. A busy, noisy, power lunch place at noon, but in the evening, calmer, smaller and sophisticated. They sat at a secluded table for two and discussed the menu. After wine had been poured and orders taken, Steve was saying he too thought it was a perfect honeymoon and he wanted to give her something to remember it by.

A robin's egg blue box with white ribbon appeared on the table. Steve put it in Liz's hand and smiled at her..."Just a little token, Lizzie Love, just a little token!" Liz, completely surprised, untied the bow and opened a flat square velvet box. There lay, connected by a narrow golden chain, six aquamarine stones, each set in gold and about an inch apart.

"When we walked through Tiffany's yesterday, I saw it and thought it was perfect for you...beautiful, smart, elegant. I called them last evening, when you were showering, and had it

276

delivered to the hotel."

"Oh, my stars! I love it! How did you know I'd love this? It's beautiful! Oh, thank you, Sweetheart! This is such a surprise. Oh, I want to put it on...now!" Liz was lifting it out of the box. It just sparkled as she reached around her neck to clasp it. "How does it look, Tarzan?" asked Liz, softly, as she moved her head around, chin lifted.

"Well, Jane, if it looked any better, we'd have to go home without dinner!" About this time the waiter arrived with the salad course. "Would you care for pepper?" he asked. There was a pause as Steve answered, grinning at Liz. " I don't think we need pepper right now, thank you."

The next morning, after a continental breakfast from room service, Liz and Steve packed to go home. "I have loved every minuet of being here with you," said Liz, "but I also can't wait to see our babies and Joey and the pirate crew. I'll bet the girls will be happy to see us. This trip has been so wonderful we should go somewhere at least once a month. Tarzan and Jane on a monthly safari...now that would be living! What do you think, Sweetheart?"

"What I think, Jane, is we're still up here, in the asphalt jungle, and don't have to leave the hotel for at least forty-five minutes!" Steve put his arms around her..."Now about the laws of the jungle..."

67

High in the sky, seats reclined, feet up with Bloody Marys in hand, Liz said to Steve, "Maybe now is a good time to discuss it."

"You mean the elephant in the room?" Steve paused, "It's your elephant, tell me what you are thinking? It's so much money...we both hesitate to consider what and how things should be done. What are your thoughts, Lizzie, how do you see it?"

"Well, first, I don't want it to be the focal point of our family, and to make sure of that we need to keep it quiet. I don't mind being rich, you know, nice house, cars, good educations for the children, vacations. That would not be unusual in Key West, but seventy-five million dollars...I don't want people to know about that.

"Second, I want you to feel like it's our money, something we share. That money came to me unearned, so I don't feel like it's necessarily just mine. I hope you will take a lead role in this, as I don't want to be the one in charge.

"Third, we can share our ideas on how to spend this money. We, together, will decide what is important to spend the money on. That is very simplistic, I realize, but, then, what do I know about big money...nothing."

Steve sat there, listening. "You have been thinking about it. I don't have all the answers, but we're in agreement that living a normal life with our children in Key West is important. I've been worrying about that too. Win will be a big help with setting up a non-profit foundation. There is going to be a lot to decide. We could just give it to a larger foundation but I'd like to see Doctors Without Borders a recipient."

"And I want to help raise the educational level here in Florida...particularly in the math and science areas," said Liz, "giving scholarships in those fields to anybody interested, even the middle class, which often gets overlooked. If we just helped DWB and concentrated our interest in Florida, I'd be happy."

"I guess we'll just see how it goes and I will try to take the lead. I know you hated all that stuff in Atlanta and this is going to be a lot of behind-the-scenes work, financial and organizational meetings. Until it is all organized, we'll just play it as it comes. Tarzan and Jane, braving the financial jungle!" Steve laughed, "Maybe we should name the foundation 'Vines' and just swing with it."

Stella picked them up at the Key West airport. They couldn't wait to see the twins and Joey. They had teddy bears for all three of them. The three women, Stell, Mia and Grace, had managed, but all were happy to see Liz return. Babies were 24/7! The pirates had made a sign for the patio, "Welcome Home Honeymooners", with lips and hearts and 'smoochie, smoochie'... written all over it. It was good to be home.

That evening, Stell went to a beach party, and Mia had a date with a navy pilot she had met through her aunt. Kirk and Iggy were sprawled across the sofas busy with their iPads. Liz was lying on the floor with the babies climbing all over her, and Steve was reading out loud about happy hippos. The 'pirates' kept rolling their eyes, but Joey was engrossed as he sat in Steve's lap looking at the pictures. "Hopos Vater, hopos!" Joey looked at Kirk, who was laughing at him. The little angel reached over and bopped him on the head. "Hopo, Kick, Hopo!"

"Yeah, Kick, hopos!" laughed Iggy. Joey slipped out of Steve's lap, toddled over and bopped Iggy on the head. "Hopos, Giggy, baa boy!" Then Joey came back and sat in Steve's lap again and calmly waited for him to continue. Joey took his literature seriously. ToJo woofed softly. He was in complete agreement.

As the story of the happy hippo continued, the front door opened and in came Stella and her date. Stell looked breathless and scared and about to cry... "I just saw our Dad! I can't believe it! It was him...I know it! Oh my God, what are we going to do?"

"Where?" asked Steve.

"At the Raw Bar...he was eating at the bar and watching TV," said Stella. "Pete and I went to get conch fritters for the beach party. We were at the take-out counter when I saw him, but I don't think he saw me!"

Kirk looked at Stella with a very uncertain expression. "Do we have to run away again, Stell?"

"No, no," Liz said quickly. "No one runs away...this is home and you are safe here! We'll get to the bottom of this, right Steve?"

Steve looked over at Pete and asked if he had seen him. "Yes sir, after Stell turned around, I took a good look at him."

"OK, right now let Pete and I run by the Raw Bar and check him out. You all stay here. He doesn't know where you are. He may not even know you're in Key West so don't panic! We'll be right back. Lock the doors and, please, someone finish reading to Joey about the happy hippos."

At the Raw Bar, Pete pointed him out...a broad shouldered man with a long gray ponytail and bushy gray beard with large forearms sporting tattoos. He was avidly watching a football game. "Let's wait till he leaves and see what he's driving," said Steve. "He could be a problem if he knows where they are and wants them back. He is the father and it might take time to get them away from him, legally. I wonder where he's staying."

"Everyone I know likes Stell and would like to help out," said Pete. "Maybe we could put a tail on him, see what he's up to. We could take turns and he'd never make us! We could call in his whereabouts...just like TV detectives. You can learn a lot from the tube."

"Well, maybe that's an idea. Let's see...oops...our quarry is paying his bill. Let's stand over here in the shadows and watch...now he's arguing with the bartender...oh, my God!" said Steve.

"He just punched the bartender in the nose! Damn...the police will be here any minute," said Pete. "This is amazing... now I know why Stell and Kirk are so afraid of him!"

As the man turned around to walk away, police sirens could be heard fairly close. He calmly walked over to a new, red motorcycle, inserted the key, and roared off. As the police were running in, Steve called one over and told him about the motorcycle and gave a description of the rider. Maybe the police would put him up for the night and tell him to leave tomorrow. Win could check tomorrow morning. Key West was a place where, if they did not want you here, they escorted you to the island exit and told you not to return. It had been done.

The police did keep him overnight. When Win called the next morning they were checking to see if the bartender was pressing charges...if not...he was free to go, with a strong suggestion to leave Key West. He did leave, but not before announcing he would come back anytime he wanted. He was not one to take pointed suggestions very well. "Suit yourself, Mac, but know, we'll be waiting for you," said the police sergeant. "We won't be this nice next time. And don't speed on the way out of Key West or the hundred miles up the keys. We'll be watching. Have a nice day."

The problem now was no one knew if Kirk and Stella's father was here by chance or if he knew his kids were here. Grace was afraid he might have seen Win's license plate in her driveway and checked with his sheriff friend to place the location. It was obvious that he did not know the whereabouts of his children, even if he thought they were in Key West. Stella would be eighteen soon and that would help their situation. Kirk could live, legally, with Stell as his guardian. Win was checking the laws of Florida and Georgia on sibling guardianship. The best plan right now was to keep Stella and Kirk out of sight. Maybe their old man was just in Key West out of curiosity. They could only hope.

68

It was interesting how close Kirk and Iggy had become. Kirk was outgoing, loud, funny and always laughing...finding something new and creative to do. He had been a big help to Iggy when he was first trying to use his new prosthesis and never far from his reach if he was needed. Now, of course, Iggy was doing well and Kirk was a big help in getting him into the groups of boys that Kirk had made friends with at school.

Iggy was more serious about things, often quiet and thoughtful. He was doing well in school, as he loved to read, and his home schooling he had taken seriously. They were different personalities, and maybe that was why they were such good friends. Kirk called Iggy, 'peg leg' and Iggy called Kirk 'red neck'.

Liz had put bunk beds in their bedroom to form an 'L' shape. Top bunk for Kirk and the bed below, coming out from under Kirk's bed to form the 'L', gave Iggy room below the top bunk to store the leg and other needs of wearing a prosthetic. They wanted pirate bedspreads and flags on the walls...and a spyglass for looking out for Kirk's dad. Stell was checking the Internet for Liz to see if anything like that was available.

There was another situation involving Iggy. He had inherited his family's home on Gumbo Limbo Lane and a few other properties owned by his great-grandmother, Mrs. Morales. Win had located their family attorney, Mr. Lopez, who had taken care of things when Iggy's parents were killed. Mr. Lopez was up in years, semi-retired and seemed happy to see that Iggy had a place to go. They talked for a while. Mr. Lopez wanted to retain the management of Iggy's properties. He said Win could handle the adoption. Win felt strongly that Iggy, while young, at least needed to be aware of the fact he had an inheritance. Mr. Lopez did not think Iggy should be bothered about any of it. The newly-formed family needed a group meeting.

Uncle Win had teased Liz that since she had arrived in Key West, his business had doubled. Now, as they all sat around the dining table in the big house, Win had more news. It seemed Iggy had a distant relative who, although he had not come to light when they were looking for a home for Iggy, now wanted to claim Mrs. Morales' property. Mr. Lopez was representing him ,and this person might want to adopt Iggy.

"Oh no!" Liz sat up in her chair and looked at Iggy, who sat there with a surprised look in his face. "That is not going to happen! Who is this person?"

"Well, that's the odd thing...nobody knows," said Win. "Mr. Lopez said he would check, but I don't want to leave it up to him. He's too old and uninterested in Iggy. I told him I would work on the adoption, but he suggested I wait and see what this unknown relative decided to do. We have got to find out who he is and what the relationship is. It's always a revelation who climbs out of the mangroves when money is involved."

Steve said, "Maybe you should check on Mr. Lopez. Could be he was planning to get part of that money when Mrs. Morales died. If you had not shown up, he would have been in complete charge of a ten-year-old's inheritance. I bet you were a surprise."

Kirk jumped in. "You know...we need to search your old house, Iggy, maybe there's a treasure hidden in there and that is why everybody wants it!" Iggy just shook his head. His life had gone from dull to amazing since he had met Kirk, and every day his life got more complicated and more interesting.

"I don't remember Mr. Lopez ever coming to our house," said Iggy. "I don't think I even know him. Maybe granny knew him. It was granny's house, and my parents moved in after I was born. My mother worked in a doctor's office and my dad managed property. After they died, I just stayed with granny. She needed somebody."

"We'll be checking into all of this, Iggy," said Win, " and I'd like to ask you to be careful when you talk to people. If anybody asks you questions about any of this, you let me know. You don't have to answer anybody's questions...it's nobody's business but yours. I've got my secretary checking on just what is in the estate. Your granny died 'intestate' so it all goes to her next of kin, and as far as we know, that's you."

There was a pause and Iggy said softly, as he patted ToJo on the back and scratched his ears, "I like living here and being with everybody. It's like I have a family again...I sure hope I don't have to leave."

"Don't you worry about it!" Steve said emphatically. "After all, who'd keep Kirk in line if your weren't here? We need you, Iggy, you're an important part of this family...and don't ever forget it!"

69

It was around three in the afternoon, the twins were still sleeping, and Joey, now up from his nap, joined the family discussion in the dining room. In his high chair with a small,open package of Cheerios on the tray, he was happy. He knew he wasn't suppose to feed ToJo, but the little angel figured no one noticed if he turned around and dropped a Cheerio over the back of the chair.

"Now, the other problem concerns Stella and Kirk," Steve said, as Kirk made a face at Iggy. "We would like to know what their old man knows about them. If he doesn't know where they are, that's fine...no problem...but if he knows, he'll be back. Stell, ask your friends, if they see a gray-haired, pony-tailed man in town, riding a red Honda cycle, to let you know. I doubt he'll go again to the Raw Bar. He might hang around the Little League games at Peter Dopp Stadium or the school. If you see him, stay out of sight and call us."

Grace spoke up. "I know a person that lives near his trailer park in Georgia. If he walked his dog by his place, he could tell if his cycle was there. He may have gone home; then again, he might be only as far as a few keys up the road."

"Well, one thing about it," said Steve, "he's not going to sneak up on anyone with that cycle of his. We're just going to have to keep an eye out for him. But don't worry; a man of his reputation would not be given the responsibility of children by any judge. But if we can avoid him till Stella is eighteen, it will be easier for us all. Now, anyone else have any comments, complaints or words of wisdom?"

"Yes," said Liz. "OK, tomorrow we move! Everything that needs to go, moves tomorrow. Kirk, Iggy and Stella are already moved, but we'll all work together to move the babies and all their stuff. Tomorrow night we'll all be together in the big house!"

"Good," said Steve. "Maybe we can adjourn before ToJo gets filled up with cereal." Steve laughed as he picked up one of Joey's hands and raised it above his head. "I just want to announce that Johann Panholzer is now an official member of our family. The papers came this morning. His grandparents want to keep close contact and hope he continues to learn German with his English. I don't know how to do that but Mia will be a help."

Everybody was clapping and smiling at Joey as he now waved both arms in the air. "Joey gut boy, ja?" said the three-year-old, happily.

"That's something I've been thinking about," said Liz. "We've got three languages here, German, Spanish and very casual English. We all need help speaking English correctly, and the best way to do that is to hear it and repeat it the right way. So don't take it personally if you are corrected...it's just the easiest and fastest way to speak English properly. At the same time, I don't want Joey and Iggy to forget their first language."

At that moment, Joey started to rattle off in German from his high chair like it was his turn to speak. Kirk said with a laugh, "That kid is funny and doesn't even know it. But nobody joins our club if they still wear diapers...right, Iggy?" Iggy looked over at Joey. "I'd give it a few years," he said. "Muchos años."

School was about over for the summer. Kirk was going to play Little League baseball and Iggy was going with him. Maybe he could play a little too. They hoped to find out as Steve talked with the coach and offered to be an assistant. The boys were also going to summer school, both on their bikes. It was going to be Iggy's big breakout summer. He was excited about the freedom he had now. He was definitely not meant to be a porch sitter.

The following evening, after a busy, busy, back and forth day, all were now ensconced in the big house. Liz and Steve had the big bedroom and bath at the back of the second floor, with a large porch and steps going down to the terrace. The twins were in the room next to them with their cribs and baby furniture. Joey and Mia shared a room because Mia spoke German to Joey and he liked that. Kirk and Iggy were together in the pirate's lair, and Stell was in her lime green and pink boudoir. Liz was elated...they were all together, under one roof, and nobody in sleeping bags.

One night after dinner, Steve was reading 'Black Beauty' to the group in the living room. He had even caught the older boys' interest with this book. The phone rang and it was for Kirk. It sounded like a man, but Liz figured it was his baseball coach. It was his father!

"I know where you are, Kirky boy, don't think you got away from me..." Kirk at this point, eyes huge, pressed the speaker button. "I gonna come and get youse home, you little turd. Ya need ta hep me fix my trailer up...you and miss goody-goody think just 'cause ya'll took up with that stupid, mamby-pamby family everything will be smooth sailin' but that ain't how it gonna be, Kirky boy, god-damn-it! I'm comin' after youse and I gonna beat the tar out of you little shits." He hung up.

"Oh my God!" said Liz, as Stella quickly ran over and put her arms around Kirk. "That's the worst thing I've ever heard!"

"Don't panic," said Steve. "We are all safe here. There is security on all doors and windows but we need to notify authorities. I'll call the police; maybe we can trace that call. We need to have Win get us with an adoption judge as soon as possible, and we need to save that call if we can." Kirk was trying not to cry, and Iggy had moved next to him. Stell still had her arms around him and her head down on his shoulder.

"He'll never let us alone...it gives him a sense of power if he thinks he's scared us. And maybe it's put all of you in danger." Stella was very upset. "He is very unstable and just likes to be mean!" Liz went over and sat next to them. "Just remember, we are all together, so don't feel like you are alone, without friends or family. We'll see this ugly thing through to the end...together. I promise!" ToJo had heard the familiar voice and crawled over to put his head in Kirk's lap. He was scared too.

70

Although the next day dawned beautiful and sunny, Kirk was afraid to go outside. Liz could see how his father had been able to affect his life with just a phone call. Since carpenters were in the attic building in storage spaces under the dormer windows and sloping sides (Liz was making her envisioned playroom a reality) she sent the boys up to help and plan for their stuff and location for their clubhouse. Kirk needed something else to think about.

If Bo Ashcroft, Stell and Kirk's dad, knew their phone number, he also knew where they lived and with whom. Steve and Liz believed he might be staying nearby, probably in a cheap motel a few keys up the Overseas Highway. It was an odd thing...both boys, Kirk and Iggy, could be in danger. Mr. Lopez had mentioned to Win that if something happened to Iggy, the other relative would inherit everything. That comment had set off bells for Win. It sounded like a veiled threat.

Late that afternoon, Steve, Liz, Win and Grace met to discuss the situation. As they sat around the new terrace of the big house, the twins in the center, babbling with each other in their playpen, they all had ideas of what to do. After much discussion they decided to hire a tutor/bodyguard. A tough, college kid who was free for the summer, needed a job and was willing to serve in both capacities. Grace offered to check with the Community College on Stock Island.

Stella was brought in on their decision. She was very relieved. She and Pete were going to tell their friends to keep up the lookout for Bo and the red motorcycle. She agreed with Liz and Steve that her dad was not after her as much as after Kirk. She was getting too old and too smart to intimidate. Stella had one suggestion though: "Make sure this tutor/bodyguard dude speaks English properly...both boys need a lot of improvement."

About a week later, Liz and Stella were waiting to meet with the young man the school thought would fit the bill. His name was Bradford Thompkins, from one of the old Key West families, and was majoring in English and Theater. As he walked from the porch into the hallway, Stella was flying down the steps, her usual way of descending, and as she looked up and saw this blond, bronzed, blue-eyed guy, she tripped and landed right in his arms, knocking them both flat to the floor!

"Ooffff ...Wow! What an entry! I'm going to have to remember that...very impressive!" said Bradford Thompkins, lying flat on his back, laughing and patting Stell gingerly on the back, as she lay on top of him. "I just can't think, off the top of my head, what play I can work this into."

"Oh my God, I'm so sorry! Are you hurt?" Stella was trying to sit up but couldn't quite figure out how.

"Just roll to the side, if you can, and we'll check for broken bones," said the young man, still laughing. "Then again, you can stay right there; I'm fairly comfortable."

"Shit, Stell, you 'bout kilt him 'fore Iggy and I got to inner'view 'em!" shouted Kirk.

"Well," said the prone young man, "I can see this is a very interesting household already...elegant English, flying females... is it safe to get up yet?" Liz, who had been standing, still holding on to the doorknob of the front door, looked aghast! "I am so sorry about all this...can you get up? Are you OK, Stell? Shall we try to make it into the living room and into chairs?"

Both Bradford and Stella were trying to get untangled and stand up. The young man put out his hand and said, "I'm Brad Thompkins, and you are?

"Dumbo, the elephant," said Stell with a sigh. Cutest dude

292

she had seen since Phil left, and she had to mow him down flat and land on top of him. She must have missed the chapter on 'The Sophisticated Greeting' in her 'What It Takes to be Cool' handbook. Stell was mortified!

As they sat down Iggy came into the room. "I'm no late? Si?"

"No, you're fine. Let's introduce ourselves before anything else happens...I'm Liz Sandford, playing the role of mom... Stella Ashcroft, playing the teenage daughter...Iggy Morales and Kirk Ashcroft, playing eleven-year-old sons and," as Liz turned around, "three-year-old Joey and his teddy bear. There are a few more babies, a husband and a dog but let's work with what we've got." Joey toddled over to Brad, looked him over carefully, then came back to Liz and climbed up into her lap.

"Well, I can see this is a very unusual family...you may call me Brad. And I assume my charges will be Iggy and Kirk?"

"Yes, the boys will be going to summer school for six weeks but after school they want to go to the beach, the park, etc., and with Kirk's abusive father around I don't want them out by themselves. I hope you have a bike. And as you have heard, Kirk and Iggy both need to speak English properly, and I'm hoping you can work with that too."

"Why don't we try it for a week," said Brad, "and then we will all decide together if I'm to continue or not...so far it seems... interesting. Maybe Kirk, Iggy and I should go outside and have a chat and they can show me around."

"Let's show'im our room first," said Kirk, "then go out to the garden and show'im the pool. I betcha he's a fast swimmer."

"Aha, a pirate's lair! Love the bedspreads." Laughing, Brad looked around the boy's bedroom. "I used to look for buried treasure too...an island is the perfect place to hide booty. Who is on the top bunk?"

"I am," said Kirk. "It's easier for me."

"So, Iggy, You've got all this room under here?" asked Brad.

"Si, I use this space to keep all my peg-leg stuff. I can do everything myself. Sometimes mis amigos call me 'the pirate'."

293

"Cool," said Brad, "you don't need help with anything? Man, that's awesome. I'm going to have to wear an eye-patch to fit in here, I can see."

After a tour of the garden, where Brad met ToJo and potential hideout spots were pointed out, the three sat on the terrace discussing summer plans. "I like you boys, I can understand your problems and I think we can work together this summer. Just remember, one of my job titles is tutor...teaching you both to speak English properly. The other is protection... we'll talk about that later. Let's go see your mom...or is she your mom?"

There was a pause as the boys thought about that...no one had asked before...they looked at each other for a minute... "Yeah, she's our mom," they answered at the same time. "She's cool." said Kirk.

"Si," responded the pirate.

71

On the new terrace of the big house, Steve and Liz sat together in the cuddle chair...a double chaise longue. Usually they had a baby or two with them, but Mia had the twins out in the triple stroller with Joey, walking the dog. The pirates were off, explaining life to Brad. For some reason, some of those jaunts often needed Stella's presence.

"Can you believe we are alone, more or less? We need to have date nights, hotel holidays, Sunday siestas, maybe even a mini, overnight, local vacation." Steve was nuzzling Liz's neck and she was squealing and laughing. "What we need is a one-month anniversary honeymoon! What do you think, Jane?"

"I'm in full agreement, Tarzan...totally." Liz was snuggling up to Steve. "But 'tis easier said than done. Leaving this bunch takes planning. But I've got an idea. I've been wanting to go up to the old beach house, which I have never seen before. Win told me the five-year lease that the Coast Guard had on it is up. They want to renew but we need to see it first. Grampa Snow bought that property and built the house about sixty years ago. I've heard about it, but it was always rented. We might like it; maybe with a little work or something we can use it. It would be perfect for the kids...their own beach!"

"I'm ready. When do you want to go?" Steven grinned. "The beach house, I'd forgotten about that place. I don't think Carl and Edie used it much. Let's go tomorrow morning...just the

295

two of us. If we start planning now maybe we can go...alone...
Tarzan and Jane in a secret hideout...ALONE!"

They were laughing when they heard the doorbell
ringing. Win and Grace walked out on the porch. Grace was
looking younger every day. Her new look and her Key West
attitude seemed to have made her into a different person.

Win had interesting news. He had been checking on
Iggy's financial situation and had found out a lot, and none of it
was good. Mr. Lopez was not in good standing with the Florida
Bar because he had been accused of stealing from clients, usually
elderly widows. Every time they got close to charging him, he
made restitution and nothing happened.

He had been handling Mrs. Morales' finances since
the death of Iggy's parents and now was ready to cash in.
Iggy's estate was surprisingly large. His dad, while managing
properties, often bought properties and rented them out. After
his death, Mr. Lopez stepped in and took over, collecting rents,
paying taxes, utilities, etc. Mrs. Morales knew nothing about
this, except nobody ever came to her for money, her lights stayed
on, her water ran, so she never questioned the situation. Mr.
Lopez, while paying the basics, was also keeping the rest of the
considerable rental income and planned to become the owner.
Iggy, he knew, was too young to know what was going on.

One of Iggy's properties was the house next door to
where he had lived with his great-grandmother. It had long-term
renters named Lopez, and looked like it had been remodeled a
bit. Win said he would be bringing charges, and maybe they
would get him this time. "It's stuff like this that gives lawyers a
bad name," said Win. "Iggy is going to do very well when all of
this is over but I think I'll wait to tell him when it is over."

The next day, after much arranging, Steve and Liz drove,
alone, up to the beach house on Summerland Key. It was
exciting not knowing what they would find when they arrived.
They turned off US1 at West Shore Drive and then turned onto
Ocean Drive. Their house was just down the road. There...the
sign said 'Windswept'; all the houses had names. They turned in,
driving through a leafy tunnel of large, old tropical trees, in a big

circle and there it was...a tin-roofed, two-story house, painted the color of tree trunks, with a lime-green glass-paneled door flanked by lime-green shutters. Before they went inside, they walked around the yard, looking at the native trees, vines and flowers, rather casually kept but beautiful. The ocean sparkled with the morning chop, and a crisp breeze gave freshness to the air. A wooden dock, built on pilings, went 150 feet into the water. Benches were built at the end under a tiki-hut roof. Sand and rocky outcroppings made the beach, and a few empty chairs set about the sand, staring out to sea.

"Wow," said Steven, "I think I can take this...a little bit of paradise in your own back yard."

"It's fabulous!" said Liz. "How did I forget about this? I love the buttonwood trees near the water. It is so picturesque. I did not think it would be this charming. Let's go inside and see what we've really got here."

There was a huge screened porch running the width of the ocean side of the house with a decked porch above it. The open kitchen was all white with white tile floors running throughout the downstairs. Most of the walls were white, with an accent wall of pale aqua running up the stairs. Beachy old wicker furniture with faded fabrics, colorful paintings, plus a wall of shelves for books and electronics, furnished the great room. There were four bedrooms, three baths and all doors to the screen porch were glass and slid into the walls, out of the way. The house seemed completely open to the ocean, and a salty breeze flowed through.

The paint was chipped in places, the appliances looked old, but it was a family house. Liz was enchanted. It was truly amazing! They could start using it right away. She'd have to tell Win...no more rentals.

Steve was out at the end of the dock, measuring the depth of the water and deciding if it was high or low tide. He loved boating and fishing, and a boat could be kept up here on davits. He was excited...he was ecstatic...he could not believe his luck! As he had lain in that hospital bed, hurting and angry, he would try to imagine something like this in his future, but usually he couldn't see it. That he actually had his dream made him feel guilty again. He thought of Allison, under the ground, no more, and he, with everything he ever wanted in life. A tear slowly rolled down Steve's face...life was not fair.

72

Liz sat down next to Steve on the bench, under the palmetto thatch roof, at the end of the dock. "What's the matter, Sweetheart...I can tell you're troubled just by the way you're sitting. My guess is...too much of a good thing?"

"You know me too well, Lizzie Love. I guess it was the boat, which we don't even have yet...that was the final straw. My life is just too perfect...a beautiful wife I love deeply, children, even though they are a mixed group, I feel like they are all mine, a great house and now this...a beach house...with a dock...for a boat! What have I done to be so lucky? Why me?"

"Oh Sweetheart, I know you're thinking about Allison but try and think about it this way...Her life was too short, but that was not your fault. Maybe fate, or luck, or the whims of the gods gave her a short life, but she was loved during her life. First by her parents, and then she was loved by you. Some people have long lives but lack that kind of love. You helped make her short life wonderful by loving her and making her happy. So those same whims have given you a longer life, still not your fault, but you have got to go on and accept that life, and all that come with it...good or bad...without guilt. All this stuff, money, houses, boats are just things. What's important are those little lives that we have taken on to raise together. Maybe that's what you were meant to do for the world...and manage the foundation to make other lives better. Maybe that is what I was meant to do too, with you. Maybe our love was in the stars!" said Liz softly.

"Ah, Lizzie Jane, you keep me sane," said Steve as he kissed her, held her in his arms for a while and, gazing out over the water, asked softly, "What kind of boat do you think we should get?" Liz laughing, said, "Maybe a Noah's Ark would be appropriate."

After an hour or so of poking around the house, checking the linens, kitchenware and etc., the two left for Little Torch Key, a few islands up the highway, and from there took the launch to Little Palm Island for lunch. This exotic resort had a four star restaurant but was accessible only by the island's launch or your own boat. If getting away for the day was the idea, this was perfect.

Back in Key West that evening after dinner, Liz and Steve met with two representatives of a non-profit foundation group at Win's office. They had flown in that afternoon and were full of information and advice. Liz and Steve could tell this was going to be a very complicated procedure. Giving money away, in the way you wanted to give it, was not simple. After the meeting, Liz and Steve talked to Win. Maybe Grace might be interested in a roll with the foundation. She was looking for something to do and she was smart, with a Master's degree and a keen interest in education. Win said he'd talk to Grace about it.

Liz was making plans for all of her family to go up to the beach house for the weekend. With Mia and Brad, it made ten. But the house was equipped with most everything except food. The twins would sleep together in their playpen, and Liz was bringing a plastic pool.

She and Stella were leaving the house for the grocery store when Stell's cell phone rang. Bo, Stella's father, had been sighted at the beach playing volleyball, his cycle parked close by. Two of her friends had spotted him. Liz called Brad right away, to give him a heads-up, then called Steve to tell him. It was a good time to leave town, even if the beach house was only twenty-five miles away. Liz, Steve, and the twins would go in the Mini Cooper with the groceries. In the SUV, Brad and Stell were in the front seat while Mia, Joey and Iggy were next and Kirk and

ToJo were in the rear. They would all be on the lookout for a red motorcycle.

The beach house had been built long before a law was passed insisting all buildings on the ocean had to be eleven feet above ground. Windswept had the first floor at ground level, which made it convenient for going in and out to the beach. The wide screened area had a porch swing at one end with lots of comfortable chairs around a large, coffee table. The other end had a dining table with eight wicker chairs. A bar was built in the middle with stools and a bar-top of lignum vitae wood, one of the hardest woods in the world. The tree had grown on the property at one time and had blown down in a hurricane. This was all in the little bio of the house, framed on the wall in the hallway.

Kirk, Iggy and Brad went immediately around the house to the end of the dock. "I bet this is where the pirates landed and buried treasure," said Kirk. "We should keep an eye out for a good spot to dig. This is really cool!" Iggy looked into the water, "Good fishing too, si? Look at those snappers!"

Brad sat down on the bench, clasping his hands behind his head, thinking...as summer jobs go, I think I lucked out. What they need here is a boat. "I'm going to check that kayak I saw by the side of the house." Brad started back down the dock to check on a brightly colored molded plastic kayak resting on sawhorses. There were two, one single and one double, perfect.

He started to drag one toward the water when Iggy started yelling in Spanish...loudly, rapidly and completely incomprehensibly! ToJo was barking and only one boy was standing on the dock! Brad went running! Iggy was pointing to the water and there, floating motionless, facedown, was Kirk! Brad jumped in...what was wrong with Kirk? He was limp and looked to be bleeding from a head wound! Brad picked him up and, carrying Kirk in his arms, walked back through the shallow water to the beach. Stella and Steve were there, waiting, but what had happened?

"Is he breathing?" asked Steve. "Put him on the dining table... Stell get a blanket and cover him to keep him warm." Kirk was breathing but still unconscious. "Brad, get my medical bag from the SUV...Liz, some clean cloths and warm water." Liz had put the little ones in the playpen for safety. Mia was holding Joey. "OK, now Iggy tell me, in English, what happened out there?"

"I don't know much...we were looking at the fish and Kirk yelled and fell over on the water. At first I thought he had just fallen and I was laughing but he didn't move and then I see the blood and I could not help him. I feel muy malo...very bad!"

Steve had the blanket over Kirk to keep him warm and was wiping his head with warm water. "It looks like he has a long, narrow, surface wound...like a bullet grazed him! But it's not deep. I've seen bullet grazes before...this is what they look like." Steve looked at Liz. "We need to get him to a hospital but he's in no danger of dying! I've put a sterile bandage on his head and we'll keep him warm but...who shot him and where is he now?"

Brad responded, "When I was getting the kayaks from the side of the house, in the distance I heard a faint motorcycle roar. I noticed because I've been checking them out if we hear one while we're biking and just now I thought, no problem, he's not up here. But maybe he was!"

"Call 911," said Steve. "Stella and I will take Kirk to the Key West hospital and you all stay here, lock the doors, and wait for the police. This needs to be reported, but I've got a feeling the shooter is long gone. Maybe you can help the police locate his position, Brad. That would help a lot." Steve went over to Liz, gave her a kiss. "I wouldn't leave if I thought any of you were in danger. Lock the doors, stay inside...Brad is staying here with you all...the police will be here soon! Kirk will be all right, I'm sure. I'll call you."

73

Steve drove while Stell sat in back with Kirk's head on a pillow in her lap. Steve was on his phone with the Highway Patrol giving a description of Bo. He could be headed up the keys and if so, he'd be easy to find on US 1. Stella kept rubbing her brother's arm.

"It's going to be OK, Kirk honey, you'll be back on the pirate ship soon." Stella was talking softly, hoping it might help bring him around. Kirk was still unconscious and very pale. Steve was now talking to the hospital, telling them they were coming and to get a specialist for a head wound.

Back at the beach house, Brad and Iggy were walking around with the police, trying to decipher where the shot had come from. There might be evidence left at that spot. A roadblock had been put out from Key West to Key Largo. The police remembered him from the Raw Bar incident...they knew he was trouble.

Liz was rocking Caroline. Tommy was already asleep as Mia put him in the playpen/crib. "This is just so unbelievable!" said Liz. "I just can't comprehend that somebody shot Kirk. Who would do such a horrible thing?" Liz and Mia were upstairs in the bedroom, talking softly. Joey was playing quietly with his Thomas the Choo Choo, going first around Liz's feet and then around Mia's. He didn't like to use the track. He wanted it to go where he wanted it to go.

Liz left them with Mia and went to check on the boys. ToJo had sniffed out a spot that they were now checking out. A cigarette butt and a dirty handkerchief were found and bagged. They were making molds of motorcycle tire prints nearby. With a roadblock, out he couldn't go far. There were a few off roads on the larger keys but they all circled back to US1. It was the only road with connecting bridges. If the shooter had been Bo, they would definitely apprehend him.

Kirk had been admitted to the hospital and was back in his room after undergoing some testing. He was still out and showing no signs of animation of any kind. Stella was so nervous she couldn't sit still. She couldn't believe it had been their father shooting at Kirk. Was he still in danger from him? The police had sent a patrolman to sit outside of Kirk's room, figuring someone had targeted him, but his own father? Stella tried not to think about it.

Later Liz, Iggy and Brad came by. Steven asked Brad to take Stella someplace for dinner. She needed a break but was reluctant to leave Kirk. Liz convinced her she needed to keep her stamina up so she could stay with him later. They were gone about fifteen minuets, and Iggy was talking to Kirk in a low voice. Kirk was getting agitated and moving his head and hands...suddenly he very softly said..."Stella...Stella"?

Iggy looked at Liz...Liz leaned over and said, "Stell's gone for dinner, she'll be back soon. What do you need, Sweetheart... we're all here."

Kirk's eyes were still closed but he was struggling to speak..."Tell Stell...I saw Dad...on the beach...with a gun. Tell her to be careful!" He seemed to relax after that, drifting back to his deep sleep.

"Well, I guess that mystery is solved," said Steve. "I'll tell the cop in the hallway to call that in. I also want to tell the doctor he spoke. I would think that is a very good sign."

"Do you think he'll be OK, Liz?" said Iggy. "Do you think he'll wake up soon?" Tears were sliding down Iggy's worried face. "I'm very sad for him. He always was there for me so I want to stay here for him. Maybe my talking to him helps, si?"

"I think perhaps he can hear us but just needs to rest his head so it can heal. You're doing all you can, Iggy, and I bet Kirk knows that." Liz put her arm around Iggy's still thin shoulders. "Don't cry, Sweetheart, he's going to come back to us...and we'll take turns sitting and talking with him until he does. After all, what would we do without 'the redneck'? He'll be back!"

Stella, when she and Brad returned, was thrilled that Kirk had awakened enough to speak but could hardly believe what he had said. "In my brain, I knew it was him but in my heart, I didn't want to believe it. I knew he had to have his way and being mean to people made him feel like a big shot but shooting his own son? He must have been slowly going crazy to do such a horrible thing!"

Brad put his arm around her. "That is the action of a sick mind, Stella. He did whatever he did because he was unable to help himself. A lifetime of boozing took a toll on his brain. When he's caught, his attorney will probably plead insanity. And he will be caught!" Brad was trying to give Stell a pep talk. "I'll stay with him tonight, if you want," he said.

"I want to stay with him, Brad, but you can stay for a while and keep me company. You can tell me about your new play. I'm tried of talking about my problems."

74

At about two in the morning, Steve woke up. As he sat up in bed, Liz said, "You can't sleep either?"

"No, I think I'll go to the hospital and relieve Stell. She must be exhausted. I'll tell her to come home and sleep as long as she can. Who knows what time the doctor will return and emotionally this has to be very hard for her...her own father! I'll call you later this morning."

Steve found Stella sound asleep, sitting in a chair, her head on the bed next to Kirk's and holding his hand. There were dark circles around her eyes and she looked haunted. "You sure you can drive home, Stell?" asked Steve.

"Yes, thank you for coming...I feel so lost...I'm not sure what to do." Stella put her arms around Steve and started to cry. Steve held her, patting her back.

"We're here for you and Kirk and we'll get through this together...we're your family now, Stell, don't ever forget that. You and Kirk are not alone anymore. We will all work through this together...don't cry. He's going to be all right and will wake up soon and be his old pirate self, so try not to worry. Go home and sleep. You need rest as much as he does."

Later that morning, Steve was sitting by the bed, watching for any signs of Kirk waking up. He smiled as he thought of Kirk, rousing himself out of his coma, to warn Stella. That gave him a lot of hope. Nurses came in and out, but Kirk so far had not moved.

Steve was standing, looking out the window, when his cell phone rang. It was the police detective who had been there before. "Dr. Sandford, we have a bit of news in this case. A red motorcycle was found, at dawn, smashed on the rocks, at the end of No Name Key Road. A body was found about twenty feet away in the mangroves, dead and mangled. We figure he was speeding down the road, in the dark, and being unfamiliar with the area, did not know the road ended abruptly at the old ferry slip. When his cycle hit the rock barrier he was thrown off and killed on impact. The deceased has a gray beard and ponytail, and we need someone to come and identify him."

"My God, what a way to go," Steve said. "I'm not happy to hear that but it sure solves the children's problem of him being a danger to them. Thanks for calling. I'll be down later this morning."

Well, thought Steve as he sat back down, this put a different light on things. The children now were orphans and therefore adoption was an option. He and Liz had worried about the father showing up and causing problems, just because he could, but that was not a problem any longer. He had better call Liz, let her talk to Stella when she woke up and see if she wanted to go with him to identify the body. And then, what should they do with the body? It was one of those situations not often covered in 'Dear Abby'.

Later that day, after Stella said she would not mind if Steve went alone to identify the remains, they talked about what to do. Stella was torn...he had tried to kill Kirk but he had still been their father. They decided to cremate Bo's body and send his ashes up to Gwinnett County to be interred next to their mother. Stella seemed satisfied with that. The police now were no longer sitting at Kirk's hospital room door.

Win and Grace were coming to sit with Kirk. Steve had filled Win in on the new situation with the children, and now the attorney was working on four adoption cases; Stella, Kirk, Iggy and Joey, and legally changing the twins' names to Sandford. Grace was very concerned about Kirk. She had been doing research on head injuries all morning on her computer. The doctors were monitoring and testing and it was just a matter of time. Kirk's head wound was not deep and he would wake up when he was ready. In the meantime, the family was going to be there and talk to him.

Iggy came often and wanted to sneak ToJo in. Stella thought it might help. To prepare, Iggy gave ToJo a good bath and a brush. Then, in the parking lot of the hospital, they wrapped him up in a towel and put him in a basket. Brad was taking a turn sitting with Kirk and opened a door at the end of the hallway.

In the room, the three of them put ToJo on Kirk's bed and whispered to the dog to lie next to him. ToJo, always the sensitive animal, did not bark but licked his face, then lay with his head on Kirk's chest, staring at Kirk's closed eyes. Stell, Iggy and Brad were all holding their breaths...would this work? As they stood there, watching, Kirk's arm lifted and draped around ToJo! ToJo gave a big sigh, a little woof and went to sleep next to Kirk. Kirk's eyes were still closed but he was smiling! ToJo the Wonder Dog had struck again.

The next day, they brought Joey and put him on the bed next to Kirk. Joey, in all his little boy innocence kept hitting Kirk on the chest and saying, "Bak up, Kick, bak up!" Finally, Joey turned to Liz and announced, "Kick nite nite, mommy." But, all of the sudden, Kirk's arm came around Joey and he was smiling again! And this time his eyes fluttered open and he looked around.

Liz leaned over, "Hello, Sweetheart, welcome back!"

Stella held his hand... "I'm so happy! Oh, my God..." Stella started crying.

"Kick bak up, Mommy," observed Joey.

Iggy leaned over. "Hola, red neck," he said, as he gave him the thumbs-up signal.

The nurses rushed in and checked his eyes and vital signs. The doctors were notified. Steve was called to come out. Kirk just lay there, calmly looking around.

"What's going on?" he asked. "Are we having a party?"

75

A few days later, Kirk came home and although he was not as animated as usual, he was happy to leave the hospital. He still had a bandage on his head, and Iggy was now calling him Scarface. Scarface and Peg Leg...Liz just shook her head. Steve kept an eye on him, but Kirk seemed willing to take it easy and just lie around. His wounds were emotional as well as physical. He and Stella talked a lot, quietly, just the two of them. His bunk bed was moved down so he was in no danger of falling. Iggy now assumed the guardian role that Kirk had always taken. ToJo, knowing something wasn't right, kept close to Kirk, trying to figure it out.

The twins were perfecting their hair pulling, biting and other social skills. Although not officially crawling, they never stayed where you put them. All electrical sockets now had guards and all little pieces of other children's toys were constantly being picked up. Just keeping the twins in sight was a hassle. They would roll, push, squirm or otherwise move apart and seemed to hide. They were happy babies and full of adventure. Now that Kirk was not out playing he was observing them more and told Liz they were funnier to watch then a TV comedy.

Iggy and Kirk would play commando with them...pulling themselves along on their elbows like infantry under fire. The babies were better at it. They would all laugh and race and tumble. Of course, the fact that Caro and Tommy put everybody's toys in their mouths made them rather unpopular at times. Joey was never pleased about sharing his choo choo with them. All they wanted to do was slobber on his trains.

Win, Steve and Liz talked with Iggy about his great-grandmother's house. It was standing vacant. Steve suggested they fix it up and rent it. The rent, after paying for repairs and updating, would go into Iggy's trust fund. A reputable real estate firm was now properly managing all his other properties. Mr. Lopez had disappeared again.

Soon Iggy's house was taking shape. Liz had decided not to paint the house but to leave it the beautiful, unpainted color of silver-gray and paint the shutters a pale blue. The front door was to be a deep coral to match some of the flowers that bloomed around the porch. After trimming some of the plants and trees but keeping most of the natural foliage, the house was shaping up to be the prettiest place on the lane.

Grace, after thinking it over, had decided to work with the foundation. She liked the direction Steve and Liz wanted to go. They decided to make Iggy's house the temporary headquarters, and Grace was busy setting up the interiors for business and a few guest rooms. She and Liz both loved doing interiors so they often took the three little ones, the three-seated stroller, Stell, Mia and whoever could fit in the SUV, shopping. Liz and Grace agreed. It might be an office, needed to function like an office, but it didn't have to look as serious as one.

One Saturday, Liz was driving down Von Phister Street and stopped at a garage sale displaying a set of twig furniture. They had quite a few pieces, and she bought them all. With coral canvas pillows, they would be perfect arranged in Iggy's back yard under the spreading guava tree.

As soon as the dining/conference table was in place, surrounded by wicker armchairs with colorful, soft cushions, the first meeting of VINE^{2}S was called. Although the name had been thrown out as a joke by Steve, it seemed to work...Very Inventive Numerical, Environmental, Engineering and Science. Liz loved it...said it reminded her that vines truly could wind their way into anything and grow and climb. She liked the metaphor.

Two other people were to attend the meeting from other non-profit organizations, and also a young woman who was being considered for the CEO position. Those three were arriving on the island by noon. The two men were staying in the guest rooms at VINE²S and the woman, in their little pink guesthouse. Lunch was being catered by Sarabeth's Restaurant down the street and served on the shady, new terrace built behind Iggy's house. It was all very exciting. There was a lot of discussion and finding out about each other and questions, but after lunch they went into the dining room for serious discussion of a mission plan.

Steve insisted Liz take the lead in the beginning as it was her money they were going to be talking about. He said he would take over but wanted it established that she was the financial source of the foundation. Liz told the group she and Steve wanted a certain percentage to go to Doctor's Without Borders but the rest to stay in the State of Florida and fund a scholarship program for any child interested in studying any kind of math, engineering or science. They wanted a total, four-year or more scholarship for any income level child who would contract to teach in their field, in public schools, for two years, and provide after-school tutoring free to all who wanted it.

"Give it a patriotic ambiance like the Peace Corps," said Liz. "A call to make our country more competitive in these fields and a mission to make Florida the science state. Publicize science competitions, bring in guest speakers for the students, make being a math, environmental, engineering or science major glamorous and exciting, something of which to be proud. Make science cool!

"I'm a novice at all of this but I hope I've conveyed the direction we would like to see the VINE²S Foundation grow. How to go about it...is your job. I'll be around, but my husband, Steve, will speak for us in all things. We are in this together, but my main job is six children. One, we just happen to be renting this house from."

313

76

Liz and Steve both liked Nora Rothanburg, the young woman being considered to lead the foundation. She seemed capable, serious and appeared to understand what Liz and Steve wanted to accomplish. She was not overly pretty but one you would classify as having her own style, gave off an air of academia, and had a fabulous resumé. Liz asked her if she liked children. She had never been married and as to children... she liked them, as long as they were not hers. But she was one hundred percent behind education for children and agreed with the scientific aspect of VINE²S.

The two men, George O'Brian, a big, bearded Bostonian and Luther Pettijohn a short, thin, youngish guy, were from foundations with similar financing structures but different mission statements. They knew the nuts and bolts of starting up this type of organization; and discussions, which included Win and Grace, went on all afternoon until they finally broke for dinner.

The seven of them walked down the sidewalk to Michael's, past the beautiful, stately houses and around ancient trees, often passing old walls with blooming vines cascading over the tops. George, Luther and Nora relished the unique casual atmosphere of the island and thought that keeping the foundation headquarters here could be done without a lot of notoriety. It could be referred to as a branch of the foundation, and Steve's 'job' was with the branch office.

Zoning in Key West was very loose, so using the house on the lane was not going to be a problem. The big houses in Key West were often guesthouses, law firms, inns, restaurants, art galleries, etc, all side by side with families living in the historic old homes.

Liz liked the idea of keeping the headquarters in Key West, but she was adamant about keeping her family and the money separate. She wanted the children to grow up in a normal way, like she and Steve had done. This money was an unusual bit of happenstance. She was willing to do the best she could with it, but it was to be a separate entity from her and her family. She would have it no other way.

They could rent the house Iggy owned next door to the one they were now using, have a larger work area and more living space for staff. Living space in Key West was so expensive that it was now a major problem for workers on the island. Being able to house your own staff was a big advantage.

The more Liz and Steve talked about it with Win and Grace the more practical it seemed. Liz could envision the decking and garden areas that would combine the houses. Parking could be built in under an archway between the homes, with living space above, like the old arch house on Eaton Street. It could all have the same classic gingerbread look as other Key West houses and those on Gumbo Limbo Lane.

Liz smiled at Steve. "I can keep a closer eye on you, here on the lane, Sweetheart...don't want you to get away."

Steve laughed, leaned over and gave Liz a hug. "Not a chance, Janie, not a chance! We'll always be entwined...by a vine...in our little island jungle."

When Earl and Phil had moved out of the big house, Elaine, their maid, had stayed. She now worked for the Sandfords. Liz had also hired Sara, Elaine's sister, to be the cook. Besides the six children, there were Liz and Steve, Mia, Brad, who was in and out, often Win and Grace, and now, Nora...Liz never knew

316

who would be sitting down for dinner. Keeping up with the meals was a full-time job. Sara, although not as exotic a cook as Phil, was still a good, healthy cook and much more flexible then Phillip. To succeed in this house you had to be laid back, and Sara was, always joking with the children and loved having them hang around the kitchen. Her cookie jar was usually full, but sometimes she found misspelled cookie suggestions in her empty container.

The twins were now always on the move. One afternoon Liz couldn't fine Caro. "Where's Caroline, Joey? Where did she go? She was sitting right here on the living-room rug." Liz was looking behind chairs when she heard a soft 'woof, woof'. ToJo was flat on the floor, beside a skirted table, staring at the edge of the cloth. Joey ran over and lifted the skirt and there sat Caro, laughing and clapping. Joey said, "Peek-a-boo," and dropped the skirt. Then Caro lifted the skirt and peeked out, "Peek-a-boo," said Joey again and laughed, Caroline squealed and ToJo woofed. Liz sat down on the floor, laughing with them. This is my life and I love it, she thought as she looked around. Oh, oh, where did Tommy go?

Steve thought they should go back up to the beach house as soon as possible. It was too perfect a spot to be spoiled by bad memories. They needed to make some good memories to replace them. Kirk was still not as active as before his accident and was not very thrilled about going back to the beach house... but that was the whole point. He needed to recover his outgoing, happy love of life. He needed to get back on the horse.

That Friday afternoon, Steve, Brad, the pirates and Joey went up in the SUV, buying kayaks, life preservers and fishing equipment on the way. Joey did not like the plain, orange life preserver they chose for him...he wanted the pink one with the drawing of 'Dora the Explorer' on it. Kirk and Iggy tried to tell him it was for girls but Joey didn't care about that. He liked Dora, watched her every morning on TV. Dora was his friend.

"Good choice, Joey," said Steve. "She will help keep you safe...right boys?...right boys?"

"Si, good choice, termite," said Iggy, laughing and giving a

317

thumbs-up sign.

"Yeah, Josephine, good choice," commented Kirk.

Joey smiled at them with his angel face all aglow. "Goot oice, Vater, goot oice!"

Liz and Grace came up in the Mini Cooper, shopping for food on the way. Stella and Mia drove Grace's SUV with the twins, the twins' stuff and ToJo. Liz just shook her head at the changes in her life. A year and a half ago, she fit all she needed into the trunk of a sports car. Now she needed three cars to go anywhere. Who could have guessed she would find a totally new life at the end of the road, literally?

77

When they arrived at the beach house, Steve and Brad started unloading the kayaks. Kirk and Iggy were carrying the paddles, and Joey was walking around with his Dora life jacket on. He did not know for what, but he and Dora were ready. ToJo barked and ran back and forth. He liked this place, lots of new spots to sniff. As the fellows put the kayaks on the beach, Kirk went inside the house with the paddles.

"Come on, Kirk," yelled Steve. "Bring out the paddles." Soon Iggy came out with all four paddles.

"I don't think Kirk likes it out here, says he wants to watch TV," said Iggy. "I don't know how this get-back-on-the-horse stuff works, but I don't think he wants to get-back-on-the-dock."

"Gotcha," said Steve. He turned back to the house and yelled, "Bring out Joey, Kirk, he wants to come out on the dock. He wants to see the fish."

Kirk stood there on the porch. Joey kept saying, "Go, Kick, dock!...Fische...see Fische!" Joey finally turned around and started running toward the dock. Kirk had no choice. He started running after Joey and then took his hand and walked out with him...looking over his shoulder at the shooting spot a couple of times. Iggy was already at the end and was yelling encouragement..."venga aqui, Scarface, vamonos, come, come Joey...let's look for fish. Si?"

Steve and Brad were watching with interest. Kirk had

319

an apprehensive expectant look on his face and kept glancing at Steve. Remounting this seahorse was not easy. Soon, he, Joey and Iggy were lying, tummy down, on the edge of the dock, looking at brightly colored fish swimming in and out of coral covered rocks.

"I'm staying out here with them if you want to go back," said Steve to Brad. "I think I heard one of the cars pull in." Steve sat on the bench looking out over the water. Little Palm Island was out to the left about four miles, Looe Key, a perfect diving spot, was six miles out at the edge of Hawk's Channel and Monkey Key was on the southwest horizon with its perfect sandy banks for fly fishing. It was a beautiful view. Waterfronts were always very changeable, but today it was peaceful...a glass calm.

Joey jumped up and ran to Steve. "Vater, fische...big, big, big fische in wasser!" Grabbing Steve's hand Joey lay back down on the dock with Steve next to him..."big, big fische!" Sure enough, there was a three-foot parrotfish swimming around the coral under the dock. Great excitement! Kirk and Iggy were discussing the right bait for fishing and if you could eat a parrotfish.

Brad left them all prone on the dock and walked around the house to the driveway on the old wooden decking surrounding the house. This walkway had been made from odd sections of the main dock that had washed ashore after various hurricanes. With another storm or two, the entire house would be surrounded with this historical record of named and dated examples of the rampaging violence of nature.

As he had hoped, Stella was there, unbuckling one of the twins. No one had noticed or commented but there was a bit of romantic tension budding between Stella and Brad.

"Hi, Stell, Mia, I'll take this little peanut so you can get their stuff," said Brad, as he reached for Tommy, then picked up the wading pool. Mia instructed, "Take that around front, under the tree, and put a little water in it. You can play lifeguard while we unpack the car."

Later that afternoon, they were all sitting in a semi-circle out on the beach, under the shady buttonwood tree. The twins, splashing and babbling in twin talk, were in the little plastic pool in the center of the group, with ToJo lying next to them. Joey, with great concentration, was pushing 'Thomas the tank-engine', around in the sand. He stopped at every shoe he came to, gave a "choo choo, toot toot", the foot moved and the little, wooden train continued its sandy journey.

Kirk and Iggy were at the water's edge, investigating rocky, tidal pools...trying to dam up the water, as the tide went out, so they could pen in some hermit crabs. Things were getting back to normal, and Kirk seemed more at ease on the beach.

Steve was burying a fire-pit in the sand. There was little wind so tonight was a good time for a wiener-roast. Liz had bought marshmallows and Hershey bars for 'smores,' and Brad had brought his guitar with him. Kirk didn't realize it, but this was a welcome-back-to-the-beach-house party for him. He was going to have good memories of the place, like it or not, and they all were working on it.

Win had arrived late in the afternoon and was sitting in a beach chair trying to hold a squirming 'Jackpot'. Tommy did not think Win's stories were as important as he used to and would rather get down and throw sand in ToJo's direction. ToJo moved out of range.

After everyone had finished their hot dogs and the 'smores were all gone, Brad announced that he, Stell, Kirk and Iggy had a surprise. Stella went on, "We thought our family needed a theme song, one that meant something. We searched through Edie's old sheet music. Brad said we needed a ballad...I wanted an old song...Kirk and Iggy wanted to sing rap. But we found an old ballad in the piano bench, the sheet music was torn and brown, and a few words had been changed, but we thought it was perfect. We have been practicing in the attic, and Brad worked with us...so here we go. Quit it Kirk! Sit, and don't make faces."

But Joey was giggling at Kirk and got up to sit between Kirk and Iggy. He wanted to be one of the boys and sat facing the circle with a big smile. Brad strummed his guitar in a loud chord and Joey looked at him in amazement. The little boy had obviously not been part of the practice session.

With Brad and Stella sitting in chairs with their backs to the water, and the three boys sitting on a log in front of them, they began the old love song. Stell was singing harmony and Brad, with the boys, was singing the lead. Joey just looked at them all in awe.

> "With someone like you, a pal so good and true
> I'd like to leave it all behind and go and find
> Someplace that's known, to God alone
> Just a spot to call our own
> We'll find a perfect peace, where joy will never cease
> Somewhere beneath the cloudless skies
> We'll build a sweet little nest, somewhere in Old Key West
> And let the rest of the world go by."

78

Everyone was applauding, Liz had tears running down her face, Steven leaned over and put his arm around her, the twins were sing-songing and moving up and down. Joey was taking bows with Kirk and Iggy... altogether, an exceptional performance.

"A perfect song for a perfect family. Don't you agree, Sweetheart?"

Steven was now standing..."Encore! Encore! Let's all sing it again. I bet Win and Grace know that song...I know it...do you Lizzie?"

Before they could answer, Joey stood up..."Joey singen... Joey singen." And in his three-year-old, clear, lilting voice, he began to sing a German song he must have heard his mother sing to him. It was a funny song and he had all the motions to go with it. Mia then translated...Joey was a hit!

"I can see he will have to join our group...maybe he'll sing lead," said Brad. Amid lots of applause and laughter, Joey took more bows.

"We'll teach him some hip-hop," said Iggy.

"He probably writes his own material," said Kirk.

It was a good way to end the summer and solve Kirk's problem. Nora Rothanburg, who had driven up with Win, was amazed at the interaction of all the people in the family.

Win explained, "This is a family of happenstance, few

are related, all seemed to have just arrived, unplanned, with a desperate need for a family, including Liz and Steve. Even Liz's twins were a big surprise. Although the children are of all ages, this is a new family. Liz and Steven have only been married for a few months and these children were forming around them even before that. The only ones who take it for granted are the twins and Joey...because they're so young."

"Well, I think it is amazing how it has all happened," said Nora. "Most things don't turn out this well. But I guess if you are willing to give away your fortune, you must be a special person."

"I think both Liz and Steve are special people. I'm working on adoption papers now, trying to get them all done by Christmas, so they can adopt the children all at once. That should give them all a full Christmas stocking." Win laughed, "Maybe Joey will remember a Christmas song by then."

School was starting soon, and Iggy, who had gained weight and grown in height, needed a new prosthesis. He and Kirk had long discussions as to what kind of motif his new leg was going to sport. After much indecision, they talked to Brad about it. "Star Wars" was a leading contender but finally they agreed that NASA, the space program, was more timeless. Iggy was getting taller and his legs were getting bigger and this would be a growing problem for years to come.

Joey loved to watch Iggy attach his 'peg leg' and wanted one. The older boys tolerated the three-year-old because he was so funny...and they could teach him to do or say anything...not always a good plan.

The twins were crawling into everything and driving ToJo crazy. They wouldn't stay put. They liked to follow Joey, he liked to follow Kirk and Iggy...again...not always a good plan. But Brad was fascinated with the challenging idea of teaching all three to speak English well. He would drop by the house after the boys came home from school and always seemed to be around. Liz was starting to notice the real reason why. Stella was turning into a very pretty girl, was popular and usually involved in something interesting. Liz was amused; the best chaperones are little children. Joey was going to start nursery school and that would help his English. In a couple of years, Liz was going to miss the agreeable 'si,' ' ja,' and 'yeh' of their present multicultural conversation.

"Liz, can you come in here a minute, please," said Steve as he stood at the door of his study.

"I am not alone, as you can see." Liz walked in with both babies and handed one to Steve. "Oh, dear, what happened? Are you OK?" Liz could tell something was wrong. He had an odd look on his face.

Steve sat behind his desk with Caro in his arms, she was cuddling her dirty, pink teddy bear. Steve looked at Liz. "My mother died! Dad just called from Japan. She had a brain hemorrhage and died immediately! I can't believe it! She was having some problems but I never thought it was serious. Dad said she was fine up until she fell down at her bridge club luncheon and never revived."

"Oh my God, I am so sorry...you must go over there!"

"No, Dad said not to come. She is being cremated and he is coming here with her ashes to be placed in the Key West cemetery. There will be a memorial service in Japan before they leave and a family service here at the internment. He seems OK, but I can hear a lot of uncertainty in his voice. Mother was usually in charge of things like this. He says to give him a few weeks because he is still trying to figure out things. It was a shock to him too. He said he might take an early retirement. They had planned to do that in a few years and move back to Key West. The Navy and friends are giving him lots of help and support, he said. He'll call back when he knows more...I'm kind of stunned by this!" Steve looked at Liz as he cuddled Caro. Liz came to hug him and the four of them had a group hug.

"Let's all go sit in the cuddle chair on the terrace," said Liz. "You need to think about this. It's so sad about your mom."

"Let's take the twins with us...they make me feel better about life and stuff. Their birth helped me recover from Ali's death. Their liveliness puts it all into perspective. Some lives are short, like Ali's, Iggy's parents, and even the twins' father. Some are long, like Aunt Norma and Iggy's great-grandmother.

Maybe even my mother. She was around sixty-five, not so old but not so young either. I think, at least, my mother had a happy life."

Liz and Steve sat there, close together, the babies climbing and baby-talking around them. The day was beautiful, the breeze soft, late summer birds were calling and Steve's mother had just died. He lay back on the chaise and closed his eyes. ToJo walked up and lay down on the terrace next to Steve. He gave a little 'woof' like he was saying, "I'm here for you, buddy."

79

The next morning, Steve ran out to the White Street Pier at dawn. It seemed to be an exceptionally beautiful sunrise. It was an odd feeling, losing your mother, whom you had seen very little of since you were seventeen. Even though she was in Japan all those years, you always knew your mother loved you, cared about you. You just understood she was your most loyal fan... whatever you did. It felt like one of your support pillars had been removed. Steve sat on the sea wall watching distant gold-lined clouds slowly swirl in a prism of sunrise colors.

Thinking about his children, and that's how he thought of them, as his children, he realized how hard it must have been to lose your mother when you were young but old enough to realize she was gone...like Iggy had been, and Kirk and Stella. Happy Joey was too young to fully comprehend his mother was gone...he still was figuring out whether Mia or Mommy was his mother...if he thought about it. Steve realized he, himself, had been very lucky.

The next day Steve heard again from his dad. He was going to retire from the Navy and there were a lot of things to wrap up. Steve offered, again, to go to Japan to help in any way he could but his dad said no. He would be in Key West soon. Liz was planning for the elder Dr. Sandford to move into the guest room or, if he preferred, the little house.

Joey was in the up-and-down process of learning to ride a bike without training wheels. Liz had been teaching him on the grass, so when he fell, it was a soft landing. Kirk and Iggy were anxious to get him in the lane where Iggy had learned. One afternoon, Steve put the playpen on the side of the little dead-end street so Caro and Tommy could watch as he, Liz, Kirk and Iggy served as coaches. The twins were the cheering crowd and little Joey was the team. The neighbors came out to watch and cheer him on.

The little lane had been quiet and tranquil until the Sandford family had grown. It was now, usually, a lane of activity. Joey was serious about learning. He wanted to ride like his big brothers. A bike rack was now in the side yard of the little house and everyone's bike was a different color. Joey's was green and purple. He said they were Dora the Explorer's favorite colors! Who knew?

After a sweaty and exhausting hour, much yelling, lots of laughing, trying and crying, Joey did it. He was now able to fly down the lane and stop without crashing. Wow! What celebrity! Everyone came over to give him a high-five...Mr. Garcia, a neighbor, gave him a kitten. Joey was thrilled! Steve, laughing, said he thought Mr. Garcia was very clever. He awarded kittens and how could you turn down an award? Liz, looking at the tiny kitten as Joey cuddled it said, "Joey, that's the prettiest little kitten I've ever seen." She then looked at Steve, over Joey's head and rolled her eyes, laughing...another family member. ToJo came over to check this out...he sniffed, woofed and then sat back down again next to the twins. He was maintaining his seniority.

Steve again had heard, via E-mail, from his father. He was arriving next Tuesday on the morning flight. To Liz, Steve said, "This is great, now I'll have a family member to bring on board. I hope he and Win hit it off. This family has two grandfathers now."

"Since Nora's bought a condo, the little house is ready

if he wants to stay there. I think he might like the quieter place but he can take his meals with us." Said Liz. "I can't wait to meet your dad. Are you and he alike? Does he have your magnetic sex appeal?"

"Are you kidding me? He's an old man of sixty-six. I hope the trip won't be too much for him. That's a lot of travel at his age," said Steve.

Tuesday arrived and Steve and Liz were driving up the oceanfront boulevard as the plane was landing. Inside they waited for the steps to be pushed into place and the passengers to descend. "There he is," said Steve. "The man in the hat."

"You mean Sean Connery with the little Japanese girl? Wow, he does have sex appeal, and the little girl is precious. Maybe he's just helping her down the steps."

They watched as the two walked across the tarmac, holding hands. Steve looked at Liz with a puzzled expression. "Hadn't heard anything about this," he said. They walked to where the travelers came through.

"Hi, Dad. I'm glad you're here at last," said Steve, giving his dad a hug. "And who is this...blue eyed beauty?" Steve was looking down into the most adorable Eurasian face with mirror image, blue eyes and dark, straight hair with bangs.

"This is Aya, Steve...your half sister!" said Dad with pride. "For later discussion of course."

Steve did a double take and then knelt down, saying, "I'm very happy to have a beautiful sister with blue eyes like mine... he blinked his eyes...she blinked hers and smiled. "How old are you, Aya?"

In perfect English she replied, "I am five and a half years old and I am very glad to have a big brother." She gave a little bow.

Liz knelt down and hugged her. "I am very happy to meet you, Aya. Welcome to your new home. I'm Liz."

"Thank you, Liz," said Aya, with another little bow.

They were all walking into the big house when Mia returned with Joey from nursery school. Joey took one look at Aya and went running toward her yelling, "Dowa da Esplora. I wove you!" He threw his arms around her waist and hugged her. Aya, with a worried look at her Papa, patted Joey gingerly on his back.

"No, no, Joey, this is Aya," said Liz. "She's come to live with us."

"Dowa da Esplora, she come to play wif me!" said Joey, confidently. And when you stopped to look at her, she did resemble his favorite person, at least in the eyes of a three-year-old.

80

Later, while Aya was napping inside, Dr. Sandford sat on the terrace of the little house with Steve and Liz. He asked Liz, and any others person to whom he was not related, to call him Skip. Though he was a bit tired from the trip he figured Steve deserved an explanation as soon a possible.

"Well", he smiled, "About five years ago your mother and I had a bit of a rough go. So we thought a short separation might do us both good. She went to Hawaii for three weeks with girlfriends and had a wonderful time. In fact, she got a whole new lease on life, took up painting and a study of Japanese woodcuts...traveled around Japan to shrines and museums to study the art of woodcuts and seemed happier than before. I was delighted. But, an incident had happened while she was away in Hawaii."

"A surgical colleague of mine, the beautiful Dr. Hana Sakura, had been working with me for a few years," continued Skip. "She was unmarried and often talked about how she never wanted to be married but would love to have a child. She was very amusing and we often talked, in a joking way, about which doctor she should choose. Operating rooms are often places of ribald jokes and conversations, and the other doctors were always offering her their services. She, in turn, would tell then what was wrong with them and why they didn't qualify. It was all in fun."

Steve's father paused, gave a little lop-sided grin and said, "We can always justify these things, can't we? But to make a long story short...she had decided on me, asked for my cooperation and discretion and...got it. We never discussed it again but about four months later she took a leave of absence and I never saw her again, until about five months ago."

"She called the ER one day and asked me to meet her in the park by the hospital. I went and was shocked to see her. She looked very thin and wan and it appeared she was wearing a wig. Chasing a yellow butterfly around the park was a beautiful, little girl in a blue dress. I knew she was mine as soon as I saw her. Talk about love at first sight!"

"Hana sat on the bench watching her daughter run and skip. She said, she's yours, you know. I told her I knew and asked her what was happening? She told me she was dying of cancer, had held out for a cure as long as she could, but now she wanted to settle things. Her family did not truly love Aya because she was part American. They were nice to her, but Hana wanted a loving home for her daughter. She asked if I could take her and if my wife could accept her and love her? I knew Dorothy could and would and I told her so. We discussed a lot of things and decided to meet the next day."

Skip chuckled as he remembered Dorothy's reaction. "Your Mom was a sport, I'll tell you, she even laughed at a few spots in my explanation and was very concerned about Aya. In fact, she told me we should take her in, it was the least I could do! She also wanted to meet Hana. So the next day we both met with Hana, talked with Aya and figured out a plan. Hana died about two weeks later, and Aya has been with us ever since. Your Mom loved Aya, as if she was her own, and did all she could for Hana before she died. I think your mother finally got the daughter she always wanted. She loved you and was so proud of you, but she always wanted a daughter too."

"That is an amazing story", said Steve. "I guess Aya has lost her mother twice. She must be a strong little girl. Does she speak Japanese? She speaks English beautifully."

"Yes," answered Skip. "Hana had sent her to a very good

332

private school that emphasized both languages. Aya is a smart little girl for five. You had written me about your interesting family here and now that I've retired, and finished traveling, I'm hoping we can be part of it. We both need a home and...Aya needs a family."

"Of course," said Liz. "We have lots of room and lots of love and you already are part of the family. We are having a group adoption next Friday, but you both already have the last name of Sandford. We're just adding to your family!"

"Don't worry any more about a home, Dad, this is it. This little house can be yours as long as you want it, and you and Aya are part of the family. Its just too bad mom didn't get to retire too. She would have loved it here."

"It's the only regret I have, son...the only regret. I will say, I think Aya did make her life happier and more fulfilled. Your mom just loved having a little girl!"

Aya came out of the little house and went straight to her 'Papa'. Skip lifted her up into his lap, put his arm around her, looked down and smiled. She looked up at him, cuddled into him, then looked at Steve and Liz with a still-tired expression.

"Why does this make me think of Joey hanging on to you," said Liz to Steve..."an anchor in a swirling sea they don't understand. Not only do you and your dad look alike, but you both have that gentle heart."

81

Friday dawned bright and clear, just another perfect day in paradise. Everyone was excited, in motion, and loud. Adoption Day! Much discussion had taken place with each child about keeping his or her family history and individuality, but being part of the Sandford Family as well.

It was about the only thing Kirk didn't joke about. His own family he wanted to forget, so he was glad to be a part of this one. He knew he and his sister were lucky and, although he had never mentioned it, he would never forget the fact that they had actually come to get him, that odd, bleak day in Stone Mountain, Georgia. One of these days, he, Kirk Sandford, would do good things for people. At least he would try. And according to 'Mom', trying hard counted!

Iggy, on the other hand, was just simply grateful he didn't have to go far. He had grown up on Gumbo Limbo Lane and knew at some point, when his great-grandmother died, he would be sent somewhere else. To be able to stay here, with people who helped him with his leg and seemed to care a lot about what happened to him, was amazing. They even told him about the property he inherited, and Steve occasionally spoke to him about it, keeping him up to date on it, even though he was just a kid.

He would never say anything to Kirk, but Iggy was very proud of owning property on the lane and renting some of his houses to Steve. He thought they were now the best-looking houses in Key West and he owned them! His life, since the day Kirk came up on his porch, had done a complete about-face. One of these days, Ignacio Hipolito Diez y Morales Sandford planned to make a difference in other people's lives. When he had enough money, he was going to make sure anyone who needed an artificial limb would get it! Maybe he could start a fund called 'Off the Porch'. Maybe Kirk would help.

Stella had often thought about her life since she picked up Liz, sitting forlornly by the side of the road. She realized life often took serendipitous turns, but she and her brother had been very fortunate...they were together and part of a wonderful, new family. She was already planning to be a doctor...she was going to do something important with her life. And Stella Sandford already knew, for a fact, little acts of kindness could have enormous consequences!

Joey was dressed like Kirk and Iggy...khaki pants and a polo shirt with the horsey on it. Blue was the only color Joey acknowledged, so his shirt was blue, Kirk's was red and Iggy's green. The twins had matching outfits, and Stella looked very grown-up in a new dress of yellow linen with pink, strappy high heels. Liz was wearing the pale aqua dress she had found to go with her perfect-for-today aquamarine necklace.

They all were ready to go. Steve's Dad and Aya were going as well as Mia, Brad, Win and Grace. Fourteen people would crowd into the judge's chambers, and six would be adopted.

After a little talk about responsibility and family values, Judge Sanchez said he thought a prayer was appropriate. "What religion are you all adopting?" asked the judge. There was a pause.

"Well, Judge Sanchez, we haven't figured that out yet," said Steve. "You see Stella and Kirk are Baptist, Iggie is Catholic, Joey's Lutheran, Liz and the twins are Methodist, Aya is Shinto/ Buddhist and Dr. Sandford and myself are Episcopalians". Steve looked around and continued..."Uncle Win is Jewish, Grace is Pentecostal, Mia, our nanny, is agnostic and Brad, our tutor, wears a red band of some type around his wrist. We'll work it out one of these days, but I don't think anyone's God is mad at anyone else's."

Judge Sanchez laughed, "Well, I can see you are a work in progress. Good luck to all of you Sandfords. Godspeed!"

Sitting on the terrace in their favorite cuddle chaise, Liz and Steve were surveying their official new family. Stella was making sure everyone included Aya. She was a bit shy at first but when Stell put Caroline in her lap, she melted. Caro flirted and cooed and laughed and pattie-caked and, of course, Aya fell in love with her. Stella told Aya they needed more girls in the family and how happy she was that Aya was part of them

"Is your mother here?" asked Aya.

"No, she died a long time ago of cancer," replied Stell.

"Mine did too," said Aya. "Is Kirk your brother?"

"Yes, and Steve is your brother?"

"Yes. He is very nice, isn't he?"

"He sure is! You are very lucky to have a brother like him and a dad like Skip. I think you'll be very happy here."

"I want to write a letter to my mother so she will know where I am. Can you help me?"

"Of course," said Stell, puzzled. "How do you do that?"

"If you will get me some paper, I have a pencil, and after I write to her and tell her where I am, then we need a candle so I can burn the paper up. The smoke will take my letter to her, and after that she can watch me. I won't be able to see her but I'll know she is there...she loves me very much. The letter is supposed to be a secret between my mother and me but...I'm not allowed to use matches," said Aya quietly.

"It will be our secret, Aya. I'm your big sister now and I'll help you any way I can."

Stella hugged Aya and said, "Any time you are ready you just come find me, OK?"

"OK, Stella, thank you." Aya gave a little bow. "I am very happy to be a little sister to a big sister." She looked down at Caroline, sitting in her lap happily chewing on a rubber doll's foot. "And I'll be a big sister to you, Caroline."

Joey came running up. "See my kleine Katze, Dowa? You want'a holer? Katze purren." Stella took Caroline so Aya could hold the purring kitten.

Skip, sitting with Liz and Steve, Win and Grace was explaining that Aya had been raised very formally and American families are so casual. "I feel, sometimes, when I'm with her that I have to sit up straighter. And that little bow, in Japan everybody bows...the cab driver turns in his seat and bows to the doorman...the doorman bows to the driver...then to the passenger getting into the cab...it is kind of like a handshake or acknowledgement." Skip smiled. "I told her Americans didn't bow, but a high-five didn't make much sense to her. In this group I'm sure she will loosen up a bit, but she is a rather quiet child. She needs a family...and young people to be around."

"Well, she certainly has a friend in Joey, if she doesn't mind being called Dowa." Liz laughed.

The photographer arrived to take family photographs. Besides an official family photo, Liz wanted candid shots of every member of the family. This was a day they were all going to remember! She planned to have each child's picture blown up, framed, and hung together in the family room.

They grouped around Liz and Steve, who were seated and each holding a baby. Joey held Aya's hand, Stella was standing between Kirk and Iggy with her arms around their shoulders, and Skip was standing behind them all as they laughed at Brad's antics. "Wait," said Liz. "Win is a member of our family as much as any one else. Come on, Win, every family has two grandfathers!"

Steve smiled as he looked over at Liz. "A perfect family, Lizzie Love, just perfect. We are very lucky. It just couldn't get any better than this!"

Liz looked over at the man she loved. With a secret little smile and a subtle bit of eye contact, she patted her tummy... "Don't be too sure about that...Tarzan!"

Acknowledgments

When one attempts to write a first novel there is little respect for the endeavor. Family thinks it's about the nuttiest thing they have heard (You're kidding, right?), and friends, you don't even dare tell. But a few adventurous souls have been available to read the first draft (Thanks, Dorothy Ann), try to correct my spelling (Thanks, Barbara), discuss content (Thanks Alice, thanks 'Termite'), provide technical support (Thanks, Birdie), show interest and give helpful advice (Thanks, Bob Morris, a real live published author), and in general be supportive or at least pretend. My daughters, Kim and Laura, thought it needed more sex but both have favorite characters. My son found it was more intriguing than he thought it would be (Mom wrote this?). And his wife, Michele, well, without her expertise I'd never have been able to get this thing out of the computer. (Thanks, Michele!!!) And Tom,...what can I say...OK, OK, I'm finished!

About the Author

Anne Yates Burst is a native Key Wester whose family goes back three or four generations on the island. A graduate of Florida State University, she has been regional editor of FLORIDA HOME & GARDEN, columnist and feature writer for the ORLANDO SENTINEL and other magazines and newspapers. She now lives with her husband in Winter Park, Florida. They have three children, Kim, Tom and Laura.

How You Can Help a Child

Iggy, one of the characters in "THE VIEW FROM THE WIDOW'S WALK", needed a prosthesis, which is very expensive; but he was fortunate to have loved ones who could afford to purchase one. Many other children in need of a prosthesis are not so fortunate. If you are interested in helping children like Iggy, please visit the **Jordan Thomas Foundation** online to learn more about the prosthetic needs of children with limb loss, and how you can help.

www.jordanthomasfoundation.org

The Flavors of Key West

Food plays a large role in books about certain regions of the country and Key West is no exception. A combination of Cuban, English and Bahamian influences, plus interpretations by many off-island chefs, gives the island cuisine an international flavor. Be that as it may...here are some of the menus and recipes that were often enjoyed in the book.

The Classic Cuban Dinner

Boliche or Picadillo...black beans and rice...plantains... tossed salad...garlic bread...Key Lime Pie

Boliche Roast

A **Boliche Roast** often needs the expert cutting of a Cuban butcher. A long horizontal hole is cut through the center of the roast and stuffed with chopped ham, hard-boiled eggs, minced garlic and seasoning. Brown roast in olive oil, add tomato paste, onions, green peppers and a few bay leaves. Cover and cook on low for about 45 minuets a pound. To serve...slice as you would a loaf of bread.

- or -

Picadillo

Try **Picadillo** as your entrée...a very Cuban dish and much simpler to prepare. In olive oil, brown chopped onion, garlic, green pepper and add ground beef. After browning, add a can of chopped tomatoes, small bottle of capers, a few bay leaves, a handful of seedless green olives and, to give it the real Cuban flavor, a small box of raisins. Yum.

Black Beans

For **Black Beans**, you can buy canned beans that are seasoned and add a little more olive oil, a bay leaf and a touch of red wine.

Plantains

For **Plantains**, buy Goya microwave ripe plantains in the freezer section...three minutes and they are the best I've ever had.

Tossed Salad

Toss a garden salad with olive oil and balsamic vinegar, make or buy garlic bread and you are ready for the dessert Grande...

Key Lime Pie

Key Lime Pie! The State of Florida passed a law that says...if you do not use REAL key limes you can't call it Key Lime Pie! And key limes are capricious...some years your tree is full and dropping on the ground, other years your tree snubs you and you get none. So...you can use key limes or try Nellie & Joe's Key West Lime Juice or fake it. Just don't tell the Governor.

Eva's Key Lime Pie

4 eggs, separated
1 can sweetened condensed milk
1/2 cup key lime juice
3 teaspoons sugar
1 9-inch graham cracker crust

Preheat oven to 350 degrees. Separate eggs. Beat the yolks in a bowl until thick. Add condensed milk and beat until well blended. Add lime juice slowly, mixing well. The custard will thicken as you add the lime juice. Pour into already baked pie crust. For meringue, beat egg whites until stiff, add sugar, beating constantly, then spoon and spread meringue over top of pie (hopefully into high and swirling peaks). Brown meringue in oven until it is a delight to the eye.

Guava Duff

About the **Guava Duff**...it is a steamed pudding... delicious...an old-fashioned, time-consuming concoction that is seldom made today. But here it is, right out of the 1949 Key West Woman's Club cookbook...good luck. (Use canned guavas if you don't have a guava tree.)

Guava Duff
3 eggs
1/8 lb. butter
1 cup sugar
3 cups flour
2 teaspoons baking powder
1/2 teaspoon nutmeg and cinnamon
2 cups guava pulp, finely sieved

Cream the sugar and butter, add beaten eggs, guava pulp and spices...beat smooth. Sift flour with baking powder and work into mixture. The dough should be stiff. Put mixture in tightly sealed and greased can...place can in vessel with water reaching 2/3 from top of can. Let steam three hours. Slice and serve with 'butter and sugar' sauce.

Butter and Sugar Sauce
1/8 lb. butter
3/4 cup sugar
1 egg

Cream butter and sugar, add yolk of egg, fold in stiffly beaten egg whites and a small portion of hot water.

Guava Tarts
Uncle Win's favorite is easier. Purchase frozen pastry sheets and thaw 30 minutes. Roll into thin 4" X 6" rectangles. Mix equal parts cream cheese and guava jelly together. Place 1 tablespoon of mixture in center of rectangle. Fold and seal edges with fork. Brush top with egg wash. Bake at 400° for 12-14 minutes, or until golden brown.

Made in the USA
Lexington, KY
17 January 2013